Postcards
from the Past

Center Point
Large Print

Also by Marcia Willett and available from
Center Point Large Print:

Christmas in Cornwall
The Sea Garden

**This Large Print Book carries the
Seal of Approval of N.A.V.H.**

Postcards from the Past

MARCIA WILLETT

CENTER POINT LARGE PRINT
THORNDIKE, MAINE

This Center Point Large Print edition
is published in the year 2015 by arrangement with
St. Martin's Press.

This is a work of fiction.
All of the characters, organizations,
and events portrayed in this novel are either products of
the author's imagination or are used fictitiously.
The text of this Large Print edition is unabridged.
In other aspects, this book may vary
from the original edition.
Printed in the United States of America
on permanent paper.
Set in 16-point Times New Roman type.

ISBN: 978-1-62899-642-5

Library of Congress Cataloging-in-Publication Data

Willett, Marcia.
  Postcards from the past / Marcia Willett. — Center Point Large Print
edition.
     pages cm
  Summary: "Siblings Billa and Ed share their beautiful, grand old
childhood home in rural Cornwall and seem as contented as they can be.
But when postcards start arriving from a sinister figure they thought
belonged well and truly in their pasts, old memories are stirred"—
Provided by publisher.
  ISBN 978-1-62899-642-5 (library binding : alk. paper)
  I. Title.
  PR6073.I4235P67 2015b
  823′.914—dc23
                                                              2015015437

To Linda Evans

CHAPTER ONE

There are two moons tonight. The round white shining disc, brittle and sharp-edged as glass, stares down at its reflection lying on its back in the black water of the lake. Nothing stirs. No whisper of wind ruffles the surface. At the lake's edge the wild cherry tree leans like an elegant ghost, its delicate bare branches silver with ice, yearning towards the past warmth of summer days. Tall stands of dogwood, their bright wands of colour blotted into monochrome by the cold brilliant light, guard the northern shore of the lake and cast spiked shadows across the frosty grass.

She stands in the warm room, staring down at the frozen, wintry scene and, all the while, her fingers fret around the edges of the postcard thrust deep into the pocket of her quilted gilet, just as her mind frets around the meaning of the words scrawled on the back of a reproduction of Toulouse-Lautrec's *La Chaîne Simpson*.

'A blast from the past. How are you doing? Perhaps I should pay a visit and find out!'

It is addressed to her and her brother—Edmund and Wilhelmina St Enedoc—and signed simply with one word: 'Tris'. She fingers the card, breaking its corner; from a room below drift a few notes of music, the lyrical poignancy of the trumpet: Miles Davis playing 'It Never Entered My Mind'. It is one of Ed's favourite CDs.

Instinct made her hide the postcard earlier, shuffling it beneath yesterday's newspaper as Ed came into the kitchen to see what the postman had brought. She made some lighthearted remark, passing him the handful of envelopes and catalogues, whilst the writing on the postcard burned on her inner eye.

'. . . Perhaps I should pay a visit and find out! Tris.'

Later she slid it into her pocket to examine it in the privacy of her own room. The postmark is Paris, dated three days ago. By now he might be in the country, driving west. How could he know, after more than fifty years, that she and Ed would still be here together?

Fifty years.

'Tris the tick.' 'Tris the toad.' 'Tell-tale Tris.' Ed, at twelve, has a whole collection of private names for their new stepbrother. 'We'll have to watch out for him, Billa.'

'Try to be nice to Tristan, darling.' Her mother's voice. 'I know it's hard for you and Ed but I do so want you all to get on together. For my sake. Will you try?'

Fifty years. She takes the card out of her pocket and stares at it.

'Billa?' Ed's voice. 'Are you coming down? Supper's ready.'

'Coming,' she calls. 'Shan't be a sec.'

She glances round, picks up a book from the small revolving table—her mother's little walnut table—and slips the postcard inside. Drawing the curtains together, closing out the two moons and the lake, Billa goes downstairs to Ed.

He stoops over the supper he's prepared, checking the sauce. The jointed chicken legs have been marinaded overnight in oregano and garlicky red wine vinegar, then cooked in white wine, and he looks approvingly at the result, now on a dish, with its sprinkling of olives and capers and prunes. It smells delicious. His cooking is capricious, extravagant and occasionally disastrous, but he likes to pull his weight. Tall and wide-shouldered in his navy Aran jersey—unravelling at the cuffs and patched at the elbows—his thick thatch of badger-streaked hair falling forward as he bends to take plates out of the bottom oven of the Aga, he looks like an amiable bear. Ed's approach to life is simple, unhurried; he hates fuss or extravagant emotion and believes himself to be inadequate in fulfilling people's expectations of him. The women who are drawn to his innate kindness, his gentleness, grow irritated by his inability to commit. He went straight to a major publishing house from university and stayed there until his early retirement, but always weekended here at Mellinpons. He cherished his authors—naturalists, travellers, gardeners—enjoyed launch parties and lunches but, in his middle fifties, with his childless marriage drifting into an amicable divorce, he decided to move back to Cornwall. His own book, published two years later—*Wild Birds of the Peninsula*—was an astonishing success, partly attributable to his charming ink drawings and beautiful photographs. *Wild Birds of the Cornish Cliffs and Coasts* followed, and now he is planning *Wild Birds of the Cornish Inland Lakes*: Colliford, Crowdy, Siblyback.

To his regret, their own lake is too small to harbour more than a few wild duck; too domestic to be home to tufted duck or great-crested grebe. Frogs in plenty come to carouse in the early spring, slipping and sliding, clasping and clambering in the shallows, their mating songs echoing eerily in the night.

Ed lifts out the warmed plates from the lower oven. Billa and he were always happiest here at Mellinpons; always glad to leave the big town house in Truro at the beginning of the summer holidays. He can remember the excitement of heading out of the city with their father driving the big Rover, their mother beside him, and he and Billa packed into the back with their favourite toys and books. Mellinpons: built as a mill in 1710, extended and converted into a butter factory by a cooperative of local farmers in 1870.

Their branch of the St Enedoc family made its

wealth from mining, and Great-grandfather bought this piece of land with its mine—now defunct—the mill and some cottages back in the 1870s. In 1939 the butter factory closed when the men were called up for war, and it lay derelict until Harry St Enedoc decided to convert it. Mellinpons was his post-war project. He'd had a bad war and afterwards took very little interest in the family business, passing more responsibility to his fellow directors, resigning from the boards of the great mining companies, until at last he moved his family out of Truro and settled in this quiet valley. He lived only six years at Mellinpons before he died.

It's odd, thinks Ed, that, though his father lived here for such a short time, his influence is still so strongly present in the butter factory. It was his idea to use the old millstone as a hearthstone beneath a granite chimney-breast, which takes up one whole corner of the hall from where it is possible to look up and up, past the galleried landing, to the massive black beams in the roof. The great window facing down the valley was his idea, too. The recess, cut into the thick granite walls, is big and deep enough to take two armchairs. It was he who named the old butter factory Mellinpons: the Mill on the Bridge.

Ed places the dish beside the plates on the huge slate kitchen table, on which the butter was once patted into blocks, glancing up as Billa comes in.

11

'That looks good,' she says appreciatively.

The kitchen is warm and full of delicious smells, Miles Davis is playing 'I'll Remember April' whilst Ed's Newfoundland—the colour of tobacco and called Bear because, as a puppy, he looked like a brown bear-cub—sleeps peacefully on an ancient, sagging sofa beneath the window. Keeping her eyes resolutely away from the mess Ed will have made at the business end of the kitchen, Billa sits down at the table. The huge dog raises his head, checks her arrival and slumps down again. His tail beats gently, just a thump or two of welcome, before he resumes his slumber.

'Don't get up,' Billa tells him drily.

'He won't,' Ed says comfortably. 'Far too much effort would be required.'

He spoons some chicken and sauce on to a beautiful old Spode plate, whose gold leaf is nearly worn away, and passes it to her. There is roasted parsnip mash in a Clarice Cliff bowl and some purple heads of broccoli in a Mason's Ironstone dish. Ed chooses his dishes for their designs and colours but with no sense of uniformity. Oddly, it works; old and new, priceless and valueless, all existing happily together. The table is only partially cleared: seed catalogues, a pair of binoculars, the latest edition of *Slightly Foxed*, as well as the diary—bursting with crucial pieces of paper containing addresses, telephone numbers and all the notes Ed makes to himself whilst on the telephone—are scattered across the black slate. A terracotta pot planted with cyclamen stands beside a pretty branching silver candlestick.

Ed fills Billa's glass with wine—a mellow South African Merlot that has been warming by the Aga—and sits down. He talks enthusiastically about his plans for seeding the small meadow with wild flowers and grasses, for planting more bulbs beneath the great copper beech, and all the while, as she nods and says, 'Mmm. Good idea . . .' her mind skitters around the words written on the postcard.

Ed notes her distraction but says nothing. She is generally more involved in her charity work for the local hospice than in his writing and drawing, his continuing development of the land along the stream and his study of its wildlife. This is where Ed reigns supreme and Billa doesn't attempt to advise him on any of these subjects.

As he clears the plates, shovelling a few tasty morsels into Bear's bowl, he reflects on Billa's marriage to the much older, well-known physicist, Philip Huxley. Ed's always believed that the relationship was based on hero-worship on Billa's side, rather than passion, and by an almost paternal kindness on Philip's. Gradually she was undermined by a series of devastating miscarriages, subsuming her grief into a growing absorption with her work as the head of the fund-raising wing of a big charitable organization for disabled children.

She'd nursed Philip through his last, long illness and then come back to live at Mellinpons. Yet even now, widowed and retired, Billa is still tough and he is glad that his expertise is outside her own areas of endeavour. They get along very well together.

Bear climbs down from his sofa and goes to inspect the contents of his bowl. He glances up at Ed as if to say: 'What d'you call this?'

'Don't you fancy it, old man?' Ed asks, concerned. 'Too much oregano?'

Billa rolls her eyes. 'Perhaps he'd rather have it on the Spode plate.'

'Perhaps he would,' answers Ed, unruffled by her sarcasm, 'but there are only two of them left. They were Great-grandmother's, as far as I can remember, and I rather treasure them. I do agree, though, that your old chipped enamel bowl is rather mere, isn't it, Bear?'

Billa bursts out laughing. 'Poor old Bear. We'll buy him a new one for his birthday. Do you want me to make the coffee or will you do it?'

Her laughter relieves some of her tension and she feels stronger again. After all, what can Tristan do to them now? That particular part of the past has long gone; finished.

But, as she watches Ed making coffee, his figure dislimns and fades and she sees her mother instead, standing there fiddling with cups and saucers, eyes averted from her children, sitting side by side at the table.

'I know it will be difficult at first,' she was saying rapidly, hands busy with the kettle, with the tea caddy. 'But I know that you'll love him as much as I do when you get to know him. After all, it is more than five years now since your father died and . . .' The kettle began to sing and she lifted it from the hotplate. 'And I want you to try very hard to understand how lonely it is for me with you both away at school . . .'

'We don't both have to be away at school.' Billa's voice was harsh with anxiety. There was something frightening, embarrassing, at the sight of her mother so nervous and beseeching. 'At least, *I* don't have to be away,' she said. 'Ed does, of course, especially now he's got a place at Sherborne, but I could be a day-girl. I could go to Truro School.'

'But, darling . . .' Their mother looked at them at last and Billa saw that she could not hide her happiness; her excitement. She stretched her hands to them, like a child at a party inviting them to join in the games. 'You see, Andrew and I love each other. I think you are old enough to understand this. I am so happy, you see.'

Ed, feeling his sister's tension, said politely: 'Perhaps we will understand when we've met . . .' he stumbled over the words 'this man' or 'him' and settled rather waveringly on 'Andrew'. 'When we've met Andrew,' he finished more strongly.

Their mother made tea, though Billa could see that her hands were shaking. 'And,' she said, in a special voice, as if this was an extra bonus, 'and Andrew has a son of his own, called Tristan. He's ten, two years younger than you, Ed, and I'm sure we shall be very happy together. A proper family again. They will both live with us here at Mellinpons.'

Billa and Ed were stunned into silence: a boy of ten. Tristan. Living here in their house.

Out of sight, under the table, Billa's hand stretched out to Ed and fastened round his wrist. They stared stonily at their mother as she came across the kitchen and put their tea on the table.

Ed pushes Billa's coffee cup towards her and stares at her, bending down a little to peer at her more closely.

'Are you OK?' he asks.

She looks back at him, frowning, and then nods. 'Sorry,' she says. 'I went off there for a minute. I was just remembering Mother telling us that she was going to marry ghastly Andrew.'

'I suppose he wasn't that bad,' Ed says. 'It can't have been easy for him, either.'

'We were just the wrong ages,' says Billa reflectively. 'Fourteen is no age to watch your mother falling passionately in love. Of course he was very attractive in an edgy kind of way, but she was so mad about him that it was embarrassing,

16

especially in public. I stopped telling her about events at school because I couldn't stand the humiliation. Girls can be so cruel.'

'It was easier for me.' Ed sits down at the table. 'Andrew was quite clued up about things like rugby and cricket. It was that little tick Tris that I couldn't stand. He was such a stirrer, wasn't he?'

Billa is silent, thinking of the postcard, panic twisting again in her gut. 'Mmm,' she says, not wanting to talk about Tristan, bending her head over her cup lest Ed should see her expression. After a moment she gets up, picking up her coffee mug. 'I'm going to check emails,' she says.

Ed continues to drink his coffee and Bear comes to lean heavily against his chair, which shunts slowly sideways across the big rug flung down over the slate floor until Bear collapses gently to the floor. Miles Davis' trumpet fades into silence and Ed stands up, bending to blow out the candles, and begins to clear away the supper. As he sorts the plates that will go into the dishwasher from the more delicate pieces—the Spode and Clarice Cliff—he broods on Billa's preoccupation. All day she's been on edge but he knows that any kind of questioning or concern will evoke a quick denial that anything is wrong. And on those rare occasions when she shares some anxiety or fear with him she'll immediately add: 'But it's fine. It's fine, really,' hurrying away from any comfort he might offer, turning the conversation.

17

Even as a child, once their father died, she shouldered her own burdens; made her own decisions. He'd relied on her so much when they were small. Her eager, passionate vitality lent colour to his quiet, subdued personality, investing it with some of her own brilliance. She made him brave, laughing at his terrors, spurring him beyond the modest limits he set himself.

After their father died suddenly, one cold March day, she was silent with shock for weeks, her face rigid with suffering. She was just nine years old, Ed was seven, and the quality and depth of her grief frightened him, diluting his own sense of loss. He subsumed his pain, his terror of death, into focusing on the life that continued to riot heartlessly around him. The cold sweet spring: how vital and generous it was, almost profligate in its abundance. He began to notice that many of the wild flowers were yellow and for the first time—the first of many—he made a list. It became a test; a challenge. It wonderfully concentrated his mind.

Catkins—he wrote in his round childish hand—cowslips, daffodils, primroses, dandelions, buttercups, celandines, kingcups. Alongside each name he drew a picture of the flower and painted it carefully, noting nature's wide range of the colour yellow: egg-yolk, lemon, cream. Pussy willow might be a bit of a cheat, being more grey than

18

yellow, but he put it in anyway. Billa watched him, clenched in her misery.

'What are you doing?'

'It's a list of all the yellow flowers I've seen,' he said, defensively, lest it might be seen as too light-hearted an occupation under the circumstances. 'Nearly all the wild spring flowers are yellow, Billa.'

He could tell that she was trying to think of some that weren't, to prove him wrong, but even this seemed beyond her—which frightened him even more.

'What have you got so far?' she asked dully.

He read his list to her and watched while she racked her brain to think of something he'd forgotten. He willed her onward, longing for the old, vital Billa who kept him up to the mark.

'Gorse!' she cried at last, triumphantly—and he felt quite weak with relief, as though some important corner had been turned. 'And forsythia.'

She spelled it for him, and he wrote obediently, although he forbore to say that forsythia was not a wild flower but a tame garden shrub. Nevertheless, his heart beat with ungovernable joy: their roles were reversed and he'd drawn her back from the edge of the abyss. But it was Dom who really saved them from their despair.

'Dominic is a kind of relation,' their mother told them. She looked uncomfortable, as though she would rather not discuss it, but Ed and Billa had been full of the news that Mrs Tregellis's grandson had come to stay with her at her cottage down the lane.

'He's twelve,' Billa had told her, 'and he came all the way from Bristol on the train on his own. And he and Ed look alike. It's so odd. Mrs Tregellis says that we're related.'

And that's when their mother said, 'Dominic *is* a kind of relation.' Colour burned her cheeks a dull red, and her mouth compressed into a thin line, but they were too excited to notice much. The arrival of Dom distracted them from their grief and gave them something new to think about.

The sharp trill of the telephone bell cuts across Ed's thoughts. As he dries his hands and reaches for the handset the bell stops and he knows that Billa has picked up the extension. It will probably be one of her co-workers from the charity. He pours himself some more coffee and takes the Miles Davis CD from the player. He puts it away, hesitating at the shelf on which other CDs are piled, and then chooses a Dinah Washington recording.

Billa finishes her conversation with the treasurer, replaces the handset on its stand and stares at the computer screen. The small room off the kitchen is now her office. An old pine washstand is her desk and Ed's tuck box, which accompanied him to school, is her filing cabinet. She is amazingly untidy. Even Ed, who is not methodical, is silenced by the disorder of Billa's office.

'However did you manage when you were working?' he asked once, awed by the magnificence of such chaos.

'I had a PA and a secretary,' she answered briefly. 'I wasn't paid to do the filing. I was paid to have ideas about how to raise money.'

Pieces of paper, books, letters, are piled on the floor, on the desk, on the Lloyd Loom chair, on the deep granite windowsill. At intervals she has a tidying session.

'Thank heavens so much is now done by email,' she'd say, coming into the kitchen with her short fair hair on end and her shirtsleeves rolled up. 'Be a duck and make me some coffee, Ed. I'm dying of thirst.'

Now, she stares at an email about fund-raising at an event in Wadebridge and thinks about Tristan. Her first instinct is to protect Ed; her second is to talk to Dom. All her life—since her father died and her sense of security irrevocably shattered— she's turned to Dom for advice and for comfort. Even when he was working abroad in South Africa, and after he was married, she'd write to him, sharing her woes and her joys. She feels inextricably linked to him. From the beginning it was as if their father had come back to them in the form of a boy.

He built dams across the stream and a tree house high in the beech tree in the wood—though not too high because of Ed still being little—and showed them how to light a campfire and cook very basic meals. All that long summer—the summer after their father died—Dom was with them. He was tall and strong and inventive, and they recognized that look of his, the way he laughed, throwing back his head, the way he used his hands to describe something, shaping it out in the air. How safe they felt with him; just as if their father was back with them—but young again, and reckless and fun.

Their mother was cool in response to their enthusiasm—and they were too conscious of her grief to want to upset her—and, anyway, Dom preferred the cosiness of his granny's cottage and the wild countryside beyond it to the old butter factory and its grounds.

'I wonder how we'll manage now,' Billa said to Dom as they watched Ed splashing in the quiet, deep pool behind the dam. 'Without Daddy, I mean. Ed's too little to be able to be in charge yet, and Mother is . . .'

She hesitated, not knowing the right word for her instinctive awareness of their mother's neediness and dependence on others; for her emotional swings between tears and laughter; her instability.

Wood pigeons cooed comfortably amongst the high leafy canopy that dappled their camp with trembling patterns of sunlight and shade; tall foxgloves clung in the stony crevices of the old footbridge that spanned the stream where tiny fish darted in the clear brown shallows.

'My father's dead, too,' Dom said. 'I never knew him. He was in the navy in the war and he got killed when I was very small.'

And here again was another wonderful coincidence. 'Our father was in the navy, too,' she said. 'He might have been killed but he was only injured. That's why he died, though. It was the injury and then he had a heart attack. I don't know what Mother will do without him.'

She didn't mention her own overwhelming sense of loss and pain.

'My mother works,' Dom said. 'She's working now. That's why I've come on my own. She says I'm old enough now.'

'I'm glad you've come,' Billa said. 'We both are. And we're glad you're a relation.'

He looked at her then, his face serious. 'Funny, though, isn't it?' he murmured, and she felt a little shock of fear—and excitement. He was so familiar, yet a stranger. She wanted to touch him, to be close to him always.

Now, on an impulse, Billa picks up the telephone and presses buttons.

'Dominic Blake here.' Dom's voice, cool, impersonal, calms her at once.

'It's me, Dom. I was just wondering if I could come down and see you in the morning.'

'Billa. Yes, of course. Everything OK?'

'Yes. Well . . .'

'You don't sound too certain.'

'No. The thing is,' instinctively she lowers her voice, 'we've had a postcard from Tristan.'

'Tristan?'

'Yes. Weird, isn't it, after all these years?'

'What does he want?'

'That's the whole point. It just says that he might come down and see us.'

In the silence she can imagine Dom's face: that concentrated, thoughtful expression that narrows his brown eyes; his thick hair, black and grey badger-streaked like Ed's, flopping forward; his straight brows drawn into a frowning line.

'What does Ed say?'

'I haven't told him. I didn't want to worry him.'

She hears the tolerant, amused snorting sound with which Dom acknowledges her ingrained sense of responsibility for Ed's wellbeing.

'You assume there's something to worry about, then?'

'Don't you? Fifty years of silence and then a postcard. How did he know we'd both still be here?'

'What's the postmark?'

'Paris. Is Tilly with you?'

'Yes. We've just finished supper.'

'Will she be there tomorrow morning?'

'She should be gone by about ten.'

'I'll come down about eleven.'

'OK.'

Billa sighs with relief. As she puts the phone back on its rest, she can hear Dinah Washington singing 'It Could Happen to You'. She passes through the kitchen to the hall where Ed is piling logs on the fire whilst Bear lies in his favourite place across the cool slates by the front door. Billa watches them, filled with overwhelming affection for them both.

Tomorrow she will talk to Dom: all will be well.

CHAPTER TWO

D om stands still, arms folded across his chest, his face thoughtful. Tristan: Ed and Billa's stepbrother. In his mind's eye he calls up the boy's face: thin, sharp, attractive; frosty grey eyes that stare with a bland challenge. Dom was eighteen when he first met Tristan Carr and never before had he been so aware of the capacity for destruction in one so young. Even now, more than fifty years later, Dom remembers the shock of that meeting; the sensation of a fist in the guts.

He was back in Cornwall with a place at the Camborne School of Mines to study mining engineering. He felt strong and proud and free, and he couldn't wait to see Billa and Ed; especially poor Billa, who'd written to him telling him about the disaster of their mother's second marriage.

'Wait till you meet the ghastly Tris,' she wrote. 'He's utterly loathsome. I'm glad Ed and I are away at school all term. Ed'll never be able to compete with Tris. Nor will I . . .'

He wrote back, trying to comfort her, to make light of her antagonism.

'He can't be that bad, can he?' he replied. 'Didn't you say he's only ten? I'm sure you're more than a match for a ten-year-old . . .'

And now, as he walked along the lane to the old butter factory, a shadow moved beneath the ash tree and a wiry, russet-haired boy stepped out into Dom's path. This boy stared for a moment—he had to look up at Dom but that didn't faze him—and then his left eyebrow shot up and his lips quirked as though in amused recognition.

'So you're the bastard,' he said lightly.

Even now, all these years later, Dom's hands ball into fists at the recollection of that meeting. Memories hurtle back, fragmented and random: the little house in Bristol where he and his mother lived with a cousin, and how the three of them huddled beneath the kitchen table when the bombs fell. His father, James Blake, was away, they told him, he was at sea, at war—and then, he was dead. Later, there was the little school round

26

the corner and, when Dom was eight and the war was long over, there was the interview at the cathedral school. He won a scholarship, sang in the choir, grew taller. And, all the while, there was a shadowy presence of someone in the background who sent money and supported them.

'He's a relation,' his mother said evasively. 'You have relations down in Cornwall. No, not Granny. Other relations. I'll tell you when you're older.' But, in the end, it was Granny who told him.

And now the memories shift and change. He was in the potager with Billa on a hot June afternoon. With the scent of the herbs and the lavender drifting on the warm air, Granny's potager was a magical place. When her husband died in the Levant mining disaster in 1919 she was twenty-one years old. Old Matthew St Enedoc allowed her to stay in the cottage as long as she could pay the peppercorn rent, so she got a job at the old butter factory and channelled all her passion into her six-month-old daughter, Mary, and the garden at the back of the cottage.

She grew the necessary vegetables—as many as she could in her small patch—but she loved flowers and, in amongst the vegetables, she planted her favourites. Delicate sweet peas climbed amongst the pea-sticks, yellow-headed sunflowers peeped from the willow wigwams that supported runner beans, lavender grew at the edges of the narrow paths. Nasturtiums tumbled over the stone wall alongside campanula, geranium and dianthus. Between the lettuces and beetroot and chard, with its red and yellow stems, grew clumps of herbs: fennel, basil, chive, rosemary, thyme.

The young widow cherished her garden almost as passionately as she cared for her child, who trundled around beside her, falling over, chasing a butterfly, sitting down suddenly to examine a stick or a stone. The child grew, attended the little village school, became beautiful—and, all the while, the rumours of another war grumbled like distant cannon-fire. And then young Harry St Enedoc came calling. His father had died and he was their new landlord. He drove a smart shiny car and he was kind and amusing. The two women were shy to begin with and then began to relax. He drank tea in the little parlour, teased Mary and complimented her mother on the delicious cake, before continuing along the lane to the butter factory.

'He's nice,' said Mary, eyes glowing, cheeks bright as the poppies in the potager.

'Yes,' answered her mother, watching her daughter with a mix of fear and heart-aching compassion. 'A bit too nice for us, perhaps.'

But Mary wasn't listening; she twirled a strand of hair dreamily and presently wandered out into the lane . . .

But on that June afternoon eighteen years later, when he and Billa were picking peas in the potager, Granny hadn't yet told Dom this story.

Billa was angry. She talked and talked as she twisted the pea pods from their stalks, telling him that her mother was going to marry this man called Andrew and that he had a son called Tristan who would live with them and that life could never be the same again. Billa was fourteen; Dom was nearly eighteen. For five years, during the long summer holidays, she and Dom and Ed had been inseparable. Today, her barley-fair hair was snagged by the leaves and her pansy-blue eyes gleamed with tears. She looked up at him, mouth trembling, and, without considering his action, Dom put an arm around her and held her close. To his surprise—and pleasure—she flung both arms round him and clung to him.

'Whatever shall we do?' she sobbed. 'It won't be the same now, will it? Everything will be spoiled.'

He held her, comforting her, and then he saw Granny watching them from the little path. Something in her face made him disentangle himself quickly, though he treated Billa gently, bringing her on to the path where Granny took control and led Billa into the cottage.

Granny made tea, listened to Billa, and then walked with her back to the old butter factory, leaving Dom with some digging to do in the potato patch. He worked hard, driving himself in the hot sunshine, until Granny came back and told him, sitting there on the little bench amongst the scents of the potager, about young Harry St Enedoc and his fast, smart car.

She explained that Harry hadn't known, that he'd gone off to war a few months before Mary, weeping and distraught, told her mother the truth about secret meetings in the woodland along the stream—and the result that was growing in her womb. And her mother thought hard and fast about what must happen. She imagined the local talk: hot gossip licking its lips as it passed from tongue to eager tongue. She thought of her cousin Susan, in Bristol. Susan had done well for herself but she had been widowed young, and was childless, and might welcome some company during these dark days of war. So Mary was sent across the Tamar, away to Bristol, to help cousin Susan, and presently, when the news spread that Mary had found a nice young sailor called James Blake and that a child was on the way, her old friends and neighbours in Cornwall were very happy for her. And when three years later, in 1942, that nice young sailor was killed at sea, well, by then it was a very common story and people were sympathetic but not shocked or even surprised.

Dom was both. He sat on the little bench, his mind whirling with this amazing story. Granny watched him. She didn't touch him and made sure to keep her voice firm and light.

And then, she went on, Harry St Enedoc came back from the war. He'd been torpedoed twice and wasn't in very good shape but he'd got married along the way and he was now planning to convert the old butter factory. He'd asked after Mary and that was when she, Granny, had told him the truth.

She sat in silence for a moment, as if remembering the shock on Harry's face. 'Oh my God,' he'd said. 'Oh my God, I never knew. I swear I didn't, Mrs Tregellis.' And she'd believed him and made him some tea and told him about Mary and about Dom—and showed him a snapshot of his six-year-old son.

Harry hadn't doubted it or denied it. He'd stared at the snapshot and said: 'I've got a little girl. Wilhelmina. And my wife is expecting another baby.' He'd looked at her then—and he'd seemed like a child himself for all his twenty-eight years. 'I can't tell Elinor,' he'd said. 'I can't. She'd never forgive me.'

And somehow things were managed between him and Granny. When old Mr Potts in the adjoining cottage died Harry put both cottages in Granny's name in trust for Dom. He paid for school uniforms and any fees over and above Dom's scholarship, and helped however he could. But he didn't go to the little house in Bristol, and Mary and Dom only came to Cornwall when the St Enedocs were away. Granny travelled by train to see her daughter and her grandson until Harry St Enedoc died when Dom was twelve and he was considered old enough to travel to Cornwall alone on the train.

Another little silence whilst Granny watched him and Dom remembered that first visit to Cornwall on his own on the train; Billa and Ed running into Granny's kitchen to meet him, commenting on how alike he and Ed were. He sat with the sun on his back and tried to grapple with the thought that Billa was his half-sister.

'They don't know?' he said to Granny quickly. 'Billa and Ed and their mother? None of them?'

But it seemed that Mrs St Enedoc knew. When Harry died, his will made it clear but Mrs St Enedoc refused to tell her children. Even when Dom began to spend his summer holidays with Granny she continued to refuse to tell Billa and Ed, despite Granny's pleas that they should know the truth.

'But I've told her that she must tell them now,' said Granny. She stood up, pausing for a moment to pass her hand lightly over Dom's bent head. 'And if she doesn't, then I shall tell them myself.'

She went away, leaving Dom sitting with his hands clenched between his knees, trying to come to terms with such cataclysmic news, wondering what he would say to Billa.

But it was Ed who saved the day: Ed, running down the lane with Billa trailing behind him, who flung himself at Dom, shouting with delight, 'I knew it really all the time. I just knew it. You're our brother, Dom. Tris might be going to be our stepbrother but you're our *real* brother.'

Dom looked over his head to Billa, who hesitated; she looked nervous and awkward.

He thought: she's only fourteen. I must deal with this. I must be the strong one.

He grinned at her. 'It's a bit of a shock, isn't it? But Ed's right. It explains lots of odd things . . . and feelings, and why we're all so close.' And he saw her relax a little.

'Dom will sort Tris out,' said Ed eagerly. 'Tris the tick; Tris the toad. Dom will put him in his place.'

And a few months later, as Dom hurried along the lane with the good news of his place at the Camborne School of Mines, the shadows moved under the ash tree and a boy stepped out.

'So you're the bastard,' said Tris.

Now, Dom comes out of his small study into the hall and glances through the half-open door that leads to the parlour that Granny kept so neat and clean. Sitting in a deep, comfortable armchair, one foot tucked beneath her whilst the other rests on the back of Dom's golden retriever, his god-daughter Tilly is watching television. Her long, thick, fair hair is plaited and she holds the end of it, drawing it through her fingers as she watches a wildlife programme. Her father was Dom's junior assistant at Camborne twenty-five years ago, when Tilly was a baby, and it is he who phones when Tilly throws up her job at the hotel in Newquay. He and Tilly's mother have just taken up a post in

33

Canada and he asks his old friend and mentor if he will look out for his daughter.

'You know Tilly,' he says ruefully to Dom. 'She was asked to organize the place and bring it into the twenty-first century and she took them at their word. She really believed they meant it and she was so excited about it. Of course, there have been all sorts of rows and now Tilly's given in her notice. Which means she has nowhere sensible to stay and she refuses to leave Cornwall and her friends and come out to us. She's sleeping on a friend's sofa. Could you manage for a week or two? She'll get herself sorted out very quickly. She won't want to be a nuisance.'

'Tilly wouldn't know how to be a nuisance,' Dom says. 'And I'd love to have her here if she wants to come. Though she probably won't.'

But Tilly does want to; and she turns up in a rather battered little car with all her worldly possessions—including her surfboard on a roof-rack—and moves into the bedroom at the end of the cottage that once belonged to old Mr Potts. She sets up her laptop to work on her CV. She already has a part-time job with a friend who is running a private scheme—U-Connect—that helps non-computerate and elderly people in rural areas to come to terms with the internet. It's still rather experimental but Tilly is enjoying it, though she doesn't quite see it as her life's work. For three nights a week she works at a local pub.

'This is just so grim,' she says now to Dom, hearing him in the doorway but not looking round. 'These huge frigate birds have flown into the gulls' nesting site and are simply walking about eating the babies while their parents are out foraging. Poor little things; they're so helpless. I can't bear it.'

'Yes,' says Dom. 'Well, it's tough being part of the food chain.'

Tilly looks round at him, frowning. 'That is just so callous.'

He shrugs. 'What d'you want me to do about it? It's how nature works.'

She stares at him. 'Why are you grumpy?'

'I'm not grumpy.' He has no intention of telling her that he's been on an excursion to the past. 'Don't watch it if it upsets you. Like a cup of tea?'

'Yes, please,' she says, turning back to the carnage. 'Oh, look. It's the bower birds. That's much better. Don't you just love them? Isn't his bower beautiful? He looks like a really camp dress designer in his atelier.'

'If you say so.'

Dom goes out into the kitchen, followed by Bessie, and pushes the kettle on to the hob. He opens the back door and lets the dog out into the cold night. The white moon hangs like a lamp high above the mist that pours along the valley floor, rising above the stream, curling across the garden;

downstream, an owl's wavering cry echoes in the silence.

Dom leans in the doorway, waiting. A hungry vixen, her lean belly low to the frosty earth, her tail dragging, slinks along the hedgeline. She pauses, turns to look at him, then vanishes up the bank. Dom waits; the kettle behind him begins to whistle.

What does Tris want? he thinks.

Bessie reappears, tail wagging, and they both go back into the warmth and the light of the kitchen.

'But what does Tris want?' asks Billa, the next morning. 'After all these years? What can he possibly want?'

They sit together at the oak gate-leg table that belonged to Granny, in the small square room off the narrow kitchen where the French window leads into the garden. Today it is closed against the bitter chill of the February day but the sunshine picks out the colours of the cushions in a wicker chair and gleams on some pieces of china arranged behind the glass doors of an old oak wall cabinet. Bessie lies by the door, nose on paws, watching a robin pecking up the crumbs that Dom scattered earlier.

'I can think of no good reason,' answers Dom, who has been awake most of the night worrying about it. He reads the postcard again. 'I see that he doesn't use your married name. There has been no contact at all, has there, since Andrew walked out taking Tris with him?'

Billa shakes her head. 'Once the honeymoon period was over the rows began. Married bliss lasted a year, maybe two. Perhaps Andrew believed that there was much more money than there actually was, though he always seemed very well-heeled. Our father left all the shares in the company to Ed and me although, by the time he inherited, Grandfather had been quite profligate. And then there was the war. Perhaps when Andrew saw that there wasn't that much cash around he decided to get out.'

'And your mother kept everything in her own control? It was odd, wasn't it, that there was no will when she died? I remember you writing and telling me something about the will.'

They stare at each other and fear flickers between them.

'There *was* a will but it was the one she made before Daddy died. She left everything to him and, if he died first, everything was left equally to me and Ed. Our solicitor thought it was odd that she never made another will after she remarried but in the end we decided that she simply hadn't got around to it . . .'

'Or that Andrew had used his own man for their affairs after they were married?'

'There was no evidence of that,' says Billa

quickly. 'Our solicitor advertised, you know. He had to do that because there was no divorce.'

'Which was odd, too.'

'Yes, well, Mother couldn't face it and there were no real grounds . . .'

'Apart from desertion.'

'Yes, but I think she always believed he'd come back. She wouldn't face the truth and by then she was already in the first stages of that terrible depression.'

'So there might be a will leaving something to Andrew.'

She stares at him fearfully. 'But he must be long dead. He'd be, what . . . ninety at least?'

'Lots of people live beyond ninety, Billa.'

'I know that,' she cries. 'For God's sake, Dom. Are you trying to comfort me or what?'

'I'm trying to think why Tris should send you a postcard after fifty-odd years and the only thing I can think of is that his father has died and something has been found amongst his papers. Remember, I was working out in South Africa when Andrew left your mother, and by the time I came home your mother was dead and everything settled.'

'Or so we thought,' says Billa grimly. 'Oh my God. What if there was a will leaving everything to Andrew?'

'Then I suppose he would leave everything in turn to Tris. But why has there been such a long silence? If Andrew knew he was a beneficiary, wouldn't he have been keeping an ear open for what was happening down here? Perhaps they went abroad.'

She shakes her head. 'I've no idea where they went. Perhaps there wasn't a will, or perhaps she didn't leave him enough to signify. She would never have cut me or Ed right out.'

'No,' he agrees. 'No, she wouldn't have done that . . .'

But he hesitates.

'What?' she says at once. 'What are you thinking?'

'I'm just painting a worst-case scenario,' he says carefully. 'Remember your mother was crazy about Andrew to begin with. Even I can remember that much. And people in love do some very silly things. I suppose we have to be prepared to think that it's a remote possibility that she made another will under a bit of pressure from Andrew and drawn up by his solicitor. Maybe she left everything to him, trusting he'd do the right thing by you and Ed. Maybe she didn't leave him much. Maybe she assumed that once the relationship was over it didn't matter so she never revoked it. But it might be enough to bring Tristan back.'

Billa drops her head into her hands. 'So what can we do?'

Dom gives a short laugh. 'Nothing. It's pure Tris, isn't it? He's creating the smoke screens, holding all the cards. We can only sit and wait for him to show his hand. You'll have to tell Ed.'

'Yes, I know. I just wanted to talk to you first. Get it straight in my head. It was a shock.'

'Yes,' he says. 'Yes, I can see that.'

'It's odd, isn't it?' she says. 'Just the three of us again. Just like it was all those years ago when Tris arrived. I must admit that it's stirred up so many memories.'

'Me too. I was remembering those first words he said to me out in the lane. "So you're the bastard." How did he know about that? OK, Ed and I were very much alike—we still are—but he couldn't have jumped to that conclusion. He knew.'

Billa shrugs. 'But that was Tris, wasn't it? He listened at doors, he pried and poked about and read letters and cards. I expect Mother told Andrew about you once they'd agreed to get married and Tris just happened to be within earshot. We had to be so careful what we said or what we left lying around. D'you remember? And then he'd tell Andrew that we left him out of things or were being unkind to him. Oh, the joy when Andrew left and took Tris with him. It was like being let out of prison.'

'We'll have to rely on Tilly,' says Dom, trying for a lighter note. 'She'll see him off.'

'Tilly's a clever girl,' Billa says. 'I wish I'd had a Tilly working for me in London. They don't know what an opportunity they've missed, those hotel people. I hope she finds something else soon. Or that this scheme with Sarah works, although I can't quite see Tilly being satisfied with that. She'll be wonderful with the clients but she needs to be a part of a bigger canvas.'

'She's certainly not letting the grass grow. She's firing off applications and someone will give in soon out of sheer exhaustion. Meanwhile she's quite happy working with Sarah. Sarah is a very switched-on girl, too, by the sounds of it. It can't be easy, trying to get a business up and running out of a tiny cottage, whilst managing two small children, and a husband in the navy who is away at sea for most of the time. D'you want some more coffee?'

'Yes, please. No.' Billa shakes her head. 'No. I shall go back and show Ed the postcard before I lose my nerve.' She stands up, hesitates. 'But what if Tris should turn up without any more warning, Dom? It would just be his style, wouldn't it? Catching us on the back foot.'

Dom thinks about it. 'I think it's more like Tris to keep us waiting now. He'd like to imagine us wondering and worrying. And that's just what we're doing, of course.'

'That's why I wasn't going to tell Ed.'

'You must tell him. I might be wrong and Tris could walk in any minute now. Ed needs to be forewarned.'

She nods, her face downcast, and Dom gets up and gives her a hug.

'We're happy, aren't we?' she asks, holding on to him. 'Me and Ed just muddling along together and you here, with the family coming to visit in the summer holidays, and your occasional waifs and strays staying in Mr Potts' bedroom. I'm terrified that Tris could do something to spoil it. He always spoiled things. Birthdays, days out, Christmas. Somehow he always contrived to poison or destroy. Just small things, a whisper in the ear, a spiteful little joke, but enough to take away the joy. I'm afraid, Dom.'

He holds her tightly for a moment, the old rage seething in his veins as it had on that summer morning long ago.

'Let's not cross too many bridges,' he advises. 'Tell Ed, but keep it light, and we'll hope that it's just another Tris tease.'

'Yes,' she says, releasing him, resisting the urge to talk in circles. 'I won't tell him I've told you first. It'll make it seem as if I'm worried. I shall pretend it came in today's post and take it from there.'

'Too late.' Dom, leading the way into the hall, picks up some envelopes. 'Postie's been.'

'Damn,' she says. 'OK then. Well, I'll wait until tomorrow morning. It's a foreign postmark and the date's smudgy. Anyway, he's going off to do some research on his book so it's not the best time to tell him.'

He helps her into her old sheepskin duffel coat with the hood, she steps into her gumboots in the

42

hall, and he and Bessie go out with her into the lane. It's icy underfoot and she goes carefully. At the bend in the lane she turns to wave to him and, in her boots and her jeans, and the big coat with the hood covering her short fair hair, she might be the teenage Billa of fifty years ago.

Dom watches her out of sight. Suddenly, instinctively, he glances the other way, where the lane curls uphill to the village. He scans the hills across the valley. Some sixth sense tells him that Tris is already here; watching.

CHAPTER THREE

Tilly drives through the deep, precipitous lanes that twist and turn, and dive and climb around the edge of the moor. There are milk-white snowdrops under the thorn hedges and glimpses of gold: the first daffodils. She pulls into a gateway, to make room for a tractor coming towards her, and sees a huddle of lambs beneath the spreading branches of a huge fir. The sunlight slices down, sharp and bright, but frost rimes the brittle grass in the black shadows of the ditch and the rutted verges are frozen and icy. As the lane tips down into the village she can see the rooks swirling like cinders in the cold blue air, their nests tossed high in the beech trees: spiky black balls caught by bare bony fingers.

Tilly parks in the small cul-de-sac near the church and takes out her iPhone to check her notes.

Mrs Anderson: widowed last year. Only daughter now lives in New Zealand with her husband—a New Zealander—and their two children. Wants to be shown how to Skype. Rather nervy and diffident.

Tilly glances at the neat little bungalow with its neat little garden. A figure stands at the window watching Tilly, who waves cheerfully as she climbs out of the car. The figure disappears, the door opens and Mrs Anderson is revealed. She is as neat as the bungalow and the garden, and the room into which she shows Tilly is achingly tidy. Mrs Anderson is talking rapidly, explaining how she's never understood computers, how her husband dealt with all that sort of thing, but now, with her daughter and the grandchildren so far away . . .

Tilly listens and nods sympathetically, and her heart is riven with the unspoken loneliness that reveals itself in Mrs Anderson's bleak eyes and in her hands that twist and twist. There are photographs everywhere: a wedding group, a beaming young couple with two small children, a much older man with the same two children, a bride displaying a set of rather prominent teeth in a happy grin, the two children again, in school uniform.

'I never thought they'd go,' she's saying, 'not with the children settled so well here at school, but there's such opportunity out there, isn't there? And then my Donald died last year just before Christmas. Three months to live when the cancer was diagnosed.'

Her eyes are bright with pain, she is brittle with suppressed grief, and Tilly longs to put her arms around her.

'They've been going on about this Skype,' she's saying, 'and Donald always meant to do it, so when I saw your advert in the local paper I made up my mind to have a go.'

Her brave smile is heart-breaking and Tilly smiles back at her.

'It's really easy,' she says reassuringly. 'Honestly. And it'll be lovely to be able to see them when you talk. Much better than the telephone, and calls are free. It helps to keep more closely in touch as the children grow. And they'll love to see Granny. Do they call you Granny or Grandma?'

Quite without warning, Mrs Anderson's eyes brim with tears which overflow and stream down her thin cheeks. Tilly stands still for a moment, biting her lips.

'Don't hug the clients,' Sarah has warned. 'I know you, Tilly; you'll get yourself into trouble and waste hours. No, I'm not unfeeling, I'm just being rational. It'll take you all day if you start doing the tea and sympathy stuff. There are some very lonely people out there.'

Sarah's voice is very clear and loud in Tilly's head as she puts an arm around Mrs Anderson's bony shoulder and holds her tightly. Mrs Anderson rests her head against Tilly and cries in earnest.

'Life,' says Tilly, staring at the photographs, 'is absolute hell, isn't it?'

'Don't forget,' says Sarah, 'that the clients pay us on an hourly rate.'

She is a small, dark girl: had been head of house, head of school, a demon on the lacrosse field. The baby, George, is slung across her shoulder as she prepares some lunch for herself and Tilly.

'I know,' says Tilly, unmoved by Sarah's fierceness. 'But Mrs Anderson is a slow learner. Poor old duck.'

'And I know what that means,' says Sarah, resigned, slotting George into his bouncy chair. 'You are hopeless, Tilly.'

'How's Dave?' asks Tilly, stroking George's cheek. 'When's he getting some more leave?'

'The ship's due back in three weeks,' says Sarah, ladling soup into bowls, allowing herself to be distracted from Tilly's weakness of character. 'He'll be home for a bit then. Not actually on leave but around. D'you want a sandwich?'

Tilly shakes her head. 'Soup's fine.' She feels more comfortable in the cheerful disorder of Sarah's kitchen than in Mrs Anderson's tidy bungalow. 'So how are we doing? Any new punters?'

'A very posh new punter,' says Sarah, sitting down at the table, pushing a wholemeal loaf on its wooden board towards Tilly. 'Sir Alec Bancroft, no less. Retired diplomat. He lives down in the village and he's a friend of my mum. He wants to organize a database for all his contacts. Hundreds of them, by the sound of it. Quite a few people wanting to learn how to send emails. Someone else is keen to do her shopping by internet.'

'Gosh!' says Tilly. 'By next week we could be millionaires.'

'Not,' says Sarah, repressively, 'if we spend hours with people because they're lonely. Time is money. After lunch we'll look at the diary.'

George squeaks plaintively and Tilly leans to tickle his cheek with the end of her thick butter-yellow plait.

But it's *my* time, she thinks. And I can afford it at the moment.

She remembers Mrs Anderson in the painfully tidy little room, staring with eager intensity at the computer screen.

'Now you simply need to let your daughter know when you're going online. Try to have a regular time each week for it. Factor in the time difference . . .'

Tilly sits up straight, cuts herself some bread, grins at Sarah.

'I'm really hoping this is going to work,' she says. 'I can't sponge off Dom for ever. Though I have to say that, after your sofa, Mr Potts' bedroom is positively luxurious.'

'And you're still pulling pints at the pub?'

'Three nights a week. Is there any more soup?'

'Help yourself.' Sarah pulls an A4 notepad towards her. 'You're keeping a record of your petrol costs, aren't you? That's our major outgoing. The ad was worth it, though. There's been a good response.'

Tilly sits down at the table and they lean together, looking at the notes on Sarah's pad, whilst George sleeps peacefully in his chair. The telephone rings and Sarah leaps up to answer it. She makes a thumbs up sign at Tilly and begins to make notes: another client.

'Did you get my message about Mrs Probus?' she asks when she sits down again. 'Her son says that she still hasn't quite grasped the finer points of emailing and isn't answering his messages. I said you'd be there about half past two.'

'She's an old darling,' says Tilly, 'but she simply isn't part of this brave new IT world. He's bought her this lovely new laptop and she's frightened to death of it. She's got about fourteen cats and she seems curiously unmoved about being unable to receive messages from her son. OK. I'll go and see what I can do.'

• • •

'Tedn't nat'ral,' says old Mrs Probus stubbornly. 'And I weren't never no good at spellin'.'

Each chair in the over-crowded living-room of Mrs Probus' small council flat is occupied by several cats. They lounge languidly, watching Tilly with indifference. A few prowl, rubbing against Mrs Probus' hair-covered trackies, opening their mouths in tiny mewling cries.

'The spelling isn't important,' says Tilly. 'Your son wants to hear from you. Of course he does. He wants to know you're OK. And you like to hear from him, don't you? Look, he's left you three messages. You haven't read any of them.'

Three or four cats circle them, tails waving, whilst Mrs Probus stares frowningly at the screen, peering at the messages, reading each one slowly.

''E don't say nort,' she mutters at last. 'Could've phoned.'

'It's quicker,' says Tilly coaxingly, scooping up a persistent tabby and stroking it. 'He can just log in and dash off a quick message to you and be back at work a minute or two later. If he telephoned it would take much longer. And anyway, when he arranged these sessions he told us that you don't always answer the phone.'

Mrs Probus looks at Tilly mischievously. 'It do depend on when he do phone, doan't it? Might be watching *Emmerdale*. Or *Flog It*. Never mind they ole messages, my 'ansome. Shall us 'ave a cuppa?'

49

Tilly wonders for how much longer she can breathe the pungent, cat-laden air, but grins back at her.

'Go on then,' she says. 'But don't you tell my boss.'

She phones Sarah from the car where she sits with the window down, gulping cold fresh air.

'Hopeless,' Tilly says. 'You're going to have to tell her son that she is email resistant and he might be wasting his money. I don't mind trying, but he needs to know. We sent him a message and I'm sure she's grasped it—she's not stupid—but her heart isn't in it.'

'He's feeling guilty,' says Sarah. 'He and his wife have divorced and she's moved down near Penzance. The kids have grown up and left home and he does this long-distance lorry driving and wants to keep an eye on his old mum while he's away.'

Tilly laughs. 'I don't think his old mum wants an eye kept on her. She's perfectly happy with her cats and the telly.'

'Very ungrateful,' says Sarah. 'I'm off to do the school run. Ben's bringing a friend home for tea.'

'OK. I shall head for home after the next appointment. It's pub night. See you tomorrow.'

Tilly drives home through the lanes, wondering if Sarah's venture will eventually make enough money to support both of them. It's fun helping her to get U-Connect up and running, and they've both been surprised by the level of the response to their advertising campaign, but can it provide enough money for two people? And does she want to commit totally to it? She prefers to work with a team of people, bouncing ideas off one another, but such jobs are very thin on the ground. She's been offered more work at the pub. It has an annexe with two self-contained holiday flats and the girl who does the changeover cleaning on Saturday mornings is leaving. The extra money will be very useful whilst things aren't going quite according to plan, though there aren't many holiday-makers around at the moment.

Tilly makes a face; her mother is not pleased with her for throwing up her job at the Newquay hotel though she knows that Dad is more sympathetic.

'Your mum just wants to know that you're in a secure place,' he told her when she Skyped to tell them that she'd given in her notice. 'She worries about you. We're a long way off and you're our only chick. Oh, I know you've got lots of friends and that you always get a job somewhere, but we really hoped that this was going to work for you.'

'So did I,' protested Tilly. 'I really did. They said they wanted the hotel to be brought right up to date and it was going to be such an exciting project. But they blocked me at every turn. Every suggestion, anything new or fresh was rubbished. They just want a yes man to take the flak. I can't tell you how frustrating it was, Dad.'

'I know, but look, Tills, you can't sleep on Sarah's sofa for ever. Go and see Dom. He'd love to have you there until you get sorted. Promise you'll go and see him. Mum'll feel happier if you've got somewhere sensible to stay.'

Despite her protestations that she is quite capable of looking after herself, Tilly is very happy to be with Dom. It was fun at first to stay with Sarah and the boys, and listen to her plans for U-Connect, but not so good once Dave was due home on leave. Anyway, she loves Dom and likes being with him: he's laid-back and detached, in a good way. And she loves Ed and Billa, too, and the old butter factory. It's such a romantic story, the way they're all related, and she's known them for ever, so it's like they're her family. It's sad for Dom and Ed and Billa that both Dom's girls have settled in South Africa, in Johannesburg, where Dom met and married their mother, Griet.

'It's odd, isn't it?' Tilly once said to Billa. 'That Dom should stay here now he's retired and Griet's dead. You'd think he'd want to be near his family.'

'Dom's a Cornishman,' Billa answered. 'He's a St Enedoc. We're his family, too. We wanted him to change his name once we knew who he really was but he was too stubborn. He's moved around the world so much with his engineering work, but there's nowhere like Cornwall as far as he's concerned. Harry's just like him. He's a true St Enedoc, young Harry.'

Tilly agrees with this. She is extremely fond of Dom's youngest grandchild—the only grandson—who comes to stay with Dom whenever he can and loves to surf and sail.

She parks beside the old shed, which Dom uses as a garage, and gets out. A path leads between lilac and hydrangea bushes to the back door where Dom is kicking off his boots. Bessie greets Tilly with delight, and she puts down her bag and bends to kiss her on the nose.

'Can you smell cat?' she asks her.

'Good day?' asks Dom. 'Lots of punters requiring your skills?'

He dusts crumbly earth from his dark green corduroy trousers, which are tucked into thick socks, and follows her into the cottage.

'Pretty good, actually,' she says. 'But is it to be my life's work? That's what we want to know, isn't it, Bessie?'

Bessie wags her tail enthusiastically.

'The question is,' says Dom, 'whether there will be enough work for you and Sarah to be able to take a decent salary each. And what happens when she moves nearer to Plymouth? The cottage is only a temporary long-stop, isn't it?'

'It's her mum's second home. When Dave was posted down from Portsmouth they got a rented house set up near Plymouth, on the edge of Dartmoor, and then the owners changed their minds at the last minute. George was due, so they decided to go into the cottage until they had time to look around for a house nearer to the dockyard. I think that's on the cards for Dave's next leave.'

'And when they go?'

'We've talked about that. We don't have the sort of client base that is going to keep coming back. Most of the things we're doing are very short term—learning to Skype or email—and we'll have plenty of notice when Sarah goes. This was a kind of trial run to test the water. The point is that she can do this wherever she is.'

'And what about you?'

'Ah,' says Tilly. 'Yes, well, the thing is that even if Sarah moves away I could carry on once we've got it all set up. If I want to.'

She smiles at Dom's expression: it's clear that Dom doesn't believe that she'll want to.

'I don't see you as a solo operator,' he says. 'You like people around you.'

She nods. This is quite true; she is certainly happier working with a team.

'I suppose I am working with people. Going to see people like Mrs Anderson and Mrs Probus.'

'It's not the same,' he says. 'Those are your clients. You can't kick ideas about with them or let off steam.'

'I know,' she answers. 'The point is that I'm

helping Sarah to get started and earning a bit along the way. She's slightly hamstrung with George so I can be useful there. If something else comes up that's irresistible then I'll go for it. She knows the score. Meanwhile I've got some extra work at the pub. Changeovers on Saturday mornings.'

Dom fills the kettle. 'I suppose there aren't many holiday-makers around at the moment though, are there? No strangers around?'

She glances at him, puzzled by the phrasing of his question. 'There are always couples having a weekend away, even in February. Or the occasional twitcher. Or really dedicated walkers. The Chough's been very popular ever since Giles Coren stayed there and did that rave review.' She glances at her watch. It takes nearly twenty minutes to drive to the pub. 'I'm going to have to get a move on but, yes, please, I'd love a cup of tea when I've changed.'

By eight o'clock the small bar is humming with laughter and conversation. Tilly pauses in her glass-collecting round of the tables and stoops to put another log on the fire in the big granite inglenook. A man is sitting alone at the small table in the corner and he smiles at her as the logs catch into flame and the sparks dance up in the sooty cavern of the huge chimney. He looks slightly unusual, slightly foreign. His deeply scored skin is tanned a pale brown, which sits oddly with his russet-grey thickly curling hair. He wears a black rollneck—cashmere, she judges—and black moleskins quite tightly cut. Resting beside his chair is a bag, a kind of soft leather satchel on a long strap, which is hooked around the arm of the chair. It is an unusual kind of bag for a man to have in Cornwall—more of a London fashion—and she wonders if he is a writer or a musician. She guesses that he's in his late fifties, early sixties, but he looks lean and tough and a bit edgy. He might be French or Italian but when he speaks he sounds English enough, though she can barely hear his voice above the noise in the bar.

'Jolly cold tonight,' he says. 'We certainly need the fire.'

She smiles at him, nodding, and he smiles back and she notices that his eyes are a bright frosty grey. Suddenly she remembers Dom asking, 'Any strangers around?' and then someone calls her name and she forgets all about it.

Later, when she glances across to the table beside the fire, the chair is empty and the man is gone.

CHAPTER FOUR

Ed sits at his desk, checking his notes, comfortable and happy in this room, which was his father's study. Here, Harry St Enedoc's presence can still be felt; here he gathered around him all he treasured most that would not be missed in the town house in Truro. His bookcase full of first editions of modern writers, the paintings by local artists that he valued, a little glass-fronted silk-lined cabinet with its three shelves of netsukes, the small tray containing six exquisite miniatures of his ancestors were all placed carefully in this room.

It was here Ed went as a child to grieve for his father; here he tried to recapture those magical afternoons when the two of them shared a private world. Together they looked at the miniatures and Ed would listen again to the stories of each delicately painted face, each history so familiar, yet never stale however often he heard it. He'd stare at his great—many greats—grandparents and their two daughters and two sons, proud that he so closely resembled the younger son. Sitting with his father in the big armchair he listened to readings from some of the books—Conan Doyle was a favourite, John Buchan another—and was allowed to handle some of the netsukes, those tiny, perfect carvings that were like toys, and make up stories and games around them. These were his own special times with his father, which his mother and Billa never interrupted.

After his father died Ed continued to go to the study. He sat at the desk in his father's chair and worked as his father had worked before him, channelling his grief and fear into things that could be contained, understood. He made lists, and painted flowers and birds and checked them against the pictures in the encyclopaedias and reference books just as his father had shown him. Glancing up from time to time, certain that his father was just there by the bookshelf, waiting for the comforting hand on his shoulder and the warm breath on his cheek, Ed used all that his father had taught him to come to terms with the terrible finality of death. Everything that represented security was here, in this small room, and whilst that remained intact he could manage. Since all business and family matters were handled from Truro, the study remained a deeply personal and private room that slowly became Ed's domain . . . until the arrival of Andrew and Tris.

'We'll have to clear out the study so that Tris can have his own room,' their mother said in that bright voice that she'd begun to use whenever Andrew and Tris were mentioned. It was a voice that implied that things were going to be such fun, and that Ed and Billa must surely be anticipating it with as much pleasure as she was. They'd met Andrew and Tris, now, and the meeting had not been a particularly happy one. Andrew was confident, proprietorial with their mother, who was so nervous that it seemed she might shatter with the strain of it all. Billa spoke only when required and looked awkward; Ed was afraid to appear disloyal to his sister, and to his father's memory, and felt deeply uncomfortable. Only Tris was at ease. He stared coolly at his putative stepbrother and -sister, stepping forward obediently to shake hands on his father's instruction, but his look was amused, calculating.

'Just you wait,' that look seemed to say.

And they don't have to wait long.

'We'll have to clear out the study,' said their mother a few days after this meeting, 'so that Tris can have his own room,' and now, at last, Ed joined the battle in which Billa had enlisted weeks before.

'No,' he said. 'No. You can't.'

They both turned to look at him: his mother with anxiety, Billa with surprise. Ed didn't care. He thought about the study; the watercolour paintings, the John Smart miniatures, the netsukes and the books. In the five years since his father died he had added his own treasures: his paints, his books, his model warships. The study was not a big room—it had been the smallest of all the bedrooms—but it was his and he would fight for it.

'But, darling,' his mother began, half-laughingly so that he would see that he was being rather silly—Ed was always reasonable, and malleable—'Tris has to have a bedroom, doesn't he? You can have some of the things in your own room and some can go down to the drawing-room.'

'No,' said Ed again.

It was the room itself, not just the things in it, that mattered. It was there that he and his father talked, read, painted; his shade was there, looking up from the desk, smiling a welcome; standing beside the table where the miniatures sat in their little glass-covered tray, pointing to each one in turn; reaching down a book from the bookshelf: 'So what shall it be today?'

'You can't do that,' said twelve-year-old Ed. 'It's Father's room as well as mine. It's all that's left of him.'

He was tall for twelve, and his resemblance to his father was startling, but he was unaware of the effect he had on his mother. She felt disloyal, belittled, frightened. He could have no idea of the fear that made her heart beat fast as she contemplated the battles yet to come. Still, she was in love and she would fight for her happiness as Ed would for his father's study.

'Then,' she said coldly, 'Tris will have to share your bedroom.'

She waited for the cry of protest, capitulation—even Billa was silent—but Ed stared back at her.

'Very well,' he said. 'We'll share.'

'How can you?' Billa demanded later. 'How can you bear to share with him?'

Ed was silent. During that meeting, once the two adults had left the children to 'get to know each other', Tris's well-behaved mask had slipped a little.

60

'Have you got a bike?' he asked Ed.

Ed nodded. His Raleigh bike—drop handlebars, three-speed—was still very new, a present for his birthday a few weeks earlier.

'Yes,' he answered, 'but I'm tall for my age so it'll be a bit big for you.'

'I'll manage,' said Tris cockily. His light, frosty eyes challenged Ed: summed him up. 'Where is it?'

Silently Ed led him to the garage his father had converted out of old outbuildings. Billa followed them, glancing back towards the house and wondering if they were being watched. The wooden doors were open. Mother's Morris Minor Traveller was inside and Andrew's new Ford Consul drophead coupé stood behind it. It looked rather flashy and self-conscious beside the station wagon. Carefully Ed wheeled his bicycle out and stood holding it, feeling awkward, not knowing quite what to say. Tris, though wiry and tough, was not very tall and the bike looked much too big for him. Nevertheless he took hold of the handlebars, pushing it further out on to the driveway. Ed let go reluctantly and watched as Tris put his foot experimentally on the pedal and then suddenly pushed off. He didn't attempt to sit in the saddle, he simply pedalled, hell for leather down the drive, and out into the lane.

Ed and Billa raced after him. When they reached the lane they saw him still pedalling ahead of them and as he reached the bend they saw him jump from the bike, leaving it to wobble and crash, wheels spinning. Ed cried out in dismay, running to pick it up, checking for scratches and damage, whilst Tris stood watching, grinning from the verge.

'Why did you do that?' cried Billa in a rage. 'Why do such a stupid thing?'

'Do what?' asked Tris. 'I fell off. You shouldn't have dared me to ride it. It's too big for me.'

They both stared at him in silent amazement.

'Dare you?' repeated Ed at last. 'We did no such thing. I warned you not to ride it.'

'Prove it,' said Tris. 'I've hurt my ankle now. Dad said you'd look out for me, seeing that I'm the youngest. He won't be very pleased.'

He turned and began to limp back towards the old butter factory.

'But he didn't hurt himself,' said Ed apprehensively, watching him go, holding his bike. 'He jumped clear. We saw him. He wasn't limping then.'

'No,' said Billa. 'But he is now, the little tick. Come on. Is it OK?'

Ed checked his bike again. There was no real damage apart from a few scratches to the front mudguard. He looked at them distressed, running his finger over them, and then wheeled the bike back along the lane, hurrying to keep up with Billa. When they came into the kitchen they saw Tris perching on the edge of the big slate table, holding an apple, whilst their mother massaged his ankle and his father turned to stare at them with those same light, frosty eyes. He had a lean, tough build and there was an almost menacing air in his quick movement.

'Not very clever,' he said sharply. 'Daring a much smaller boy to ride a bicycle several times too big for him.'

'Oh, don't blame Ed, Dad,' Tris said. 'I needn't have done it. And I'm fine. Really I am.' And he took a big bite out of the apple and smiled sweetly at Ed and Billa over his bulging cheek.

'That's a good boy,' said their mother, putting Tris's sock back on to his thin, narrow white foot, and touching his russet hair lightly. 'No harm done.' She looked mortified, hardly glancing at Ed or Billa, her lips pressed tightly together as she turned away.

'Well,' said Andrew, 'boys will be boys, I suppose. And we ought to be getting back to Bristol. How about a cup of tea before we set off, Elinor?'

'How can you possibly share a room with him?' demanded Billa later. 'How can you bear it? Thank God I'm a girl and he can't share with me.'

'It's better than him having Daddy's study,' said Ed. 'I'll manage somehow.'

Now, as he looks around him at his father's beloved possessions, Ed's mind is still so full of that scene that he is hardly surprised when Billa opens the door with some letters in her hand and says: 'The post has just come and, guess what, there's a postcard from Tris.'

He stares at the card, at the cyclist in his blue jersey and shorts bending over the drop handle-bars, and his stomach gives a little lurch.

'But what does he want?' he asks.

'I don't know,' she answers, watching him. 'I've made coffee. Come down and have some.'

Following her out on to the landing and down the stairs, Ed is filled with apprehension.

'But why should he care how we are? Why should he want to see us?'

She has put the coffee on the old carved sea chest they use as a table, in front of the hall fire. Bear comes padding out of the kitchen to see if there's anything going and Billa gives him a small tasty treat, which he crunches with evident enjoyment. He licks his chops and settles down at some distance from the fire.

'I was remembering,' Ed says, 'just then, when you came in. I was remembering the first time we ever met him and how he rode my bike.' He holds out the card. 'Do you remember?'

'I remember everything,' says Billa bitterly, 'though I hadn't made the connection with your bike. That was the first sortie, wasn't it, and Mother was always on his side. She was so obsessed with Andrew that Tris could do no wrong. It was so bloody unfair.'

Ed watches her. Her sudden anger reminds him of those miserable days and how their lives were turned upside down.

'Thank God we were away at school,' he says. He puts the postcard down on the chest and they both read it.

'A blast from the past. How are you doing? Perhaps I should pay a visit and find out!'

'We can simply refuse,' says Ed. 'If he phones we'll just say no.'

'*If* he phones,' says Billa. 'He might just turn up.'

'Even so,' says Ed, 'we don't have to ask him in. He has no rights here.'

Billa is silent for so long that he glances up at her; her face is preoccupied, almost grim.

'What?' he says.

She shakes her head. 'Nothing. Drink your coffee.'

'I expect it's just one of his silly teases,' says Ed hopefully, but he can see that Billa doesn't accept this suggestion. He thinks of how his mother's second marriage altered his life; of how much he missed his father, and of how he began to fear change; to cling to what was safe and known. He thinks of the odd longing to write and illustrate books for children—magical, enchanting books—which he has always denied for fear of being perceived as inadequate; a laughing stock. He drinks his coffee, which tastes as bitter as missed opportunities, and an old, familiar anxiety settles around him, chill as a damp cloak.

CHAPTER FIVE

S ir Alec's house is a warren of small rooms and unexpected staircases. He comes to meet Tilly at the front door, which opens directly on to the precipitous village street, and takes her into the first of the small rooms. An elderly yellow Labrador rises creakily from a beanbag to greet her and she stops to smooth the broad head and murmur to him. His tail wags rhythmically, gratefully, and Sir Alec smiles approvingly.

'I see that you speak dog,' he says. 'That's splendid. Poor Hercules loves to have visitors. He misses my wife dreadfully.'

Tilly has already been briefed.

'Sir Alec's wife died quite suddenly last year,' Sarah said. 'I've already been to see him since he's just down in the village and he's an absolute duck in a right old mess, despite the fact that he has a cleaner who goes in twice a week. Remember that you're there simply to set up a database for all his contacts. His wife used to do the Christmas card list and it came as a terrible shock to him so he wants to mechanize the addressing system. You're not there to tidy up, Tilly. The database will take ages as it is. He's got hundreds of friends all over the world and he stays in touch with all of them.'

When Sir Alec leads her through into his study

Tilly takes a breath: it is almost as untidy as Billa's office. There are piles of newspapers, towers of books, heaps of letters.

'I know,' he says, glancing at her apprehensively, pulling a humorous face. 'Pretty chaotic, isn't it? Shall we manage, d'you think?'

'Of course we shall manage,' she replies warmly. 'And look at that view.'

The long sash window looks out across the uneven, grey slate roofscape of the village to the coast. Beyond the cliffs, curving away to the west, the sea surges in, strong and muscular, smashing itself against the steep granite walls and pinnacles of rock. A fishing boat, plunging in the swell, chugs on its course for Padstow with a cloud of seagulls screaming in its wake.

'It's glorious, isn't it?' He comes to stand beside her at the window. 'Very distracting when I'm trying to work.'

He looks at her. Tilly sees they are much the same height but his erect military bearing makes him seem taller, gives him a presence, and his eyes are friendly.

'Sarah was rather shocked by the state of the room. She was very polite but I could tell. She said I might find it easier if I were more organized.'

Tilly gives a snort of amusement. 'I do rather see her point.'

'It comes of having secretaries, d'you see? I've been spoiled. Always someone keeping you up to the mark, reminding you, tidying up after you. And Rose, bless her, was wonderful.' He sighs, not self-pityingly, just in remembrance of things past. 'Do you know our curate, Clem Pardoe?'

Tilly is taken aback by this apparent change of subject. 'I don't think so.'

'Ah, splendid fellow, Clem. Wonderful with Rose at the end. He still comes to see me just to keep me on my toes. Or perhaps I should say on my knees. It was he who showed me your advertisement. He used to be in IT in London, d'you see? "This is what you need," he said. "Phone them up and make an appointment." So I did.'

'Well, let's make a start,' says Tilly, turning away from the window and bracing herself at the prospect before her. 'Sarah tells me you have a very big address book.'

He chuckles. 'We lived abroad for most of our lives. Made lots of friends and I like to stay in touch.'

'We did, too,' says Tilly. 'Still do. My father's a mining engineer. He and Mum are in Canada.'

'I expect you miss them.'

'Yes, but I'm used to it. I was at school here and I've got lots of friends in Cornwall.'

'Like Sarah? She said that you were at school together.'

'Yes, although actually it was her sister that was my best friend. Sarah's older than I am but she always looked out for me and I often went home with them for exeats if it was too far to travel for Mum just for a weekend.'

'And where do you live now?'

'I'm staying with my godfather, Dominic Blake. He was my father's boss for a while down at Camborne and he's putting me up until I find another job.'

'Isn't this your job?'

'It's one of them. We've got a bit of a way to go yet before it's up and running properly.' She makes a little face. 'Perhaps it's a bit ambitious to think that it might work at all.'

' "Ah, but a man's reach should exceed his grasp, Or what's a heaven for?" ' exclaims Sir Alec.

Tilly stares at him. 'Sorry?'

He smiles. 'Browning,' he says. 'Nobody reads him nowadays. Never mind. Let's get down to work.'

'He told me all about the curate and then quoted Browning,' Tilly says to Sarah later. 'I utterly love him.'

Sarah rolls her eyes. 'And talking of the curate,' she says, 'I've had a phone call from the convent.'

'The convent?'

'Chi-Meur. Well, it's a retreat house now but there is still an Anglican community of Sisters, just three or four of them, but hanging on. Anyway, the retreat house needs someone to organize a new website.'

'It seems a bit odd. A website for a convent.'

'It's not for the convent. It's for the retreat house, to encourage people to come and stay. You'd have to talk to them to find out exactly what they'd need and what they offer. Quiet days, courses, that kind of thing. The administrator is secular so you won't actually be dealing with the nuns. I can do it, if you like.'

'No.' Tilly shakes her head. 'I'll be fine. I'm good with the nutters.'

Sarah is best with small businesses: builders in a muddle with their filing, decorators confused with their accounting, garages needing a system to deal with their VAT returns. She is efficient, firm and—though she fears that Tilly will be inclined to waste time with their clients—Sarah knows that Tilly is the best one to deal with people like Mrs Probus and Sir Alec. They make a good team.

'You shouldn't call them nutters,' says Sarah reprovingly.

'Yes, but I mean it in a good way,' protests Tilly. 'I like nutters.'

When she gets back, she parks the car and, on an impulse, walks up to the old butter factory, looking for Billa. She's very fond of Billa. The older woman's toughness, her dry sense of humour, her deep attachment to Ed and Dom; all these qualities make her very attractive. She talks to Tilly with a directness that the younger woman appreciates.

The late afternoon glimmers with primrose light, green and palest gold, and she can hear a strange chorus: hoarse, rasping, resonant. On an impulse she walks round the end of the house and along the path beside the stream. The lake is full of clouds and, at the water's edge, all among the clouds, are the frogs. Scrambling, crawling, brown-blue bodies in shiny mounds and oily heaps, they clasp each other, singing. The cloud reflections break and reform as the ripples disturb them, spreading across the lake, drifting away into the shadows beneath the willows.

In the new woodland along the stream, where Ed has planted beech and spindle trees, bluebells and daffodils, Tilly sees Billa wandering slowly towards her with Bear following at her heels. Billa's head is bowed, her arms are folded beneath her breast as if she is holding herself together, and—even at this distance—Tilly can see that she is deep in thought. Bear pauses to examine an interesting scent and follows it away from the stream, jogging quietly on its track, nose to ground. Suddenly a hen pheasant breaks cover from a patch of dead, brittle bracken; she runs squawking ahead of him and then rockets upwards, wings threshing, soaring to safety in the fields beyond.

Billa turns to watch, disturbed by the sudden commotion, and sees Tilly who waves and hurries to join her. Billa raises her hand in response and then puts both hands in the pockets of her sheepskin duffel coat, straightening her shoulders as though she is trying to relax.

'I heard the frogs,' Tilly says, hoping she isn't intruding on some important train of thought, 'and couldn't resist coming to see them. There are going to be millions of jelly babies. I used to love coming here when I was little and taking them off in jam jars.'

'Ed still does,' says Billa wryly. 'He's doing his bit to save the planet. Last year, when we had all that freezing weather, he put lots of them into his tadpolarium, those big plastic containers, and then released them when they'd grown legs and were big enough to withstand the cold or the likelihood of being eaten by birds. You'll be able to help him.'

Tilly bursts out laughing. 'I think that's brilliant. Does it really work?'

Billa shrugs. 'Who can tell? There seems to be even more than usual this year, so I assume it did.'

Bear comes up behind and overtakes them, disturbing the frogs who dive into the clouded depths in a gelatinous swirl of mud. He pauses to watch them and Billa calls to him.

'No swimming today, Bear. Too cold, and you'll frighten the frogs. Come on.'

He turns rather reluctantly and pads on huge

paws towards the house; with his lazy, sinuous swagger he looks just like the brown bear for which he was named.

'I've had an email from this friend in London,' Tilly says, 'saying that she can recommend me to her boss for a job and I can't decide whether to go for it.'

'What's the job?'

Tilly makes a face. 'IT. Corporate. All among the suits. I've done it and I know it's not really what I want but I can't decide if I ought to try it.'

'Why "ought"?'

'Well, it's very nice of Dom to let me use Mr Potts' bedroom but I feel I'm kind of sponging.'

'Do you pay anything?' asks Billa in her direct way.

Tilly shakes her head. 'He won't let me, but I buy food and wine and stuff. Of course, Dad's asked him to look out for me.'

'Does that bother you?'

'Not really. Dom doesn't patronize me. He sees what I'm trying to do and he respects it. He says he likes having company and someone doing his ironing. Actually, I'm loving it. The thing is, Dom treats me like I'm a friend who's got a problem and he's just helping out. He isn't fatherly.'

'And how is it going with Sarah?'

'Pretty good. The advertisement is getting a really positive response, but it's difficult to fore-tell the future and I suppose that now jobs are so thin on the ground I ought to go for the one in London.'

'Even though you don't want to do it and it's not where you want to be?'

'You don't think, then, that it would be a responsible thing to do?'

Billa smiles at the expression on Tilly's anxious face. 'If you had a family to support I might give you a different answer. Right now I think you can afford to give U-Connect a chance so as to help Sarah out while you're waiting for what you really want to come up. You're lucky to have Dom but he's lucky to have you, too, so it cuts both ways. And you're still working at the pub?'

Tilly nods. 'I've been offered a few extra hours a week on Saturday mornings and I've got some money saved, which helps keep the car on the road, but I really just want to be certain that Dom isn't feeling . . . you know . . . pressured.'

'Dom's loving it. My advice is stick with it, stay positive about U-Connect, but don't be distracted from what you really want to do. In a way, the hotel job was ideal for you. You relish a challenge, the opportunity to work with people. Don't go for second best because it didn't work out. Keep watching for the right opening and, meanwhile, I think it's great that you and Sarah are making a success of U-Connect. It's always good to strive for something.'

' "A man's reach should exceed his grasp"?'

Billa raises her eyebrows and draws down the corners of her mouth. 'Browning? I'm impressed.'

Tilly laughs. 'There was another bit but I've forgotten it. Sir Alec said it. You'd really like Sir Alec, Billa. Ex-diplomat. He's lovely. Shall I introduce you?'

'I'm not above meeting lovely men. I imagine this is one of your clients?'

'I'm doing a database for him. He's a bit up the creek now that his wife has died and he needs some organizing. He lives in Peneglos. You know? Where Sarah is.'

'I don't know the village. It's a bit off our radar over on the coast there. But yes, bring him to tea. We can show him the tadpoles. Ed'll love it.'

'I might just do that. He and Ed would get on brilliantly. Piles of books everywhere.'

'How old is he?' asks Billa, suddenly suspicious.

'About the same age as Dom,' says Tilly evasively. 'Probably a bit older, but you don't think about his age when you're with him. He's really fun. A wonderful voice and nice twinkly eyes.'

'Hmm,' says Billa. 'A lovely man with a wonderful voice and twinkly eyes. Can't wait. Got his phone number?'

'Customer confidentiality,' says Tilly primly. 'You'll have to contain your excitement.'

They part at the door and Tilly walks down the lane to Dom. She feels confident again; certain that she's doing the right thing in giving U-Connect the chance to grow, for Sarah's sake if not her own. She opens the door, shouts a greeting and drops her bag on the chair in the hall. All is well.

CHAPTER SIX

The second postcard arrives the next morning. Billa takes the post into Ed's study but he isn't there, though his laptop is switched on and a CD is playing Jacques Loussier's interpretation of the Allegro from Bach's 'Italian' Concerto. She drops the other letters on to his desk and turns the postcard over, barely glancing at the picture.

'On my way. Tris.'

The postmark and the stamp are French; the date is smudged but she makes it out to be three days earlier. He could be here at any moment; driving up the lane, knocking at the door. She turns the card to look at the picture, a reproduction of a Victorian artist, and a strange, complicated emotion pierces her heart. A dog—a terrier—sits gazing out, head on one side, ears pricked. Its pointed, foxy face has an enquiring, intelligent expression; one paw is raised as if it is poised for action.

'Bitser,' murmurs Billa.

The past is crowding upon her so strongly and unexpectedly that her heart beats fast, her eyes burn with tears and she swallows several times.

She feels the rough rasp of Bitser's wet tongue on her hand, the warm weight of his body in her arms. Bitser, that adorable, impossible puppy, was given to her as a birthday present from her father less than two years before he died.

There had always been dogs, well-behaved, good-natured gun dogs, but this was the first time either she or Ed were allowed a puppy of their own. He was brought in to birthday tea in a hatbox immediately after Billa had blown out her eight candles whilst everyone sang 'Happy Birthday to You' and clapped. The box was set down on a chair and Billa stared at it, hearing strange rustlings and small whimpering noises. Her father was smiling at her, indicating that she should remove the lid. She did so very warily, and there was a puppy of indeterminate parentage scrambling around in a nest of tissue paper. Billa gave a cry of joyful disbelief and lifted the warm wriggling body out of the box. Ed was beaming with pleasure and pride that he'd managed to keep such a secret; her mother clapping and laughing; her friends crowding round with cries of envious delight.

'He's a very nice first-cross,' her father was saying. 'Bits of cairn and bits of Jack Russell . . .' and so he became Bitser.

'What a funny-looking dog,' said Tris. 'He's a mongrel, isn't he?'

Bitser didn't like Tris. He growled when Tris slipped out a quick foot to kick him or teased him with a biscuit, offered and then snatched away. Tris never did this when a grown-up was looking but managed to time the reaction so that what they actually saw was Tris pretending to stroke Bitser, who was growling by now, or even snapping. Tris would look at his father, mouth turned down, pretending sadness and Andrew would say: 'Bad-tempered brute, isn't he?' which made Billa rise in hot defence of Bitser.

'Tris is teasing him again,' but Tris shrugged wide-eyed innocent surprise at such an accusation, and their mother said, 'Take Bitser outside, Billa.'

Their mother and Andrew decided that Bitser was jealous of Tris and needed to be taught that Tris was now part of the family. Gradually small privileges were withdrawn. Bitser was no longer allowed to sit on the sofa in the drawing-room, he was banished to the laundry room at mealtimes and was banned from Andrew's car. Nobody could stop Billa from taking him upstairs to her room at night, however. Bitser would curl up at the foot of the bed and Billa sat beside him, stroking him, trying to make up for these new puzzling exclusions.

'But what shall I do,' Billa asked Dom as the long summer holiday drew to an end, 'when I go back to school? Mother has always been glad to have Bitser around when we're away. He used to sleep in her room. But she won't need him now she's got Andrew.'

She sounded bitter. It was still a shock to see Andrew going into her mother's room at night; to see him in the morning through the half-open bedroom door, half-naked and unshaven in the rumpled bed, drinking coffee whilst her mother perched beside him, laughing at some remark. He'd see Billa passing and raise his cup almost challengingly to her whilst his other hand held her mother's wrist, and Billa blushed scarlet and scuttled away, confused and embarrassed by her own reactions.

Just as Ed withdrew to the study so Billa clung more to Bitser; their father's gift to her. She began to wage her own war, which was, of necessity, directed more against their mother than their chief tormentor, Tris.

'Do you remember . . .' she'd begin—and then it might be anything that involved Bitser and their father. Her mother grew to dread this casual, conversational opening—but it was the only weapon Billa had in her armoury of self-protection against the dismantling of her past.

So she went to Dom, Bitser rushing ahead, and 'What shall I do?' she asked him. 'Could you have Bitser with you?'

The potager had an autumnal feel about it now. The sunflowers' heavy heads drooped, though the sweet peas still carried their blooms amongst the pea-sticks. Pumpkins and gourds were fattening, and the bright flowers of the nasturtiums trailed across slate paths and beneath the hedge.

They sat together in the soft September sunshine and Billa longed to lean nearer to Dom, to feel the comfort of his arm round her.

'I can't have him,' Dom was saying wretchedly. 'I'm sorry but I can't, Billa. I'm going to be in lodgings in Camborne and, anyway, what would happen to him all day while I'm at college? Your mother will look after him, surely? She always has in the past.'

'Andrew wasn't there then,' said Billa bitterly. 'And nor was Tris.'

Dom looked at her and she saw that he, too, felt a longing to hold out his arms to her and share her misery. She managed a crooked smile.

'Well, I'll just have to trust her,' she said.

Ed brought Bitser with him to the station to see her off to school and she stood at the train window for the last glimpse of Ed standing with Bitser in his arms. Ed held up Bitser's paw and pretended to wave it. It was the last time she saw Bitser. The letter arrived nearly three weeks later.

'I don't know how to write this to you, darling Billa, but I think you would want to be told that we've had to put Bitser down. He bit Tris quite badly and the vet agreed that he was getting untrustworthy. I am so sorry . . .'

• • •

Now, Billa stares at the postcard: Bitser stares
back at her, ears cocked, paw raised. She wonders
how long it has taken Tris to find a card that
would so surely pierce her heart with pain.

'On my way. Tris.'

'What is it?' asks Ed, coming in behind her with
Bear at his heels. 'Are you OK?'

She passes him the card and he studies it,
frowning. Then he gives a little laugh, affectionate and sad.

'It's Bitser to the life,' he says. 'Gosh, that takes
me back,' and he turns the card to see who has
sent it and the smile drops from his face in an
instant. He stares at Billa, shocked and angry. 'It's
like a declaration of war,' he says at last.

She nods. 'They didn't even bother to bring his
body back to be buried with the other dogs,' she
says. 'They left him with the vet. The last time I
saw him was with you at the station.'

She remembers Bitser, wriggling in her arms;
she remembers pressing her cheek against his
smooth head before passing him to Ed. And with
this memory comes the painful reminder of those
children that she couldn't bring to birth, who
wriggled, fish-like, swimming away in their
amniotic liquid to disappear for ever.

'I can begin babies,' she had said to Dom, 'but I
can't finish them.' And this time he did hold out
his arms to her and hugged her. Billa wept as she

81

had never wept: for her father, for Bitser, and for her babies. Dom held her, his cheek against her hair, thinking of their father; the man he never knew.

'What shall we do?' Ed asks now. 'First the bike and now Bitser. Don't tell me these are friendly notes suggesting that we meet up to reminisce happily about the past.'

Billa shakes her head. 'But what can we do? We don't know where he is or what he plans. As usual he has us over a barrel.'

'They got everything they wanted.' Ed drops the postcard on the desk. 'And then they just packed up and left.'

'Not everything.' Billa glances around the study; at the paintings, the little cabinet of netsukes, the miniatures, the shelves of books. 'How he hated you having this.'

'But he couldn't touch it,' says Ed with satisfaction. 'He was far too clever to go in for straight destruction but he tried everything else. It was as if the room defied him and won.'

'Has it occurred to you,' says Billa carefully, 'that there might have been another will?'

Ed frowns at her. 'What?'

'Supposing Mother left something to Andrew in a will that we never found because Andrew had it?'

'What kind of thing?'

'That's the point. Supposing she was besotted enough at the beginning to leave him Mellinpons, thinking that he'd look after us.'

'She'd never have done that.' Ed is ashen-faced.

Billa shrugs. 'We have to think of everything. Why is Tris coming back? Has he discovered something that might be to his advantage? If Andrew persuaded her to make a will with his own solicitor we'd never have known anything about it. Perhaps Andrew has died recently. He'd be well into his nineties but it's quite possible that he's lived this long. And suppose Tris has found some document . . .'

'But then he or Andrew would have come back when Mother died. Why wait until now?'

'I don't know. But I think we need to be ready for anything.'

'Oh my God.'

'Can you think of any reason why Tris should want to see us again? After fifty years?'

Ed shakes his head. 'So what do we do?'

'We try to think like he does and be prepared.'

'But what if he has some . . . some real claim? Is it possible after all this time?'

'I don't know. I might talk to Dom to see if he knows anything about the legal situation. I don't want to do anything until we know a bit more. Do you agree?'

'I suppose so.' Ed looks uncertain. 'It's just awful to think that he might have some hold over us.'

Bear sits heavily on Billa's feet, leaning against

her, and she bends to hug the huge dog, comforted by his weight and presence.

'I'll phone Dom,' says Ed. 'And then we'll make a plan.'

CHAPTER SEVEN

Tilly drives between the tall pillars at the convent gates and stops beside the Lodge, wondering if someone might come out to question her. She feels oddly nervous; still trying to think of ways that she might promote a retreat house and wondering how to behave, should she meet any members of the religious community. The front door of the Lodge remains closed, nobody comes to challenge her, so she sets off very slowly along the drive, towards the ancient granite manor house set amongst its gardens and orchards at the head of a steep valley that looks west to the sea. There are a few people wandering along the path amongst the trees, a woman sitting on a bench, her stretched-out feet almost in a golden pool of crocuses that washes over the grass. These, Tilly guesses, must be the retreatants.

The drive passes in front of the house, curving round towards some outbuildings, but Tilly stops to look at the mullioned windows and the heavy oaken door. Already she is imagining the photographs she will want for the website. The nervousness is receding and she is beginning to feel excited. As she dawdles there, words forming in her mind, a small, slight figure appears from the direction of the outbuildings. She wears a long blue habit, a green cotton scarf tied at the back of her neck, gumboots and a black fleece.

Tilly's anxiety returns but she lowers the car window and smiles at the enquiring face with its bright, intelligent eyes.

'Hello,' she says uncertainly. 'I'm Tilly from U-Connect. I'm looking for Elizabeth.'

The nun beams at her. 'Have you come to help us?' she asks. 'Oh, how wonderful. Put the car round there,' she gestures at the corner of the house, 'and we'll go to find her.'

Tilly obeys. In the stable yard the Coach House has been converted, but there is room for the car in one of the open-fronted barns and she pulls in, switches off the engine and climbs out.

'I am Sister Emily,' says the small figure at her elbow. 'What have you got there?'

She looks with keen interest at Tilly's laptop case and Tilly can't help but smile at her eager curiosity.

'It's my laptop and stuff,' she says. 'I'm supposed to be helping you to create a new website for the retreat house. I'm rather nervous, I can tell you. We've never done anything like this before.'

Briefly she wonders if Sister Emily, too, might quote Browning at her, or some encouraging religious text. But Sister Emily simply laughs with delight.

'Neither have we,' she says. 'Isn't it exciting?'

Tilly laughs too. 'Yes,' she agrees, and suddenly all her fears vanish and she sees that it *is* exciting. 'It's utterly gorgeous here,' she says. 'We'll need lots of lovely photographs for the website.'

She follows Sister Emily in through a door that leads to the kitchen and looks around with delight at the low beamed room, the big, ancient ingle-nook with its Aga, the pots of flowers on the deep-set stone windowsills.

'The community has moved into the Coach House,' Sister Emily is saying, 'but we are still very much a part of all that is happening here. Would you like some coffee while I look for Elizabeth? It's Fairtrade coffee,' she adds, as if this is in some way reassuring.

'I'd love some,' says Tilly, relishing the warmth of the kitchen and the quiet atmosphere, though there is clear evidence of industry. A saucepan of soup simmers at the back of the hotplate and a batch of bread stands on a grid. The smells are delicious.

She sits at the big table, whilst Sister Emily makes coffee, and feels no requirement to make conversation. The silence is companionable, and somehow natural. She takes the mug of coffee with a smile of gratitude and Sister Emily disappears through a door that leads into the house. Tilly sits quietly; her terrors are quite gone as she waits for Elizabeth. Her mind has cleared, ideas begin to form, and she is filled with confidence.

'So what was it like?' asks Sarah, making tea. 'Lots more lovable nutters?'

'Totally fantastic,' says Tilly, ignoring the sarcasm and picking George up to give him a cuddle. 'I've met Sister Emily and someone who does the cooking called Penny. And Elizabeth, who is helping them out with their administration. She's quite computer literate but not into websites. I've got some ideas but I need to think about it. It's such an amazing setting, isn't it, looking west to the sea?'

'It's breathtaking,' agrees Sarah. 'A perfect spot for a retreat, I should think.'

'Elizabeth gave me a list of the kind of courses they offer. They want to encourage what they call "led retreats", which are organized by independent groups looking for a venue. And then there are people who simply want to come and be quiet on their own, just to walk and read but maybe join in the Daily Offices, which the sisters have in the chapel. Sister Emily calls them Holy Holidays. I need to go back again with a camera. Dom's got a really good one so I shall ask to borrow it.'

'Great,' says Sarah. She is pleased with Tilly's enthusiasm, glad that she's overcome her nervousness of the convent and is being positive. 'Have you made an appointment to go back?'

'No, I thought I'd check with you first. I'm with Sir Alec tomorrow morning for a session. I could go on after that since it's so close.'

Tilly swings George round so that he chuckles and tries to grab her hair.

'Come and have lunch after Sir Alec,' says Sarah, putting mugs of tea on the table. 'I'll phone and see if you can go along afterwards.'

'OK,' says Tilly. She holds up one of George's chubby fists and dances with him, swaying and twirling. 'George and I are going in for *Strictly* next year, aren't we, George?'

'You are completely crackers,' Sarah says, resigned. 'Drink your tea and put George down before you make him sick.'

'He won't be sick,' says Tilly, but she puts George in his bouncy chair and sits down at the kitchen table. She feels light-hearted, as if she's passed some kind of test and is on the brink of something exciting, and it's good.

Sarah watches her rather enviously. Tilly has always been a free spirit and, just at the moment, Sarah has a sudden and uncomplicated longing to be free of her own responsibilities and duties. This is quite out of character and confuses her: she likes to be in control, hands on. She was teased at school: 'Our Natural Leader,' the girls would cry when Sarah had been commended yet again for her initiative. She didn't care; she was popular enough to withstand such teasing with confidence.

Just now, though, when Tilly was dancing with George, she'd wished that she, too, could simply put George back into his chair, drink some tea and walk out of the door, as Tilly would presently. These emotions confuse her and make her feel guilty. She adores George, she would die for him, but sometimes she absolutely longs to close the door on him and walk away from all the other duties that pile toweringly behind him: getting Ben—with all the right belongings—off to school and home again, buying food, preparing food, washing, ironing, keeping the garden tidy. The list is endless. She misses Dave; misses his quick humour, his practicality, his arms round her.

Her mother has little patience with these moments of despair.

'If you can't manage, darling,' she says briskly, 'you shouldn't have taken on this new job.'

Her mother, a naval wife—widowed now—is a tireless committee woman who has brought up three children. She is proud of Sarah but doesn't allow whingeing. She quotes the old naval maxim: 'If you can't take a joke you shouldn't have joined.' And most of the time Sarah manages very well indeed; it's just that sometimes she has those moments, when George has a fever and doesn't sleep and then disturbs Ben so that she's awake most of the night, when she'd love to hear Dave saying: 'Don't worry. He'll be fine. Just try to relax and I'll bring you a cup of tea . . .'

But even when he does, she can't quite relax. He's good with the boys but she likes to keep an eye, to check that he's doing things the way she likes them to be done. Sometimes he gets cross with her.

'It might not be your way,' he'll say, 'but that doesn't mean to say it's wrong. It won't be the end of the world if their routine is different now and again. Lighten up.'

He doesn't understand that it's necessary for her to remain in control; this way she can feel secure, knowing that everything is mapped out so that she can manage properly. At the same time, she sometimes feels aggrieved that Dave doesn't pull his weight or appreciate what it takes to keep the household running smoothly. She accuses him of taking her for granted—oh, not directly but by meaningful sighs, irritated glances, impatient gestures—but when he suggests that he should take the boys out, cook the lunch, do the bedtime routine, she can't quite allow herself to sit back and let him. She needs to check that he's doing it properly, and so the old arguments start up again.

She'd like to unburden herself to Tilly but can't allow herself the luxury. Tilly is like a younger sister; she admires and respects Sarah. She'd lose face if she admitted these feelings to Tilly, who would never begin to understand anyway. How could she? She has no responsibilities. Everyone loves Tilly; everyone wants to help her, to be her friend. Just sometimes Sarah feels a real irritation that Tilly gets it all so easy and wonders why she offered Tilly the job with U-Connect. If she's honest, it wasn't just because Tilly had walked out of the job in Newquay. The truth is, it was because Tilly is good at this kind of work; people take to her, they trust her, and she's good for the business. Sarah gets very slightly tired of clients phoning to say how brilliant Tilly is but she bites her tongue and agrees that Tilly is sweet, clever, funny or whatever it is that has impressed them. And she's very fond of Tilly, of course she is. It's just today, after a really bad night with George and then not being able to find Ben's latest nursery school project . . .

'Are you OK?' Tilly asks, and her look is so anxious, so loving, that for a brief moment Sarah considers breaking down and howling loudly, just like George did all night.

'I'm fine,' she says brightly, eyebrows raised a little as if she's wondering why Tilly should be so misguided as to ask. 'Just planning ahead, getting things sorted in my head. Lunch tomorrow, then, after Sir Alec?'

Poor old Sarah, thinks Tilly as she drives away. So uptight and serious. All those baby books when Ben was born.

'I wonder how our cave ancestors managed without Gina Ford?' she'd said to Sarah, trying to lighten her up, and Dave roared with laughter but Sarah didn't see the joke.

'A routine is absolutely essential,' she said tightly, and Tilly didn't dare to look at Dave lest they should laugh again and upset Sarah. Dave was very good with her, trying to defuse tension when Ben refused to eat or sleep at the prescribed times, but Sarah was not to be deterred from her chosen path.

'It's best,' he said privately to Tilly, 'to let her do it her own way. After all, I'm away a lot of the time. She needs to do what's right for her and Ben.'

This was very sensible of Dave, but Tilly detected a less tolerant view once George was born. Dave hoped that by now Sarah would be more laid-back but this hadn't yet proved to be the case. When his last leave was over and it was time to go back to sea, Tilly suspected a note of relief in Dave's voice when she dashed over to say goodbye to him.

'Keep an eye on her for me,' he said jokingly to Tilly, and Sarah made a face to show how ludicrous such an idea was.

Tilly drives on through the dusk, brooding about Sarah, wishing she could think of a way of de-stressing her.

When she arrives at the cottage Dom is peeling vegetables for supper.

'I've just had an idea,' she says, stooping to hug Bessie. 'I could take Bessie to see some of the older clients. A kind of Pet as Therapy. What d'you think? Not Mrs Probus because of the cats, and Mrs Anderson would worry about dog hairs, but I can think of a few old dears who would love her. You'd like that, wouldn't you, old doggle? And I could take her to meet Hercules.'

'Hercules?' asks Dom, peeling on peacefully. 'Does he want you to help him with his twelve labours? Does he need to use Google to get advice on cleaning out the Augean stables? Or does he want to Skype the Stymphalian birds?'

'Very funny,' Tilly says. 'He's Sir Alec's dog. A yellow Lab with perfect manners. Bessie would love him and she'd be company for me in the car.'

'Get your own dog,' says Dom. 'I need her here to be company for me.'

'I'd love a puppy,' says Tilly wistfully. 'But it would be a bit tricky while I'm here, wouldn't it? Training it and stuff.'

'Don't look at me,' says Dom. 'I'm too old to cope with a puppy. So how were the nuns?'

'Utter bliss,' says Tilly. 'I've got some really good ideas. Dom?'

'Mmm?'

'Do you think I could borrow your camera tomorrow?'

'First my dog and now my camera. Anything else you'd like?'

'I'm sure I'll think of something. Supper smells good.'

'Pheasant stew,' he says. 'I found one in the freezer yesterday. So pour me a drink and tell me about the blissful nuns.'

CHAPTER EIGHT

Dom walks in the stony, narrow lanes at the edge of the moor above the cottage, and all around him he can hear the rushing of water; pouring off the fields, flooding the ditches, streaming from muddy gateways, disappearing down drains that are half-blocked with twigs and leaves. The sky is a jigsaw of cloud-shapes and colours: stormy indigo, curded cream, lustrous gold, a tiny patch of rainbow. Blown by the south-westerly winds, they lock together and drift apart again. Hail clatters suddenly and then—just as unexpectedly—sunshine washes the drenched landscape with brilliant light.

As the lane climbs steeply towards the bleak moorland, the thorn hedges give way to walls; uneven, rough-shaped chunks of granite piled together, stretching for miles in a network of rocky boundaries squaring the small, untidy fields.

Bessie carries an old, broken branch, which she refuses to drop. At intervals Dom attempts to take it from her so that he can throw it for her to fetch.

Each time she dodges away from him, turning her head so that the twigs catch scratchily against his sleeve or his hand, dropping down on her front paws whilst her tail waves with excitement, encouraging him to play.

'Daft bitch,' he mutters, grabbing for the wet, decaying wood, but she bounds away from him, running up the lane towards the open moorland. He follows more slowly, thinking of Tris's postcard, remembering Bitser, and Billa's distress when she knew he was dead.

'I don't want to go home,' she'd written to him from school. 'It isn't home any more. If it weren't for Ed I'd ask one of my friends to invite me for the holidays. But I can't leave Ed . . .'

He can recall his own sense of frustration at his inability to help them. He'd written regularly to them both, gone back to the cottage as often as he could during their holidays, but the small family unit had been broken up and only their friendship remained untouched: their friendship and the study.

Because the contents were precious to him, Harry St Enedoc had a lock made for the study door and always kept the key with him. Ed and Billa were only allowed in when he was there and they learned to respect his treasures. Ed copied his father's example. He kept the study locked, and the key with him, and his mother—still impressed by Ed's defence of his father's memory—allowed this rather eccentric behaviour. After all, the study was a small room, it wasn't needed; thus she explained it away to Andrew, who having seen Ed's models and collections as well as the treasures, agreed that a boy of his age needed a bit of private space of his own. To compensate, Tris was given the cheese-house: a small stone and slate building where he could keep his own personal belongings. He complained, of course—that it was outside, cold in winter, damp —but in this instance his protests were ignored.

He retaliated by slowly taking over most of the bedroom he shared with Ed so that, on his return from school, there wasn't much more than the bed left to him.

'I don't care,' he told Dom. 'It's the study that's important. I only sleep in the bedroom. I hate him, though.'

This remark, coming so matter-of-factly from the gentle, peaceable Ed, shocked Dom more than he liked to admit. He wanted to agree with Ed, to say, 'So do I,' but he restrained himself, hiding his own hurts. Dom could understand why Elinor St Enedoc had never liked him, but soon it was clear that she'd told Andrew the whole story and he took care to snub Dom whenever he saw him. Tris went a step further.

One cold day in late autumn he met Dom bringing a load of logs back from the woods. There was a long-standing agreement between Granny and the St Enedocs that she should have logs for her fire and Dom pulled them along, piled and strapped on an old sledge, as he always did. When Tris stepped into his path he was obliged to swerve to avoid him but Tris stopped him with a question.

'Are you allowed on our land?'

Dom stared at him; pulled up short by a gut-churning mix of disbelief, anger and humiliation.

'*Your* land?' he asked witheringly, weighting his voice with contempt.

But Tris was a match for him. 'Well, it's not your land, is it? Your grandmother only owns the cottage because your mother was a whore.'

Instinctively Dom reached for him but, even as Tris feinted a dodge, Dom knew that this was what he wanted; he wanted a violent physical reaction so that he could run home shouting, 'Dom hit me.' Just in time Dom drew back and, as he stepped away, he saw the disappointment in Tris's face. Seething with fury, he picked up the sledge's rope and walked on.

A scatter of hail jolts Dom back to the present. Bessie has dropped her stick in favour of a scent that leads her along the base of the wall. He wanders behind her, thinking of the postcards, trying to see behind them to Tris's real purpose— and beyond that to the old question: why did Andrew leave so suddenly?

Dom never quite believes the story of the quarrel: a quarrel apparently so violent that Andrew packed his and Tris's belongings and walked out, collecting Tris from his school on the way upcountry. A few days afterwards a letter arrived simply stating that it hadn't worked out as he hoped and that it was better for everyone to make the break now. Billa reported this to Dom, overjoyed at this sudden release, but anxious for her mother.

'She's off her head,' she said. 'Completely distraught. She can't seem to understand it at all. It's come right out of the blue. She simply won't take the letter seriously, of course. She thinks he's coming back.'

What, thinks Dom, did Andrew want that he didn't get?

It's reasonable to believe that he married Elinor simply because she was a rich widow, but why leave her? He was comfortable, well provided for, his child cosseted—and certainly Elinor was in love with him. His inexplicable departure is still as suspicious as Tris's postcards.

Dom calls for Bessie and turns for home, but he takes the path through the woods that leads into the grounds of the old butter factory and skirts around the edge of the lake. Bear appears from behind the stand of dogwood and comes to greet Bessie, tail waving. The two of them were brought up as puppies together and they are good friends. An old wheelbarrow stands nearby, a collection of tools in its rusty lap, and Dom looks around for Ed. He is working at the lake's edge but he straightens up when Dom hails him. Dom gestures towards the house and Ed waves back in acknowledgement.

'Shan't be long,' he shouts, and Dom walks on and goes in through the back door, calling as he does so.

'In here,' answers Billa, and he opens the door of her study where she sits, elbows on desk, her laptop open in front of her. 'Oh, good. An excuse to stop. Coffee?' She looks at her watch. 'Oh, gosh, nearly lunchtime. I didn't realize it was so late. Have you seen Ed anywhere?'

'He's down by the lake,' Dom says, 'but he's on his way.'

Billa gets up and leads Dom into the kitchen.

'Scrambled eggs? Bacon sandwich?'

'Scrambled eggs,' he says. 'And bacon. No sandwich.'

'I can manage that,' she says. 'Where's Bessie?'

'She stayed behind to play with Bear. How's it going?'

She shrugs; makes a face. 'Oh, you know how it is. This Tris thing's like a cloud hanging over us. We're going along and then suddenly we remember the postcards and think: oh my God, what's he up to? If he's going to turn up I just wish he would so we can get it over with.'

Dom sits down at the big slate table, watching

Billa cracking the eggs into a blue and white striped jug, fetching bacon from the fridge.

'I was thinking up there on the moor,' he says. 'Trying to remember what happened when Andrew left your mother. Can you remember anything about it?'

Billa snorts derisively. 'Are you kidding? I certainly can. It was up there with one of the best days of my life.'

'I wasn't thinking so much of the relief of being without him and Tris. I mean the actual leaving, and how your mother reacted. I mean, it was so sudden, wasn't it? Was it term-time? I can't remember the details now.'

Billa pauses in her beating and seasoning of the eggs to look at him.

'It was term-time,' she answers slowly, thinking back. 'I'd been home on an exeat. Just me, not Ed or Tris, and I hadn't been very well . . . a sore throat, I think it was.' She hesitates again, remembering. 'It was Andrew who said I ought not to go back. He said I looked as if I might be sickening for something. They had a row about it. Yes. That's it, of course. That's what the row was all about.' And now it comes back to her, fresh and raw: her mother beating eggs for breakfast, as she, Billa, is doing now, and Andrew sitting at the table just where Dom is.

'And I,' Billa says, 'was still in my dressing gown and whining about going back to school . . .'

• • •

'Of course she must go back,' her mother said irritably. 'It's probably just a little cold.'

It hadn't been a successful weekend. On Saturday Andrew had received several phone calls that made him distracted and rather short with her and her mother. He wouldn't say what they were about, just something to do with business, and Billa could see that her mother was getting more and more concerned about them. Each time the telephone rang, Andrew hurried to take the call, mumbling into the receiver lest he should be overheard.

'Whatever is it, darling?' she asked at last. 'It's clear that something's worrying you.'

Billa, pretending to read a book, watched them from the corners of her eyes. It was a chilly November day with a dull, grey canopy of cloud that leaked rain. The fire had been lit in the hall and Billa sat in one of the armchairs, her feet tucked beneath her, huddling over her book. Her mother sat on the sofa watching Andrew, her eyes suspicious.

'It's nothing,' he said shortly. 'It's my broker talking about some of my investments.'

'On a Saturday afternoon?' Her mother raised her eyebrows disbelievingly. 'How devoted of him.'

Perhaps, thought Billa, she thinks it's another woman. There had been other moments like this

101

one. The honeymoon year was over and Andrew was increasingly restless; going off at short notice, remembering engagements at the last moment.

'It's that crisis that's blown up in Argentina,' he answered. 'I've got a lot of shares in the livestock markets.'

Her mother shrugged slightly, clearly only half believing him but not quite able to say so. 'I'll make some tea,' she said. 'Do stop sniffing, Billa. Don't you have a handkerchief?'

Andrew gave her a sympathetic look behind her mother's back and, for once, Billa responded to it. She didn't feel terribly well, and now she felt aggrieved as well by her mother's indifference.

'Poor you,' said Andrew lightly. His eyes remained fixed on her but grew almost speculative, and Billa frowned.

'What?' she asked.

He shook his head but he looked as if he had had an idea that might solve a problem for him.

And it was the next morning, as her mother prepared breakfast and Billa stood by the Aga, shivering and still feeling sorry for herself, that Andrew said that Billa shouldn't go back to school and the row started.

'Of course she must go back,' her mother said irritably. 'It's probably just a little cold.'

'But you can see that she feels awful,' said Andrew. 'Poor girl. She's been feeling off colour all weekend.'

Billa was surprised into silence by Andrew's partisanship. Usually he couldn't wait to bundle her into the car and drive her back to school. Her mother, however, seemed almost angry at his concern. She looked at her daughter as if suddenly aware of her sixteen-year-old shapeliness in the old but clinging dressing gown. Instinctively Billa pulled the collar higher around her neck.

'She'll be better back at school,' her mother said coolly. 'Don't fuss, Andrew. She's my daughter. I know what's best for her.'

'Yes, you've made that very clear,' he answered. 'And Ed's your son, and this is your house. Everything's yours, isn't it, Elinor? Well, I think I'm getting rather tired of being a kind of lodger in my own home. But of course, it isn't my home, is it? It's yours.'

'What nonsense,' her mother said, clearly taken aback. 'You've been completely at home here.'

He laughed derisively. 'How can you say that? Billa and Ed make no attempt to hide how much they dislike Tristan, and they treat me as if I'm an intruder . . .'

'No,' her mother said. 'No, it isn't true. I know it isn't always easy in the holidays—'

'Easy? That's an understatement.'

He was standing now, his voice growing louder, shouting her mother down when she tried to speak, but a small part of Billa was puzzled: it was as if it wasn't quite real. She felt that Andrew's anger was being manufactured, pumped up, for a reason she couldn't understand.

'I've had enough, Elinor,' he was saying now. 'It just hasn't worked out. We've simply got to face up to it.'

He strode out of the kitchen, shutting the door behind him, and the two women stood together in shocked silence. Billa looked at her mother. She felt that somehow this was all her fault but, as she began to speak, her mother dropped the egg-beater and ran out of the kitchen. Billa heard her racing up the stairs and then the raised voices from the landing and the bedroom. Crouching by the Aga, Billa listened to the footsteps, to her mother's pleading voice and Andrew's angry one. Presently they came downstairs and she heard the hall door open; her mother was weeping now, begging him to stay. From the window she saw Andrew putting suitcases into the boot of his car, her mother clinging to his arm, trying to prevent him. He pushed her away, got into the driver's seat, and the car moved off down the drive. Her mother stood quite still, staring after him.

'She was devastated,' Billa says. 'There had been a few rows but she clearly wasn't expecting anything like that.'

'And you felt that he was, how did you put it, manufacturing his anger?'

'Yes.' Billa frowns, remembering it. 'It sounds

odd, doesn't it? But it was like he was picking a quarrel deliberately so that he could storm off. But why would he do that?'

Dom shakes his head. 'I'd like to know what the telephone calls were about.'

Ed comes into the kitchen followed by the dogs. His jeans are tucked into thick socks and pieces of twig cling to his jersey. Bessie goes to Bear's bowl and begins to lap at the water; Bear joins her and they drink amicably together.

'You look serious,' says Ed. His cheerful expression fades and alarm takes its place. 'Oh, no. You haven't had any more postcards?'

'No, no,' says Billa quickly. 'No, we were just re-enacting the leaving of Andrew and Tris.'

'Sounds like a rhythm and blues number,' says Ed. 'Dolly Parton. "The Leaving of Andrew and Tris".'

'I still wonder why Andrew went off so quickly,' says Dom. 'If, for instance, he knew that he was a beneficiary under Elinor's will, why would he walk away like that?'

'So you think Tris's visit has nothing to do with any kind of inheritance?' asks Billa hopefully.

'No, I'm not necessarily saying that. I'm just trying to think of everything. To be one step ahead. I'd like to know why Andrew found it necessary to disappear so quickly and completely after some rather urgent telephone calls.'

'Oh.' Ed looks at him, eyebrows raised. 'Do you

think Andrew had a shady past and it was a case of "Flee at once—all is discovered"?'

'Well, I do wonder a bit,' admits Dom. 'It was just so final, wasn't it? And neither of you believed that things were that bad between them.'

'The first rush of blood to the head had passed,' Billa says, 'but I wouldn't have said that things had irretrievably broken down. There were a few rows in the holidays but there always had been, and that was usually to do with us children rather than Mother and Andrew. But I think Andrew was growing restless. Dashing off on his own. Looking back, I wonder if Mother suspected him of being unfaithful.'

'Well, it might have been just that,' says Dom. 'Maybe he'd found a better prospect somewhere else and he was looking for the opportunity to make the break. Maybe she was phoning him and giving him an ultimatum.'

The telephone rings and Ed answers it. 'Hang on,' he says into the handset. He turns to Billa. 'Tilly is asking if she can bring Alec Bancroft for coffee tomorrow. She says he can't wait to see the tadpoles.'

Billa laughs. 'She's impossible. Yes, of course she can. Tell her, eleven o'clock.'

Ed repeats the message, looking puzzled, and puts the handset back on the stand.

'But there aren't any tadpoles yet,' says Ed. 'It's much too early. It's only frogspawn.'

'It's just Tilly's joke,' says Billa. 'Don't ask. Let's eat this before it gets cold.'

She spoons scrambled egg on to plates, with slices of crispy bacon, and the three of them sit together at the big slate table as they have so many times before. The dogs clamber on to the old, sagging sofa and settle comfortably as if they were still puppies. The kitchen is warm and peaceful, Bear begins to snore and Billa teases Ed about yet another hole in his jersey.

Dom remembers how the two of them welcomed him as their brother, accepted him so joyfully into their lives, and how happy they were until Tris arrived. He remembers Ed saying, 'I hate him,' and Billa weeping over Bitser's death. He hears Tris's words: 'So you're the bastard' . . . 'Your mother was a whore,' and he thinks: I can't allow Tris to spoil what we've got now. Not again. I'll kill him first.

'Don't look so grim, Dom.' Billa is smiling at him, guessing his thoughts. She looks cheerful and confident and happy. 'I really cannot see how Tris can do us any harm after all this time. He's probably hundreds of miles away, bored out of his mind and thinking up ways of being his old tiresome self.'

Dom nods, smiles as if in agreement, takes a handful of grapes from the fruit bowl; but he doesn't believe it. Every instinct tells him that Tris is already here, waiting.

CHAPTER NINE

'So that's great,' Tilly is saying to Sir Alec Bancroft. 'Coffee tomorrow. Would you like me to pick you up?'

'Oh.' He seems surprised by her offer. 'That's very kind but I'm sure I'll find it. You've given me good directions. But you'll be there?'

'Yes, of course. I want to see Hercules when he meets Bear. Well, I ought to dash off if that's OK.'

Before he can answer there is a knock at the door and Sir Alec gives a little shrug of apology and goes out to answer it. Tilly hears him talking, a voice answering, and then he comes back.

'It's the curate,' he says. 'I think I told you about Clem, didn't I?' and he steps aside to allow Clem to come into the room.

Tilly isn't prepared for a tall, lean young man with short gilt-fair hair and an attractive smile. She feels confused, almost indignant; he isn't her stereotypical idea of a curate—though she isn't sure what is—and he is casually dressed in jeans and an old Barbour jacket. Sir Alec introduces them and they shake hands. She suspects that Clem is amused by her confusion and she is relieved that Sir Alec has taken control of the conversation, talking about the retreat house, so that she can pull herself together.

'I'm just going up to Chi-Meur,' Clem is saying, 'so I thought I'd drop in on the way to see how you're getting on.' He looks at Tilly and his eyes crinkle up teasingly. 'How's he doing with his database?' he asks. 'Has he got past the letter A yet?'

'He is a complete technophobe, actually,' Tilly answers, entering into the spirit of the thing, rather surprised at herself. 'But you knew that already, didn't you?'

Clem grins at Sir Alec. 'He still uses a quill to write his letters,' he says to Tilly. 'Did he tell you? It was Rose who was the keyboard queen. She was terrific.'

Once again, Tilly is surprised. He talks about Rose with great affection and no sense of embarrassment. She glances at Sir Alec to see if the reference has in anyway upset him but he is grinning too.

'Cheeky young devil,' he says. 'But it's true. She'd got it all covered. Emails, Skyping, texting. But I'm coming on, aren't I, Tilly?'

'You know how to switch on and log in,' she agrees.

'And how many lessons has that taken?' asks Clem. 'Or shouldn't I ask?'

Tilly laughs and then suddenly feels slightly shy. 'I must dash,' she says. 'Sarah's expecting me for lunch. Goodbye,' she says to Clem. 'See you tomorrow,' she says to Sir Alec.

It is only after she's in the car that she remembers that she will be going to the convent after lunch; to Chi-Meur. She wonders if Clem will still be there.

'I've met the curate,' she says casually to Sarah. 'Do you know him?'

'Clem Pardoe? Yes, he popped in to see me just after George was born and now he comes in for a cup of coffee from time to time. Dishy, isn't he? He reminds me of Hathaway in *Lewis*.'

'He seems nice. Not quite how I'd imagined a curate.'

Sarah laughs. 'Were you thinking very pale and young and nervous? I don't think curates are like that any more. Clem was in IT in London. He came down to Cornwall when his wife died.'

'Wife?' Tilly experiences an odd little shock. 'He's married?'

'Was married. She died having their baby whilst Clem was at theological college. He gave it up so he could earn money to look after the baby and then when Jakey was about three Clem took a live-in job at the convent as a handyman, gardener, whatever. He was ordained quite recently and he helps at the retreat house while he does his curacy. It's Clem who's pushing for a really good website.'

Tilly rearranges her ideas about Clem. 'How awful,' she says. 'About his wife, I mean.'

'Awful.' Sarah glances slyly at Tilly. 'Apart from anything, it's a terrible waste. He ought to get married again.'

'Well, don't look at me,' Tilly says at once. 'Can you see me as a vicar's wife, let alone a stepmother?'

Sarah snorts. 'To be honest I can't see you as any kind of wife or mother.'

'Thanks,' says Tilly, secretly hurt but not showing it. 'I must admit I have no ambition to be either.'

She is tempted to make an unkind remark about Sarah's not being much of an advertisement for the domestic scene, but resists. And, to be fair, Sarah has a point. Domesticity, timetables, rules and regs have never been Tilly's strong point.

'Anyway,' she says, 'he's probably got a girl-friend.'

Sarah shakes her head. 'Not as far as I know. He doesn't strike me as someone who gives his heart easily and he's completely devoted to Jakey.'

'And living in a convent isn't actually particularly conducive to having a relationship.'

'Oh, he and Jakey moved out of the Lodge when Clem was deaconed. They're in the new vicarage down the lane. We're part of a team here so we don't have our own vicar and the vicarage was empty so they've let Clem have it.'

'You know a lot about it,' says Tilly, slightly irritated by Sarah's almost proprietorial attitude.

'Mmm.' Sarah makes a smug little face. 'I rather like Clem.'

Tilly laughs. 'Well, don't tell Dave.'

'Oh, Dave likes him, too. Great sense of humour.'

'Right,' says Tilly, giving up. 'Well, I'd better make a move or I'll be late. And if I see Clem I'll give him your love.'

'You do that,' says Sarah.

Clem is the first person Tilly sees as she drives past the house. He stands outside the open front door with a small group of people: an elderly cleric, two of the Sisters and a younger woman with a rather boho appearance and a mane of tawny hair. Tilly parks the car in the barn, picks up Dom's camera and walks round to the front drive. Clem comes to meet her; his smile is friendly, almost intimate, rather as if they share some secret joke; some common aim.

Sister Emily greets her as an old friend. 'This is Tilly,' she says to the small group. She speaks with pride and delight, indicating that Tilly is some-one special. 'She's helping us with the website. Putting us on the map. And this,' she says to Tilly, 'is Mother Magda. And Father Pascal, who is our chaplain. And Janna, who looks after us most wonderfully and imaginatively.'

They all smile at Sister Emily's description, and Tilly experiences a great sense of family, of unity, amongst them all. For a brief second she has a huge longing for her parents, far away in Canada. She shrugs it off quickly, responding to the introductions, displaying the camera.

'I've got permission to take photographs,' she says, 'for the new website. I've got some ideas already, but if anyone has any suggestions . . . ?'

Mother Magda looks rather anxiously at Sister Emily and Father Pascal as if for inspiration. Janna smiles rather shyly, as if she's not certain that she is qualified to give an opinion.

'The orchard looks beautiful when the blue-bells are flowering,' she says hesitantly.

'And when the trees are in blossom,' agrees Sister Emily quickly. 'Though that won't be quite yet.'

'We'll need one of the chapel,' suggests Father Pascal. 'How many are we allowed?'

'As many as you like,' says Tilly. 'The website needs to be updated regularly so there is always something new for people to see. We could post events and things like that. Perhaps even have a blog. And I was thinking about what Sister Emily called Holy Holidays rather than the actual retreats and quiet days. I had this idea of doing a little video.'

'Oh?' Clem looks at her quickly, eyebrows raised; interested. 'Of what?'

'Well, last time I was here I walked down to the beach. It's so beautiful. I thought I could do a video clip showing people how they can simply walk out of the door and on to the cliffs or down to the sea.'

'How exciting,' exclaims Sister Emily. 'Could you do all that with your camera?'

'I think so,' says Tilly cautiously. 'We could show the walk in different seasons with a little voice-over.'

They gaze with respect at Tilly and her camera.

'Sound as well as pictures,' says Sister Emily thoughtfully. 'Just like the television. You could describe the flowers . . .'

'And the birds,' says Janna suddenly. ''Tis wonderful out on the cliffs when the seagulls are raising their chicks. They sound like babies crying.'

'Yes, well, I'm not quite up to David Attenborough,' warns Tilly, 'but I could have a go.'

'And our little acer grove in the autumn. And the azalea walk.' Pink with excitement at the thought of the possibilities, Sister Emily clasps her hand together in delight. Mother Magda sees Tilly's apprehension and steps in.

'I think this is Clem's department,' she says firmly. 'It all sounds very exciting and we shall look forward to seeing the results, but Clem is our expert. We'll leave him and Tilly to discuss it all.'

She smiles at Tilly encouragingly and moves away, taking Sister Emily and Janna with her.

Father Pascal smiles at Tilly, raises a hand in farewell to Clem and goes to fetch his car.

'Right then,' says Tilly. 'I think this is where I start showing initiative, isn't it? Am I allowed in the chapel?'

'This is a good time, actually,' Clem says. 'It should be empty. I think your video is a brilliant idea.'

She flushes with pleasure at his praise. 'Just a thought,' she says casually. 'Could you show me the chapel? Or are you rushing off somewhere?'

'I think I've been detailed off to help you with this,' he says. 'Come on in.' He pushes the heavy oaken door open and leads her into the hall. A small group of people stand at a table where cards are for sale, and a door stands open to the library, but Clem leads her out by another door and along a passage. He opens the chapel door gently, reverently, and looks inside. He turns to smile at her and pushes it wider so that she can go in. She stands just inside, looking at the beamed roof, the plain stone altar, the simple wooden crucifix on the wall behind it, the mullioned windows flooded with sunshine. The sanctuary light glimmers in its stone niche and candles have been lit in the terracotta bowl at the foot of the carved statue of Our Lady. There is peace here.

Tilly glances sideways at Clem, who stands silently, his hands clasped, head bent a little. She wonders if he is praying—and then he looks at her and she feels an odd sense of fellowship. He speaks quietly but quite naturally to her.

'What would you like to start with? The altar?'

She speaks quietly too. 'Could I just walk about a little? Get the feel of it?'

His nod, his little shrug, say: go ahead, and she walks forward, marvelling at the simplicity, looking through the viewfinder to get some ideas. She takes a photograph of the statue and the candles, and another of the altar with its vase of daffodils. Presently she smiles at Clem, indicating that she's all done here, and they go out together.

'I'm just trying to get inside the head of someone who might be drawn to the idea of a Holy Holiday,' she tells him, as they pass through the house to the hall. 'I have to say that I'm not much of a churchgoer'—she thinks it's best to get this into the open—'so it's a difficult one for me, but I can imagine if you'd been bereaved, say, or you needed to be alone, that it might be rather appealing. You've already got some nice photos of some of the guest rooms and the library, but I think we need to go a step further.'

'I agree,' he says. 'The current website's a bit pedestrian; a bit obvious. That's why I thought they should bring in someone with some fresh ideas.'

'Well, we're not that experienced,' Tilly admits, 'but I hope we can make a difference. Could

116

anyone here manage a blog, d'you think? You need to keep a website fresh, change it a bit so that people look at it regularly.'

He looks thoughtful as he opens the front door for her. 'I'm not sure. How much would you charge to do that?'

Tilly makes a little face. 'That would depend on Sarah.' She glances slyly at him. 'Perhaps you should have a word with her.'

'Perhaps I should,' he says blandly. 'Would you be happy to do it if she agrees?'

Tilly is caught off balance. 'Well, I suppose so but, once we've set it up, you need someone who is very clued up to what's going on here. Seriously, it ought to be someone in-house really.'

'I think there's a room going in the Lodge,' he suggests.

Instinctively she glances down the drive to the little stone house by the gates. He watches her, amused, and she bursts out laughing.

'Thanks, but no thanks,' she says. 'Sarah told me that you used to live there with your little boy.' She decides to get this out into the open, too. 'It looks rather nice.'

'It was good,' he says. 'But I have to be part of the parish now I've been ordained deacon. I want to come back when I've finished my curacy and be chaplain here. Or warden.'

'Would you live in the Lodge again?'

He nods. 'Better for Jakey. It's being let at the

moment in return for the work I used to do: gardening, general maintenance and so on. We're very happy at the vicarage in the village but it'll be good to come back.'

'So it's definite, is it? That you'd come back?'

'Assuming the retreat house is making enough to pay me a salary. Obviously the diocese would cease to pay me at that point.' He grins at her. 'That's why I suggested that they called you in to get the website going. It's pure self-interest.'

She can't help laughing. 'But you said that Father . . . Pascal, is it? You said he's the chaplain.'

'He is, but not full time. Several other local priests help out. But I want to be really hands-on, to try new things, and reach out to people.'

His face is serious now, intent, almost that of a visionary, and just for a moment Tilly is moved by his clear sense of vocation. He looks at her questioningly, wondering if she's understood, and she nods, gives him a little smile.

'No pressure then,' she says lightly. 'I'll have to do my best, won't I? And you'll have to persuade Sarah to lower her rates.' She hesitates, decides to take a chance. 'Have you got time to do the walk to the beach with me? Just to confirm whether it's a good idea for the video and whether a voice-over will work?'

'OK,' he says. 'But we won't start from here. The visitors will use a side door where they can keep boots and coats and stuff. Let's start there. It takes the path through the azaleas.'

'The one Sister Emily mentioned? She is great fun. I utterly love her,' says Tilly.

'You and me both,' says Clem.

CHAPTER TEN

A lec Bancroft wakes early. He lies quite still, missing Rose's warmth beside him, preparing to do battle with those demons of loneliness and fear that lie in wait for these first vulnerable moments when memories and the heartaching sense of loss make him weak. The winter, his first without her, has been long and dark but now the year is climbing slowly into the light.

He gets out of bed, knowing that action is the best way to keep the demons off balance. There is coffee to be made, Hercules to let out, but first he draws back the curtains. Above the distant rough-edged tors, little fleecy clouds are sun-streaked; to the west a ghost of a moon still hangs in an indigo sky.

'There's nowhere like Cornwall,' he hears Rose's voice murmuring in his ear, and his hands tighten briefly on the thick material of the curtains.

She was an unconventional, and sometimes exasperating, wife for a diplomat, but life was fun with Rose around. It was she who found the cottage, close to the village where she'd been born and brought up, and insisted they buy it to use for home leaves.

In Madrid, or Hong Kong, or Tanzania, in a succession of consulates and embassies, they'd invariably lived with a menagerie of animals—puppies, donkeys, goats—rescued from drowning, starvation, execution. She'd argued with local dignitaries, questioned the motives of mission-aries, encouraged everything that was bohemian and artistic.

Alec drags on his dressing gown, searches for his slippers, and goes downstairs and through the kitchen to where Hercules sleeps in the plant room. This conservatory is Rose's true legacy. The quarry-tiled floor is covered with rugs brought from Africa, the steamer chairs are draped with alpaca shawls, bamboo tables sag with the weight of books, and plants are everywhere: in big ceramic tubs, in wooden planters, in terracotta pots along the low slatted shelves beneath the windows. Hercules' bed is beneath one of these shelves.

'We must have a dog,' said Rose once they were home for good, unpacked, settled in. 'And I know just where to find one.'

Rose knew everyone around Peneglos: she knew where to get dry, seasoned firewood, the best local sausages, the right cuttings for their coastal garden—and the perfect Labrador puppy.

Hercules was a delightful, good-natured puppy

and now he is an arthritic, benign old gentleman. He raises his head as Alec comes in and his tail beats the side of his basket in welcome.

'Good fellow. Good old boy.' Alec bends to fondle an ear, to pat the broad yellow head, and then straightens up and goes back into the kitchen to switch on the kettle. He thinks about the visit to the St Enedocs. He is looking forward to it: they sound good fun, and the old butter factory is intriguing.

'You're going to meet a new friend,' he says to Hercules, who has come in search of his morning biscuit. 'A Newfoundland. Twice your size, my boy.' He makes coffee, gives Hercules his biscuit, and opens the kitchen door into the garden where he waits while Hercules goes out across the grass to lift his leg against the trunk of the flowering cherry tree by the wall.

'Not on the daffodils, you wretched hound,' Rose shouts from somewhere behind him, and Alec smiles reminiscently.

He can hear a disputation of rooks arguing about territory in the beech trees at the edge of the churchyard. The coffee is hot and strong, and he sips gratefully and thinks about Clem and Jakey down in the vicarage. He remembers Clem's appreciative lift of the brows after Tilly had gone, and the little silence.

'Pretty girl,' Alec said tentatively.

Clem simply nodded but his eyes crinkled up

121

in that now familiar, but rather unsettling way that indicated that he knew exactly what Alec was thinking.

As Alec makes toast, puts the marmalade on the table, he reflects on Clem's ability to connect with how he, Alec, feels since Rose died. He was shocked when Clem explained that his own wife had died in childbirth; moved by the way that Clem is able to identify Alec's need to talk about Rose, to keep her alive in his daily living, whilst attempting to accept her absence. Clem doesn't use a hushed, reverent voice when he talks about her, or behave as if Alec is some kind of invalid who needs special treatment and sympathetic looks. Instead, Clem talks openly about his own feelings; the emptiness in his and Jakey's lives.

'Madeleine and I were together for such a short time,' he says, 'that you might think that it would be much less painful—but there was Jakey. I couldn't bear it that Madeleine wouldn't see him growing up. All those special times—his first smile, learning to walk, playing Herod in the Nativity play—and being unable to share them with her. Each new development reopened the wound and revived the pain. There's a Madeleine-shaped hole in our lives.'

Alec grabs the toast as it is flung out by the temperamental toaster, puts it in the hand-painted china rack and carries it to the table. He is getting used to laying the table for one instead of two; to making coffee in the small cafetière. Talking to Clem comforts him—and now he has Tilly's visits to look forward to—and he is going to meet some new friends.

Later, as he drives away from Peneglos, inland towards the moors, he is aware of an almost forgotten sense of adventure. He talks to Hercules, who sits with his ears pricked as if he too is aware that this is not quite like the usual journey to see old friends in Padstow or to shop in Wadebridge. Meanwhile, Alec rehearses in his head the important things that Tilly has told him about the St Enedocs.

'It's only fair that you have a bit of a background,' she said. 'Billa's husband died a while back. Philip was quite a lot older than she was and you get the feeling that it was a kind of semi-detached marriage. They had no children. He was a scientist and seemed to live in the lab, and Billa just kind of immersed herself in charity work. She looked after Philip for several years when he was ill and when he died she moved back to the old butter factory. Ed had retired by then to do his own books. He was in publishing. So they just carried on together rather as if nothing much had happened, if you see what I mean. It's like they've always been there. Ed used to come down from London nearly every weekend and Billa often joined him. Ed didn't have children either. He

123

married a divorced woman who already had two teenage children with a very hands-on father. He and Gillian didn't last very long.'

'Perhaps,' Alec remarked at this point, 'neither of them was particularly good marriage material. Not all of us are.'

'Their father died when they were very young and then their mother remarried and it was an absolute disaster for Ed and Billa. At least, that's what Dom says. Ed and Billa never talk about it.'

She explained about Dom.

'I'm not gossiping,' she added anxiously. 'It's not a secret. It's just that he and Ed are so alike that you might make some remark and it could be a bit embarrassing.'

He was more and more intrigued.

'And they call it The Old Butter Factory?' he asked her. 'Like The Old Bakery? Or The Old Schoolhouse?'

'Actually it's called Mellinpons. It means the Mill on the Bridge, but the locals still call it the old butter factory. We all do.'

'I can't wait to see it,' he said. 'And to meet Ed and Billa and Dom.'

'And Bessie and Bear,' she reminded. 'Don't forget the old doggles.'

Now, as he turns off the A39 into the lanes at the edge of the moor, he concentrates on Tilly's instructions. Across the valley he can see a hamlet, which he thinks might be his destination. A small hatchback is parked rather carelessly in a gate-way and a man stands with his back to the car, binoculars raised to his eyes, staring across the valley in the same direction. He turns quickly, lowering the glasses as Alec negotiates the narrow space left between the hatchback and the thorny hedge on the opposite side of the lane. He raises his hand to the man, indicating that all is well, leaning to look at him and gets a glimpse of russet-grey curly hair, light frosty eyes. Then he is past and driving on, whilst the man has turned back and raised his binoculars again.

As he sees the old village pub, the Chough, he remembers Tilly's directions: 'Go past the Chough, carry on up the hill and turn left. Then it's straight on for a couple of miles before you turn right . . .'

Nearly twenty minutes later he is passing Dom's cottage—he recognizes it from Tilly's description—driving over the old stone bridge, pulling rather cautiously into the gateway of the old butter factory. He can see at once that it had been a mill but before he can take in much more Tilly comes hurrying out to meet him with a huge tobacco-brown dog at her heels.

'Goodness,' murmurs Alec to Hercules. 'You've certainly met your match with this fellow, old boy.'

He gets out of the car, waving to Tilly, just as a woman comes out of the door behind her. She is not very tall, very slim, in jeans and shirt and a scarlet padded gilet. Her short fair hair curls attractively and she looks very relaxed as Tilly makes introductions whilst keeping an eye on Bear. Alec lets Hercules out of the car and the two dogs begin the usual sniffing ritual of greeting.

'Don't worry about Bear,' Billa says. 'He's far too lazy to get uptight with another dog.'

'And Hercules is far too old,' says Alec. 'Bear's a splendid fellow, though, isn't he?'

'He's very special,' agrees Billa, 'though not everyone's idea of a domestic pet.'

Alec laughs. 'I can see that. He's like a Shetland pony.'

'I knew they'd like each other,' Tilly says triumphantly. 'Good boys, aren't you?' She strokes them lovingly. 'Dom's bringing Bessie up in a minute for some coffee.'

'Rather like the chimps' tea party,' Billa says to Alec, 'only with dogs. Come and meet Ed.'

He is taken into the hall where the log fire burns brightly on the old millstone, and he can see up past the galleried landing into the rafters, and he exclaims with delight.

'Ed can tell you the history of it,' Billa says. 'He's got lots of old photographs. The land rises behind the house to the first floor. Upstairs there are big double doors that open out from the gallery. They were there to allow the lorries to come in so the milk could be poured from the churns into the vats, which were down here.

Before that it would have been horses and carts bringing the milk.'

'It must have taken great vision to convert it,' says Alec.

'It was my father's vision,' she says smiling.

Her smile is tinged with sadness and Alec remembers Tilly telling him that their father died when she and Ed were very young.

'A wonderful memorial?' he suggests, and he is relieved when she smiles at him more openly, almost with gratitude.

'It was good to come home,' she admits, 'when Philip died. Tilly tells us . . .' She hesitates. 'I am so sorry to hear that your wife died last year.'

Alec is pleased that she is so direct. 'We'd been together for a very long time,' he answers, 'and it seems very odd to be alone. We bought our little cottage at least thirty years ago so that we had a foothold in Cornwall whilst we were travelling around so much. When we retired our sons wanted us to buy something much bigger but I'm glad now that we didn't. The cottage has so many memories and it's more than big enough now for an old boy like me on his own.'

'I was lucky to be able to come back to Ed,' she tells him. 'And to Dom; that's our brother who lives down the lane. Oh, here is Ed . . .'

A tall man comes out of a room on the galleried landing and hurries down to meet him, and when Dom arrives a few minutes later with his golden retriever, Bessie, everything is easy and Alec has begun to enjoy himself.

They have coffee and brownies by the fire in the hall and then go to look at the lake, with the three dogs racing around them. When Alec tentatively suggest that they all go to the Chough for lunch everyone agrees with enthusiasm.

'We haven't been to the Chough for months,' Dom says. 'We tend to walk down to our local so that we can drink. You know that Tilly pulls pints at the Chough? She says that it's very trendy these days.'

Billa drives Ed and Dom; Tilly travels with Alec. Tilly is flushed with happiness that everything has gone so well. She twists round in her seat to praise Hercules—who is now exhausted—and Alec looks sideways at her with affection. He sees her smoothly soft skin, the thick butter-coloured hair, her brightly laughing eyes and he suddenly wishes, with an aching, poignant longing, that he was young again.

'No fool like an old fool,' he hears Rose mutter, and he grins ruefully to himself.

The pub is quite busy but they get a table near the fire and Alec goes to the bar to order a round of drinks. While he waits, the inner door to the lounge opens and a man looks in; it is the man from the lane, the man with the binoculars. He glances at Alec with indifference but when he sees the St Enedocs at their table an odd, wary look crosses his face and he withdraws quickly and closes the door.

Alec thinks about it, gives a little shrug, and presently forgets all about him.

Bear lies on the cool slates in the hall, exhausted after his morning with Hercules and Bessie. The house is silent, everyone has gone out, and he is quite alone. Usually he likes to go along for the ride but today he is content to rest, to stretch his big body out on the cold stone floor and sleep. He dreams that he is running, chasing and being chased in his turn, and his great paws twitch and he makes grunting noises. Suddenly the noise of the back door opening disturbs him from his sleep; the dream fades and he lies, waiting. He is too tired to get up and go out into the kitchen to welcome his people home so he stays, stretched out and relaxed, listening. He hears footsteps moving around in the kitchen, cupboards doors opening, closing, and moments of silence. The footsteps approach the hall and the door is pushed wider open. Bear prepares to get up but he sees that the man who is standing in the doorway is a stranger. He can smell all sorts of emanations coming from this man: excitement, tension, anxiety. There is something else that Bear doesn't like, doesn't trust, and he moves suddenly, heaving himself up. His deep growl is formidable. The stranger sees him and steps backwards.

'My God,' he says very quietly. 'OK. OK. Good fellow. Sit. Stay,' and he backs out again, closing the door before Bear can approach him. He can hear the stranger moving about in the kitchen again, then the back door closes and there is the sound of footsteps moving away down the drive. Bear goes to the kitchen door, tries to push it open, but it is firmly closed. His water bowl is in the kitchen and now he can't get to it. Bear sits down again, leaning heavily against the door; he slides down and stretches out. Soon he is asleep.

'You forgot to lock the back door and you closed the kitchen door,' Billa says to Ed. 'Poor old Bear's been stuck in the hall with no water.'

'I might have forgotten to lock the back door,' says Ed, 'but I didn't close the kitchen door. I never close it if we're leaving him here.'

'Well, I certainly didn't,' says Billa. 'Poor old fellow. He hasn't stopped drinking since I let him out. Perhaps Tilly closed it. Or Alec.'

'I like him, don't you?' says Ed. 'He made me feel very insular. Bit like Dom, living all over the world.'

'I like it that he didn't brag about it, though. It wasn't a travelogue or an endless recital of anecdotes.' She takes a deep happy breath. 'It was just such fun. He's like one of us. Tilly was right when she said that we ought to get together. Have you seen my mobile? I'm sure I left it here on the table.'

Ed shakes his head. 'You usually take it with you.'

'I know but I remember thinking I wouldn't bother. We all went out in such a muddle that I just left it on the table. Damn. I can't bear it when I lose it.'

'Check your study,' he says. 'I know you think you left it here but clearly you didn't.'

He picks up the letters from the kitchen table. Billa must have opened the end-of-year statement from their accountant before they went out, though she doesn't usually put it back into its envelope, and he glances down the column of figures of the company's accounts.

'If you've seen this I'll file it,' he says as she comes back from her study, looking irritated.

'I haven't looked at the post today,' she says crossly, 'and my mobile's not there.'

'Phone the pub,' he advises. 'Just check. It's worth a try.'

She sighs impatiently but takes the directory from the shelf and turns the pages. As he wanders away into the hall she can hear her voice, explaining, asking the question.

'Any luck?' he calls, and she comes into the hall looking puzzled.

'He says that a man handed it in just now. Says it was down the side of the chair I was sitting in. That's really weird. I was absolutely sure I left it here.'

Ed shrugs, raising his eyebrows, making a face calculated to tease her out of her irritation.

'Oh, stop it,' she says. 'I am not losing my marbles. Damn. Now I'll have to go and get it. Oh, wait. It's Tilly pub night, isn't it? She can pick it up for me.'

Ed sighs with relief. The panic is over and he wants to restore some of their earlier good spirits.

'I'll light the fire,' he says. 'Looks like we've got a card from young Harry. Or have you read it already?'

'I told you I haven't looked at the post.' For some strange reason she feels scratchy, unsettled, all her happiness sliding away.

'Well,' Ed says pacifically, looking at the slit envelope, clearly not believing her, 'read it now. Maybe he's coming home.'

Dear Ed and Billa,

How's everything with you? I've been staying with friends in Canada for a few weeks but Dom will have told you that I'm on my way home to see you all. I had to send this card because the chap on the front looks just like Bear. Don't quite know yet when I shall be in Cornwall— probably in the next week or so—but I'll stay in touch as I move on.

Lots of love, Harry

Billa's spirits lift again; the card restores her happiness.

'Look at this,' she says to Ed, who is breathing life into the fire with the bellows. 'Harry says he might be home next week. Dom said he was working his way here by degrees. It'll be so good to see him.' She holds the card so that Ed can see the picture of the big brown bear. 'He says it reminded him of Bear.'

'I wouldn't want to hug that chap,' says Ed. He is relieved that Billa sounds happy again and he experiences a moment of very real pleasure at the thought of seeing Harry. He's particularly fond of Dom's grandson. 'Have you thought any more about us leaving Mellinpons to Harry?'

Billa lets the card fall on to her lap. 'I think about it quite a lot,' she admits. 'After all, there's nobody else to leave it to, except Dom. It's quite right that we made him the beneficiary in our wills, after all, he is our father's eldest son. At the same time, Dom's older than both of us and he'll never need Mellinpons. I think it would be really good for it to go to his grandson. Dom's cottage will go to his two girls and, let's face it, they'll simply sell up. Of all of them, Harry's the only member of the family who's ever likely to come back to Cornwall. I just worry about whether it might cause trouble in the family. That Harry's been singled out, I mean.'

'But we hardly ever hear from the others, do

we? Only through Dom. Harry's spent holidays and weekends here when he was at Oxford. He Skypes us and sends emails. He's the only one of Dom's grandchildren who has any real interest in us. Clearly Dom must leave his property between his daughters but we can do as we like.'

Billa nods. Secretly she's rather surprised that Ed feels so strongly; usually he's very aware of people's feelings and how they might be upset. In this case it is clear that his love for Harry is stronger than his inhibitions.

'I wish Dom had changed his name to St Enedoc,' she says. 'After all, his mother simply picked a name out of a hat to go on the birth certificate as his father. James Blake didn't exist. I don't blame her—back then it was a very difficult situation to be in—but once the truth came out Dom could have simply changed it.'

'I think that it's because our father never acknowledged him. He refused to see him. I think that Dom's found that very hard and that's the reason he wouldn't take his name.'

'He made it clear, though, in his will, didn't he?' says Billa. 'The cottages were left for Dom and funds to make certain he could continue with his education. Of course, Mother couldn't bear the sight of him, which didn't help. And ghastly Tris calling him a bastard and his mother a whore. God, Dom was so angry. That's why I'd like to leave Mellinpons to Harry. To kind of make up for things. I know it's silly but he looks so like Dom. Well, like you, too. When I see Harry it's like time has swung backwards and we're all young again. And he is our great-nephew.'

'And the girls are our nieces,' Ed reminds her. 'It's a bit of a problem, but, in the end, it's our decision.'

'Maybe seeing Harry again will push us into taking the final step,' suggests Billa.

Ed nods, smiles at her and goes upstairs, taking his letters with him.

She stands the card on the top of the chest and stares at the picture of the brown bear. Since they've come back from the pub she's been feeling unsettled, like a cat with its fur rubbed the wrong way, and it's not just to do with losing her mobile. Clearly, she must have snatched it up and dropped it into her pocket on the way out while everyone was discussing who would travel with whom, and which cars to use, and whether Bear and Bessie ought to go. Even so, she can't remember doing it and she still has that odd feeling—as if she's being watched: spied on.

Bear comes to sit beside her, leaning against her legs, and she strokes his head, pulls his soft ears. He pants a little, and gazes at her intently. She smiles at his expression and puts her arm around his neck.

'Look,' she says, picking up the card. 'It's one of your relatives,' but Bear isn't interested in the card. He, too, seems ill at ease, restless.

'Come on,' she says at last. 'I thought you'd still be exhausted after all that dashing around earlier but I think you need a walk.' She shouts up the stairs to Ed. 'Bear and I are going down to the lake,' and they go through the kitchen and out into the sunshine together.

CHAPTER ELEVEN

The weather changes slowly, gently. As the east wind swings round to the west a silver curtain of rain is drawn across the peninsular, drifting, swinging, obscuring the hills and the sea. Trees, half-hidden by mist, appear as ghostly twisted semi-human shapes; old woodland gods with untidy tresses of ivy trailing from their outflung arms. Silver drops of moisture hang in the hedgerows where thorn and ash and oak have grown for a thousand years.

Coming in from the greenhouse Dom hears a woodpecker drumming in the woods and stands still to listen, his heart quickening with pleasure at this forerunner of spring. He kicks off his boots, pauses to give Bessie a rub with the old towel he keeps inside the door for this purpose. She stands obediently and then bounds away from him into the kitchen, tossing the leather bone she's holding in her mouth, daring him to reach for it. He does, just to please her, and immediately she jerks her head away, keeping the bone out of his grasp, bowing down on her front legs with her tail waving happily. He seizes the bone suddenly, catching her off balance, and tosses it through the open door, down the hall, where it lands all amongst the post on the doormat.

She bounds after it, scattering the envelopes, and he goes to rescue them, picking them up and taking them back to the kitchen. He drops them on the table and then turns to look again, his attention caught by the picture lying half-covered by an envelope. He picks up the postcard and stares at it in disbelief. It is a reproduction of Toulouse-Lautrec's *Rue des Moulins Brothel*. The model stands with her back to the artist, her chemise hitched up, half-exposing her right buttock, her dark stocking rolled down to her knees. It is almost touching in its ugliness, its humanness, but Dom stares at it with the sense of having received a blow to the heart. He knows what he will see when he turns it over.

It is addressed to Dominic Blake. Opposite the address, Tris has scrawled: 'Staying with friends in Roscoff for a few days. See you soon. Tris. PS I thought she'd be just your type.'

Dom turns the card over again and stares at the picture of the prostitute. He is so shocked, so angry, that he feels that he might explode. His hands begin to shake and with an enormous effort he takes control of himself. He sits down at the table, willing himself to be calm, telling himself grimly that this is exactly what would please Tristan most. If he were to have a stroke or a heart attack, how pleased Tris would be—especially if he were to be found dead clutching a postcard of a prostitute.

Dom almost laughs out loud at the thought. It is madness to allow this foolishness to drive him to the edge of an almost killing rage. He sits at the table and stares at the card, analysing his anger. Tris hits where it hurts most: at Dom's deep-down insecurity. Despite the fact that he has been loved, successful in his field, has a thriving family, despite all these things, there is still a part of him that is unresolved, unhealed. He cannot come to terms with his father's refusal to see him; he never spoke to him, never touched him. He supported him financially, provided generously for his future, but he rejected Dom as a person, as his son.

Silently he pieces the familiar jigsaw together. He knows now why it was only after his father died that he was allowed to visit his grandmother in Cornwall. Back then no particular reason was given for his mother refusing to accompany him on that first momentous journey; in 1952 children had much more freedom and independence, and it was seen as an adventure. Anyway, his mother had to work and there was cousin Susan to keep an eye on. Dom, just having celebrated his twelfth birthday, was old enough now to go to see Granny. He remembered how his mother hugged him on the platform at Temple Meads, giving him a kiss, telling him to be a good boy. He'd glanced round quickly to see if there might be any boys from his school, embarrassed by her emotion, and then he'd suddenly felt an uprush of love for her, a momentary pang at the prospect of being so far from home, and had hugged her too. Then the London train came roaring in, and they were enveloped in billowing clouds of steam, the sour stench of soot and the noise of screeching brakes, and his mother ran to speak to the guard to ask him to make sure that Dom got off at Bodmin.

Dom sits at the table, staring back across the decades at that boy in grey flannel shorts and a faded blue Aertex shirt, all set for adventure. He remembers he had a book specially for the journey, an Arthur Ransome—*Swallows and Amazons*? *Pigeon Post*?—and a bottle of ginger beer and a packed lunch: cheese sandwiches, an orange and a bar of chocolate.

'Don't,' his mother cautioned, 'eat the chocolate all at once. And try not to be messy with the orange. Got a handkerchief? Good, then. Don't forget to use it.'

He'd stood at the window in the corridor, waving until he could see her no more, and then entered the compartment the guard had shown them. He was slightly overawed by the other passengers:

two matronly, middle-aged ladies in smart tweeds on their way back from a few days in London, a young, sharp-faced man in a cheap suit who looked like a travelling salesman, and an older, military-looking man with a bushy moustache, who was half-hidden behind *The Times*. Tentatively Dom stepped amongst their feet—two smart pairs of court shoes, a scuffed pair of black lace-ups, and one pair of highly polished brogues —and hefted his shabby bag on to the shelf above his head. The two women stopped talking to watch him, their expressions kind, motherly.

'Travelling alone?' one of them asked brightly. 'I expect you'd like a window seat. Move up, Phyllis. He can have mine.'

They moved along, ignoring his protests, whilst the young salesman winked at him and the older man frowned slightly, rattling his paper, as if implying that Dom was too old for such childish favours. The young man grinned, tipping his head towards the old soldier as if inviting Dom to join in the joke, and Dom cautiously smiled back. He sat down and stared out of the window, not wanting to be engaged in conversation, wishing he'd thought to get his book out of his bag. This journey was life-changing: his first step into an adult world. He'd begun to realize that there were other influences beyond the small world of home and school. At school he elaborated the story of his father's death in the war so as to fend off questions about his family, but he asked his mother why he had no relations on his father's side: no aunts or uncles, or grandparents or cousins. She was always vague: his father came from the north, he'd been an orphan. There was Granny, of course, and some distant relatives down in Cornwall.

Granny occasionally came to visit in the school holidays but never during term-time. She never came to hear him singing in the cathedral choir or to cheer him on athletics day, so that watching his school friends' groups of family he'd feel oddly lonely, though there were several other boys whose fathers had died in the war. Often his mother was working and cousin Susan was deemed to be too old to attend school functions so he was used to being alone. But he had friends, good friends, who invited him to their homes—though very few were invited to the little house in St Michael's Hill—but still he'd felt lonely until he'd met Billa and Ed in Granny's cottage, and for the first time in his life he'd experienced an overwhelming sense of homecoming.

Dom stands up, fills the kettle and sits down again. Bessie settles on her rug, stretching out and sighing. He remembers now that the book had been *The Picts and the Martyrs*—his favourite of all Arthur Ransome's books—and as he sits, remembering, the scene slips again into his mind.

The tweedy women were predisposed for conversation: where was he going? Who would be meeting him? How old was he? He answered politely but wondered how they would respond if he asked them the same questions. All the while he was aware of the unspoken partisanship from the young man sitting across from him. He was now studying a racing paper but Dom saw his mouth twitch into a smile, his eyelid drop in a brief conspiratorial wink. Dom was warmed by the sensation of friendship. It made him feel grown up. The military-looking man, on the other hand, reminded him of Major Banks who taught geography. Dom surreptitiously smoothed his hand over his newly cut hair and kept his feet in their rubbed leather sandals under the seat. He was confused by these tensions. He knew that if the young man and he were alone a conversation would start up, they'd joke together, and perhaps get out their sandwiches. Alone with the older man, he'd call him 'Sir'.

Instead, he smiled at the two women and stood up to retrieve his book. *The Picts and the Martyrs: or Not Welcome at All.* He stared at the paper cover. He'd never noticed the second part of the title: *Not Welcome at All.* He thought of his arrival in Cornwall and how it would work being alone with Granny. They'd never been alone together before: how would it be? He felt anxious, and he studied the cover of the book to distract himself. It was a familiar, well-loved book and he tested himself by looking at the small printed photographs scattered over the pink paper cover and identifying them with those same pictures inside the book: here were Dick and Dot in the stone hut in the woods, and here was their little boat, the *Scarab*. And this one was the skull and crossbones over Dick's bed. Dick was his favourite character, especially in this book about mining; Dom, like Dick, was good at chemistry and physics and fascinated by geology. Dom opened the book and began to read. The first chapter began with Dick and Dot on a train journey and its heading was 'Visitors Expected'. Dom experienced another twinge of apprehension. He was the expected visitor and, just for a moment, he wished that he too was on his way to see Nancy and Peggy, and that Timothy would be meeting him at Bodmin station in a squashy hat, with lots of plans for his mining project up in the hills.

The amazing thing was that, almost as soon as he'd arrived at Granny's cottage, he'd been catapulted into his own Swallows and Amazons kind of country. Ed and Billa appeared in the kitchen—'They live just up the lane,' said Granny casually—and Billa had looked from him to Ed and back again, amazed at the likeness. 'I think you're related in some kind of way,' Granny said, even more casually. He was never invited to the old butter factory—'Mother isn't very well because of Daddy dying'—and it didn't really matter at first because Billa and Ed took him to their hearts and he felt at last as if he had a real family. He was home. He loved Cornwall, the moors and the mines, and that he—no matter how distantly—was related to a family who had been connected to mining for generations. The joy lasted. Puzzled and hurt though he was by the complete rejection of Elinor St Enedoc, the joy remained with him. She'd drive by in her Morris Minor Traveller, staring straight ahead, a hand briefly raised to Granny or to Mr Potts, if either should happen to be out at the front of the cottages. Ed and Billa would wave furiously from the back seat, as if trying to make up for her coolness, but everything changed when their mother married again.

Now, Dom remembers the scene in Granny's potager; he relives his confusion when Billa, overcome with misery at the prospect of Tris as a stepbrother, flung herself into his arms. He remembers Granny leading her away and, later, how they sat in the sun while Granny told him the truth. How angry he'd been, knowing that for all those years he'd been lied to, and then Ed had come rushing down the lane followed by Billa, who was watching him apprehensively.

'Mother couldn't stop crying when she told us,' Billa said later. 'She said that your mother . . . seduced Daddy because he was rich.'

They'd walked in the wood where each holiday they'd made their summer camps, carefully not touching; Dom with his hands in his pockets, Billa's arms folded beneath her breast. He was silent. It must be hard for Billa. She wouldn't want to think that her father had loved his, Dom's, mother. His mother must be seen as the villain of the piece: the witch, the whore.

'So you're the bastard' . . . 'Your mother's a whore.'

Dom picks up the postcard, crumples it in his fist, and then—just as suddenly—smooths it out again. He thinks of his anger, his shame; the rejection by his father that lies like a canker beneath everything he has achieved, waiting to destroy it.

And he thinks: I wonder what happened to Tris to make him like he is?

He turns his head away as if rejecting the thought; it is easier to hate than to understand: to judge rather than to allow compassion a foothold. Secretly he is shocked at the level of his rage. After all, fifty years have passed: why should this postcard, the foolish message, generate such terrible fury? Of course, there is something uncomplicated about such a reaction; something oddly pure and virtuous, almost self-righteous. Tris is insulting his, Dom's, mother; he is making that simple, innocent act of lovemaking into something disgusting and evil. And he is smearing Dom at the same time; he is implying that Dom is less of a man, less worthy, less

145

lovable because of it. Dom faces this implication. He believes it because it is how his father saw him; not good enough for his love or public acknowledgement. He and his mother were cast out because they were beneath his contempt.

'So you're the bastard' . . . 'Your mother's a whore.'

Dom turns his head again and looks at the card. Just why does Tris want to hurt, to destroy? Where did Andrew and Tris come from, and where did they go? He knew the potted history: Andrew met Tris's mother in France, she'd died when Tris was four, and the two of them continued to live in France for the next six years. Andrew had just sold his business when he met Elinor at a party in London. He'd made some very good investments and he was looking for somewhere to live, having decided that he wanted to continue to educate Tris in England. The facts, such as they were, bore this out. Tris was at a prep school in Berkshire, both of them were bilingual, and Andrew never seemed short of money.

Dom puts his head in his hands. He wonders exactly what Andrew and Tris were doing in France for those six years of Tris's life, and he thinks about how readily, how easily, Andrew walked away from his marriage to Elinor, snatching Tris from his school along the way. He thinks of the postcards of the bicycle, of Bitser. What did Tris see when he arrived at the old

146

butter factory that had made him hate them all so much? Security? A family home? Stability? Was it just one step too far along the disjointed path of his young life?

Dom sits back in his chair, stretches out his legs and sticks his hands in the pockets of his quilted waistcoat. His fingers make contact with a small card and he brings it out and looks at it. There is a name, 'Sir Alec Bancroft', and a telephone number.

'Come and see me,' he said. 'Come for coffee. Hercules and I enjoy having visitors.'

Suddenly Dom feels very tired; his anger has evaporated but he feels old and vulnerable. He stands up and reaches for the telephone.

'Bancroft.' The voice is calm, steady, confident.

'It's Dominic Blake,' Dom says. 'I know Billa and Ed have invited you to dinner for a return match, and I shall see you then, but I wondered if I might take you up on that offer of coffee.'

'Splendid,' says Alec at once. 'I'd like that very much. When can you make it?'

They agree a date and Dom puts the phone down. He feels stronger again; as if a burden has been lifted from his shoulders. He looks at the postcard and puts it in his pocket. It no longer has the power to enrage him but he doesn't want Tilly to see it, nor Billa nor Ed.

He turns his mind deliberately to positive things; he thinks about Harry's visit and is filled with anticipation. He must check his room, make up his bed. Knowing Harry, he might simply turn up at any time—and it will be so good to see him again. The bad moment has passed but the question remains: what does Tris want?

CHAPTER TWELVE

S arah puts the sleeping George in his cot, looks down at him for a moment and then goes out and down the steep, narrow stairs. She likes the little cottage, where they came in such haste when the plans for the rented house they'd organized fell through, and where she's spent so many family holidays. It's familiar, cosy, and it's a good place to be, just for now, with a new baby, and Ben very happy at the nursery school at Padstow.

At the bottom of the stairs, in the comfortable rather shabby sitting-room, Sarah hesitates. She would like to collapse on to the sofa, read a book, sleep, but there is a pile of ironing to be done. Resolutely she brings the ironing board from its cupboard under the stairs and sets it up in the kitchen, pours water into the back of the iron and turns the dial to 'steam'. She fetches the laundry basket from the tiny utility room and begins to sort through the tangled assortment of clothes. At one level this act of self-discipline boosts her sense of pride, but at another she suspects that it might be more sensible to lie on the sofa and rest. She is so tired, and George won't sleep for very long, and then she'll have the school run and Ben, weary and demanding after his day at nursery school. He's been playing up just lately, jealous of her attention to George and inclined to whine.

'When's Daddy coming home? I want Daddy to read to me . . . bath me . . . play trains . . .'

The iron steams and hisses as she pushes it wearily over creased and crumpled cotton. Her back aches from carrying George, who screams every time she lays him down, and she longs to burst into tears and scream back at him. The trouble is, everyone expects her to be strong, to lead, to cope, and just lately she feels that she might suddenly explode, smash things, get in the car and drive and drive.

The knock at the door is the last straw: she cannot manage even speaking to anyone at the moment. She puts the iron carefully on the stand, goes into the hall and opens the door.

Clem stands there. 'Hi,' he says. 'If it's a bad moment just say so.'

Sarah is filled with conflicting emotions. Clem is probably the one person in the world she can cope with just at this moment. He will ask nothing of her; he will bring his own brand of comfort and courage into her little world. But she feels exhausted. She's so tired that she might not be able

149

to live up to her own standard of bravery. She has always been strong in front of Clem—the tough naval wife and loving mother—and today she might just not be able to manage that level of control. She doesn't want to lose face in front of Clem. She likes and admires him—and slightly fancies him—and she'd hate it if he were to lose his good opinion of her.

'You look tired,' he says, concerned. 'Don't worry. It's nothing special. Just thought I'd see if you were OK. I can't stay long, anyway, Jakey will be home from school soon.'

As he makes to go she is seized with disappointment.

'No, no,' she says quickly. 'Well, I am tired but it would be good just to talk to another adult for a change. Ben and George are wearing me down at the moment.'

He follows her into the kitchen. 'I know the feeling,' he says sympathetically. 'There was a period of my life when Jakey was small that I seemed to be able to communicate only at the level of a three-year-old.'

She turns quickly, to agree with him, and her unguarded movement jolts the ironing board and the iron topples from its stand. She gives a little scream and, quick as a flash, Clem seizes the flex before the iron hits the slate floor. He hauls it up, stands it on the draining board and switches it off. Though nothing has happened and everything is safe, Sarah is suddenly overcome with foolish panic; she feels weak and trembly.

'Hey,' says Clem, concerned. 'It's OK. No problem. All over now.'

She manages a smile. 'Sorry,' she says. 'It's just . . .'

He takes her upper arm in a strong grip. 'Sit down,' he says. 'You look exhausted. Come on, sit here.' He pushes her down on to the sofa. 'Can I get you something? Tea?'

She shakes her head; his grasp makes her feel odd—feminine and rather helpless—and she is sorry when he lets go of her arm. She smiles waveringly up at him. He's very attractive, and part of the attraction is that he really does understand. He's brought Jakey up, he's had to try to be both mother and father, and he knows how lonely and exhausting it is in a way that Dave can never begin to contemplate.

'Sorry,' she says, deciding that perhaps a little feminine weakness is just as appealing as strength and courage. 'You caught me at a low moment. The boys are a bit demanding just now.'

'When's Dave back?'

'Oh, a couple of weeks yet.' She shrugs, allows a measure of indifference to creep into her voice, so that he can see that she doesn't expect Dave to be a great deal of help. She gives a little, light laugh. 'He can be almost as demanding as the boys when he's just back from sea.'

Clem raises an eyebrow, amused. 'I expect he can be,' he says.

Sarah feels confused, embarrassed. She wonders if Clem thinks she's hinting at Dave's sexual appetites, and she can feel herself getting hot, her face burning, but she can't laugh it off as she might have done on other visits. Today she is too wound up, too tense, and his friendship—respect? affection?—is too important to her. That silly incident with the iron has upset her out of all proportion.

'At least,' he is saying quite calmly, 'you'll have another adult to talk to. That's what I used to miss. Oh, there were people at the office, of course, but when I got home and the nanny had gone it was just me and Jakey.'

'That's just it,' she says quickly, regaining her composure. 'It's that long desert between getting home from school and bath-time. Sometimes those few hours feel like weeks.'

'And it must be harder with two.'

'Yes. Yes, it is.' She is eager to develop the theme, to build on this empathy, to elicit sympathy and admiration. 'Ben sees that George gets attention because he's a baby and so he's regressed a bit so as to vie with him.'

'Yes, I can see that would be rather wearing,' Clem agrees, and she smiles bravely; he's so kind, so sweet, so attractive . . .

'I expect Tilly is a comfort, isn't she?'

Sarah's smile wavers just a little. 'Tilly?'

He shrugs, glances away, as if slightly embarrassed. 'You seem to be very good friends as well as working together. She was telling me. You know, about being at school together, and how she loves Ben and George.'

Sarah's smile vanishes. She sees now that he has come simply to talk about Tilly; he is yet another of her conquests. She tries to control a bitter uprush of jealous bile but spiteful words spill out before she can stop them.

'Tilly hasn't a clue,' she says. 'She's very sweet but pretty hopeless when it comes to children. In fact, she's pretty hopeless with anything domestic.'

This time his raised eyebrows are not accompanied by amusement; he simply looks surprised. Sarah is convinced that he also looks disappointed, not at Tilly's inadequacies but in her own disloyalty at disclosing them. Before she can defend herself, George begins to cry and she, too, would like to scream with frustration.

Clem raises his hands, makes a sympathetic face. 'I'll head off,' he says.

Sarah senses his relief, his readiness to escape, and can only nod in agreement. He lets himself out and she gets up, takes a few deep breaths, and goes upstairs to George.

Outside the door Clem also takes a few deep breaths. He was getting a bit out of his depth there, he tells himself. Poor Sarah's clearly exhausted. It's time Dave came home.

He walks away, into the village and down the hill towards the vicarage. His pastoral relationship with Sarah and Dave has slowly morphed into friendship: they are his age, they have small children, and it is good to share with them at this easy level. They get on very well and he's had some good times with them. Lately, Sarah's looked after Jakey for an hour or two after school when there have been late meetings.

Perhaps, he thinks, it was unwise to mention Tilly, though he can't quite see why. After all, the two girls are good friends; they work together. Certainly Sarah was very nervy just now for such a down-to-earth, capable girl. But there might be several reasons for that. The trouble is, Tilly is under his skin: there's something about her. Sarah's tart response surprised him: it was almost as if she were jealous of his interest in Tilly. With some younger women he's cautious; careful that his visits are seen to be purely pastoral, but Sarah has never been remotely vulnerable or needy, those dangerous qualities that can turn very quickly into emotional minefields. And, anyway, she's very happy with Dave, who's a great guy. It must simply have been a bad moment; she's probably over-tired and missing Dave.

Clem looks at his watch and glances behind him. The school bus is almost due and Jakey will be home. Immediately he remembers Sarah's words: 'Tilly hasn't a clue . . . when it comes to children or anything domestic.'

His thoughts about Tilly are confused. She is pretty, witty, fun. He is strongly drawn towards her but all his instinctive caution is holding him back. He remembers how, after Madeleine died and he returned to London with Jakey, he'd picked up again with old friends, girls who were quite content with a simple physical relationship—to begin with, anyway. He soon realized that a young man with a small son triggered emotional responses from women, and these relationships became more complicated. For himself, emotional muddles and casual fumblings had never been his way and it was with relief that he moved to the Lodge at the convent; it was almost like taking a vow of celibacy. He could immerse himself in the hard work in the grounds and the house, whilst looking after Jakey, and nothing else was demanded from him except the growing desire to pursue his original vocation.

Now, as he thinks about Tilly, it's as if he's woken from a dream in which his private feelings have been kept deep frozen and this thawing process is very painful. He is confused, anxious—but he can't wait to see her again.

He lets himself into the vicarage just as the school bus pulls up. The modern vicarage is a sixties-build bungalow on a small plot. He misses the stone Lodge, with all its character, but the bungalow is yards from the beach and is very easy to keep clean. Several of Jakey's school friends live in the village, so there are very useful baby-sitting options close at hand, and he loves being able to ride to the beach on his bicycle unsuper-vised whilst Clem works in the small garden and strolls out from time to time to keep an eye on him without spoiling Jakey's sense of independence.

The bus has turned and chugs away, back up the hill, and now Clem can hear the children, their cries as piercing as the seagulls that scream above their heads. He opens the front door and waits for Jakey to part from his friends and appear through the wrought-iron gateway. He sees him come in; a small blond boy with his Spiderman rucksack slung over one arm, his face alight with some joke he's just shared with one of his friends, and Clem's heart expands with love and pride and fear.

He thinks about introducing Jakey to Tilly, how the relationship between them would begin, and he is seized with such terror and doubt that his new-found confidence is utterly destroyed. How could he take such a chance? Why should a girl like Tilly be interested in a curate with a very low salary and a seven-year-old boy?

'Daddy,' shouts Jakey, seeing him in the door-way. 'Guess what? I got a gold star for spelling.'

He dumps his bag inside the door, begins to root about inside it, and pulls out a small certificate, which says that Jakey Pardoe has got ten out of ten for his spelling test. He holds it up triumphantly, beaming. One of his front teeth is missing. Clem looks down at him and doesn't know whether to laugh or cry.

'Well done,' he says. 'I knew all that hard work would pay off. That definitely deserves a piece of cake. Come on. Let's see what's going.'

Jakey kick-boxes his way round the hall, making 'wham' and 'pow' noises at his imaginary assailant and then follows Clem into the kitchen.

CHAPTER THIRTEEN

The taxi driver turns his cab in the gateway, raises a hand to Harry and drives away down the lane. Harry watches him go and then turns back to survey the old stone cottage with relief and affection. Standing here in the sunshine he feels as if he has come home. This cottage, which was once two dwellings but has been made one, the familiar scrawl of the granite tor against the sky, the broken outline of a ruined engine house, the bleached wintry woods along the stream, all these seem to be knitted into his heart.

Despite the fact that Dom's old Volvo is parked by the outbuildings, Harry senses that there is nobody at home. For one thing, Bessie would be barking by now to announce his arrival. But he doesn't mind. He likes to arrive unannounced; to take them all by surprise. This is probably because he always has such a wholehearted welcome and he thoroughly enjoys the expressions of delight, the cries of pleasure.

'They spoil you,' his sisters say, rather sourly, but he doesn't mind that either. Back in Jo'burg he is the youngest of the family, just one amongst his siblings and their cousins and numerous aunts and uncles. He knows he's lucky to have such a big, successful family—clever lawyers and wealthy bankers—but here is where he feels truly at home, most valued.

'You're a Cornishman,' his mother said to him, reluctant but resigned, a few years ago when he was about to go to Oxford to read Geology. 'You're a little St Enedoc,' and she'd told him the whole story about his grandfather and Billa and Ed. It was as if she'd given him a present; his whole world had turned and slid gently into its appointed place. Then he understood why this odd stone cottage, the old butter factory and the wild north Cornish coast meant so much to him; then he no longer felt rather lonely and out of joint. He didn't feel envious any more of his blonde sisters and their cousins; he looked like Dom, like Ed. He was a Cornishman; a St Enedoc.

He read everything he could find about the family and Cornwall and its mining history, and when the time was right he announced that he was going to train as a mining engineer at the Camborne School of Mines as his grandfather had before him. Nobody argued or tried to dissuade him; they'd all seen the writing on the wall.

'He'll come back,' they assured each other. 'Plenty of good mining jobs here once he's finished in Cornwall and got it out of his system.'

Now, Harry takes his bags round to the back door, tries the handle, and then leaves his luggage in the porch. He strolls along the lane to the old butter factory, listening to the rush and tumble of water and a robin singing in the hedge. The sun is shining in its pale, cool, English way, and he exults in the freshness of the air and the slip and slide of the little chill breeze over his warm skin. He is invigorated, alive with excitement: he is home.

As he crosses the stone bridge from the lane he sees that someone is at the kitchen door and he calls out, thinking it might be Ed. The man turns at once, his hand dropping from the door handle. Harry doesn't recognize him but smiles at him anyway. The man smiles back. He could be anything between fifty and sixty, lean and tough-looking with russet-grey curling hair. He's carrying a leather satchel and Harry assumes he's delivering leaflets. As he gets closer he sees the man is staring at him curiously, one eyebrow quirked almost in amusement, as if he recognizes him. He has very pale, frosty grey eyes and a tanned, deeply lined skin.

159

'Hi,' Harry says. 'Nobody around?'

The man shrugs. 'I've no idea. I was just delivering something.'

He watches as Harry opens the door and goes in, calling out, but there is no answer, no Bear coming out to greet him, and when Harry glances back the man has gone. He stands for a moment in the kitchen, wanders through into the hall and looks up and up past the galleried landing to the beams above. He loves this space, the sense of airiness and light. The ash on the old millstone hearthstone is still warm and there are two empty coffee mugs on the chest that Billa and Ed use as a table.

Harry goes back through the kitchen and stands outside, listening. He can hear the whine of a chainsaw and he sets off along the stream into the woods. Soon he sees them: the two brothers working together, taking some dead branches from a tree, the two dogs—one golden, one brown— playing together nearby. Bessie is the first to see him. Barking, tail waving, she runs to greet him, and he drops down to one knee so as to fling his arms round her while she licks his face vigorously, wriggling and whining with excitement. Bear comes to investigate at a slower gait, acknowledging this favourite member of the family with a majestic air and accepting the homage due to him as Harry strokes his head and murmurs to him.

Ed and Dom have stopped work to see what the dogs are doing, and now their shouts reach Harry and he waves. With the dogs beside him he breaks into a run towards his grandfather and his great-uncle.

'Hi,' he shouts back. 'I'm back. The prodigal son has come home.'

Tris walks past Dom's cottage and along the lane to his car, which is parked deep in the shadow of an ash tree. Even now he won't hurry, though his heart beats rather faster than he likes to admit to and his breathing is uneven. He is still in shock at the sight of the boy, so like Dom when he, Tris, first met him fifty years ago.

He hears Elinor St Enedoc's voice: 'It's so humiliating, Andrew. Having the boy so close. Of course, Harry never spoke of him but he supported him—them—financially. You can imagine how I felt when I first saw him.'

'You poor darling.' His father's voice was tender, emollient. Then a slight pause and a change of tone: curious, prurient. 'So what was she like, his mother?'

There was a little rustle, as if Elinor had drawn back from his father's embrace, and her voice was sharper.

'Oh, the usual little tart, I imagine. Out for his money, of course. Well, she's had enough of it. When Harry died he left both the cottages in trust for the boy as well as money to pay for the rest of his education. Naturally Billa and Ed adore him.'

161

And again, 'It's just so humiliating to have Harry's bastard living next door.'

Peeping through the crack in the door, Tris could see Elinor in his father's arms, being comforted. He walked straight in, enjoying the slight embarrassment, the hasty drawing apart. It was like a game, seeing just how far he could push his luck. He hated the pretend life that he and his father lived but there was no choice.

'The police would take you away from me,' his father had told him, way back. 'Nobody must ever know. Do you understand? It was a terrible accident but it's too late now to do anything about it. You must promise, Tris.'

And he promised, nodding very fast, trembling a little, lest his father might lose his temper and strike him, too. He could still hear those thumps and cries and then the sudden silence. From where he crouched on the stairs, he had seen his father come out of the pretty drawing-room and look about him. He stood, rubbing his hands over his face, his shadow stretched across the hall, and then he went out quietly into the dark garden. Quick as light, Tris slipped down the stairs and into the drawing-room. His mother lay huddled, her eyes half-opened, but when he touched her, called to her in an urgent half-whisper, kissed her, she didn't move. A patch of her blonde hair was dark and sticky, and he put out a tentative finger to touch it. He heard his father coming and quickly, quickly, he slipped behind one of the long damask curtains, wiping his fingers on the silky lining. Grunting and swearing to himself, his father edged the body into a large swathe of sacking, wrapping it, covering it, before heaving it into his arms and carrying it away. Tris had run upstairs, climbed into bed, pulled the blankets over his head: waiting for the footsteps at his bedroom door.

'A terrible accident has happened,' his father said, sitting on his bed. His voice was ragged, his breathing laboured, and Tris tried not to shrink away from the heavy hand on his small shoulder. 'Maman fell and hit her head. She's dead, Tris. Now listen. If anyone should find out the police will take you away from me so we're going away, now, tonight, to a country where nobody will ever know and we shall say that she died of an illness. Do you understand me, Tris? You must promise.'

And he promised, nodding quickly, hearing those thumps, frightened of the look in his father's eyes. He was just four years old.

Standing by the car, Tris listens to the sound of the chainsaw, hears it stop. A dog is barking and he can hear voices raised in welcome. He wonders who the boy is: a nephew, a grandson, a more distant relation? He's taken Tris by surprise. From his vantage point across the valley he'd watched Billa drive off, seen Ed and Dom and the dogs mustering for a stint in the woods, and decided to chance his arm at getting into the old butter factory and having another look around.

Now he gets into the car, puts the satchel on the passenger seat, fits the keys into the ignition. He's never known why it's so important to take risks. Once, someone very close to him—one of the very few people he'd ever trusted—said that it was his way of taking control of his own life. He'd been manipulated, lied to, pushed from pillar to post, and here was an opportunity to feel in charge. Quickly he discovered how easy it was to manipulate in his turn, to frighten and influence people. It began as a game but it's a game that has become an addiction: he needs the high that comes with testing his luck.

Even now, he's still feeling the charge that resulted when he turned from the back door to see the boy coming towards him. Though Tris's heart is still out of control, and he can hardly breathe, he laughs: it's all worth it. He drives slowly, peering through the trees along the stream. He can see them now: the happy group. Standing together, the boy's arms gesticulating, the older men watching him, the dogs weaving round them. Their body language says it all. The engine idles whilst Tris watches, the laughter fading from his eyes. How he'd longed for just such a scene as this when he was young. Someone shouting with delight as he approached, faces lighting up with joy, arms opened in welcome. The weight of the secret, the fear of the exposure, excluded true intimacy between him and his father, and the other women that his father chose found Tris an unnecessary extra. Soon the relationships broke down, or circumstances arose that made it vital to move on: the spectres from the past, or his father's paymasters, appearing, threatening any hope of security or peace.

Still he watches. It was under this very tree that he stepped out to confront Dom all those years ago. The older boys at his school had been very happy to explain to him the meaning of the words 'bastard' and 'tart', and armed with the knowledge he opened fire at the first opportunity. 'If you're not one up you're one down.' It was his motto; his mantra. How easy it had been for his father to frighten a small boy into acquiescence; to threaten him with the prospect of an orphanage or a foster home. It was a relief to go away to school at eight; to become anonymous, to have the rough, unquestioning companionship of other little boys who—because his father always had money to spare—asked no difficult questions about the past and whose mothers were kind to him because his own mother had died when he was small. They invited him for exeats and part of the holidays. His father worked abroad, was often called away, but life had become simpler. And then the St Enedocs had come into his life.

Watching the group under the trees, Tris wonders

whether his father had really fallen in love with Elinor or whether she was simply good cover for him. Either way, it had been disastrous for Tris. He'd hated coming all this way from his school in Berkshire for holidays and exeats; he'd hated having to explain this new situation to his friends. Once again, everything was being destroyed and it was clear that Billa and Ed were not inclined to welcome him with open arms. He didn't really blame them; he could see that they wanted this disruption to their lives as little as he did. He'd seen their antagonism at once and—as was his way—he'd opened fire first. 'If you're not one up you're one down.'

Round one, with the bicycle, went to him, but he was never able truly to win with Ed. Ed played by different rules. He neither complained nor attacked, he merely withdrew into that little study of his, his fortress, and pulled up the drawbridge. Occasionally he'd show Tris his treasures—those beautiful miniatures, oh, how proud Ed was of those miniatures, the tiny netsukes, the paintings— but then the door was shut again and locked. Never once was he able to get into that room alone but, even if he had, he wouldn't have damaged those things. Even then, their delicate beauty touched a chord and he resented being treated as if he were a vandal.

Tris puts the car in gear and pulls away. As he drives past Dom's cottage he laughs out loud at the thought of Dom receiving the carefully chosen postcard. He thought long and hard about that one, knowing exactly what would touch the spot. 'Your mother was a whore.' Why was it so satisfying to see the rage in Dom's face that day so long ago in the winter woodland? Was it because his own mother had been wiped out, denied? No mourning for Tris. No grieving, no talking, no adjustment: just a deep weight of misery and loss like a stone on the heart. What wild, savage pleasure there was in hurting Dom. Yet Dom, in his own way, was in control. He, like Ed, refused to strike back, and Tris was denied any real satisfaction. Only with Billa was there any success. Billa rose to every provocation like a starving trout to a fly. How she'd loved that dog. Love, physical affection, privileges—everything denied to Tris was poured out on to that bad-tempered little terrier.

One day he'd taken Bitser for a walk, along the stream, through the woods and up on to the slopes of the moorland. It was a wild March day with the wind blowing from the west and, running in the wind with Bitser beside him, he experienced a new sensation. He felt light and free. He believed that everything could change and he could have a home again and be happy. Then the clouds rolled across the sun, great drops of rain fell, and he turned to run home. But Bitser had found a scent and was digging, he wouldn't come when Tris called him, so he grabbed Bitser, pulled and tugged the hard, round solid little body, and Bitser turned and bit him hard. Shocked with pain, blood pouring from the wound, quite suddenly Tris was utterly desolate. The swing of spirits from joy to despair was terrible. Stumbling home in the rain, nursing his bloody hand, he looked for some kind of revenge and found it. Billa never forgave him.

Tris thinks about Billa. He doesn't quite know why he took her mobile when he got into the old butter factory. Simply because he could, knowing it would cause irritation? How amusing it had been to drop it into the chair where he'd seen her sitting earlier. And what a shock that had been to see the little group all together at the table by the fire. Anyway, he'd taken some numbers from the phone, just in case.

As he pauses at the junction in the village and turns right up the hill, he thinks again about the group in the wood. After all, nothing has changed. The St Enedocs still have what they always had: family, love, homes, their dogs.

'This is your last journey, Tris,' his doctor warned him. 'You know that, don't you? Not much more time.'

Time for one last game, for one last roll of the dice. Tris drives to the Chough. He goes up to the little flat, carrying his satchel, and lets himself in. He pours a tumblerful of water, takes his bottle of capsules from the satchel and collapses on to the bed.

CHAPTER FOURTEEN

I f only I'd known I could have had the fatted calf ready,' says Billa. 'As it is, it's going to have to be rack of lamb.'

It is a tradition, on Harry's first night, for them all to have dinner at the old butter factory. The warm, comfortable kitchen with the great slate table is perfect for a family gathering. Ed is lighting all the candles and pouring the wine. Bear is on his sofa with Harry beside him, his heavy head on Harry's lap. Bessie is curled on the floor at his feet. Tilly laughs at them and takes a photograph on her mobile phone.

'We'll send it to your mum,' she says to Harry, and he grins at her, delighted that she is here too, sharing the homecoming.

He likes Tilly, approves of her gorgeousness and slightly wishes he were older. At the same time he knows her so well, and their companionship is so easy and comfortable, that he is content simply to add her to his Cornish family. She is an older sister, without the sibling tensions and rivalry, and he loves to be seen with her at the pub, at the beach; she adds to his street cred.

Ed has finished filling the glasses and says: 'Let's drink to Harry. Great to see you.' They all raise their glasses to toast him and Tilly takes another photograph.

Harry raises his own glass in return. 'So come on,' he says. 'I've heard some of the news. What else has been going on?'

'Tilly and the curate have fallen in love,' Dom says teasingly, and Tilly gives a cry of protest.

'We have not,' she says, turning pink. 'That is absolutely not true. And don't do that,' she adds as Dom winks at Harry. 'Just stop it.'

'And jolly good luck if they have,' says Billa, putting plates to warm in the bottom oven and taking a quick drink from her glass. 'Clem is very dishy. He is the Anglican Church's new weapon. His services are packed with women, so Alec Bancroft tells me. Lucky old Tilly, that's all.'

Tilly looks slightly mollified and Harry bursts out laughing.

'Who's Alec Bancroft?' he asks, pulling Bear's ears and blowing on his nose so that he shifts and grunts in his sleep.

'*Sir* Alec Bancroft, please,' says Dom. 'And he is Billa's new best friend. That's where she met the curate. Canoodling with Sir Alec over at Peneglos.'

Billa remains undisturbed by these revelations; she simply takes another sip of wine, aware that Harry knows that Dom is being silly because he is happy. They are all happy because he has come home.

Harry sighs with pleasure. 'Come on then,' he says. 'Tell me all. I've got six months' worth of news to catch up on, remember. Let's start with Tilly's curate.'

Later, unpacking in his bedroom at Dom's cottage, he has another sense of homecoming. During their childhood holidays, his sisters shared one of the bedrooms in Mr Potts' half of the cottage but he has always had this room to himself; the one boy amongst all the girls. He looks at the familiar books on the white painted bookcase: Arthur Ransome, Rudyard Kipling, John Buchan. These are Dom's books but Harry feels that they are his, too. An elderly teddy bear—also Dom's—shares a small wicker chair with a more modern bear—Harry's—and a whole series of small model cars are arranged in an old tray on a table in the alcove. Harry looks at these treasures whilst Tilly leans in the open doorway, watching him.

'I suppose it all seems a bit childish,' he says defensively, 'but I like it.'

'My room's the same when I go home,' says Tilly. 'It's the sense of continuity, isn't it? This was Dom's room when he was a boy, now it's yours and one day it'll be your son's.'

Harry blinks a little at this concept and then shakes his head. 'The cottage will be sold up by then,' he says. He can't bring himself to say 'when Dom dies' but it is implied.

Tilly watches him sympathetically, biting her lip, wondering what to say. 'But you'll still keep all these things,' she suggests. 'Wherever you are.'

'Of course I will,' he agrees at once, but he is unsettled by the prospect of not having this space, this special corner in the world to return to whenever he has the need.

Tilly, who feels rather the same about Mr Potts' bedroom, hastens to change the subject.

'And I am not,' she says emphatically, 'in love with the curate.'

He is distracted, just as she hopes he will be. ' "The lady doth protest too much, methinks," ' he says, opening one of his bags. 'Anyway, why not? Billa obviously approves.'

'I know, but come on. I've only just met him.'

'But you like him?'

'Sure, I like him. Clem's got a little boy of seven,' she adds casually, glancing away from him, as he turns to stare at her, his hands full of shirts.

'A little boy? Is he . . . divorced?'

'No, no.' She shakes her head. 'His wife died when Jakey was born.'

'God, how awful.' Harry looks shocked.

'Mmm. Anyway, you see the problems to the relationship developing? A curate, a widower, and a father. That's just Clem. Then there's Jakey. I like Clem a lot, though.'

He stands holding the shirts, wondering what to

say. It does, indeed, seem a pretty big undertaking. His twenty-one years haven't provided him with the experience to help her with this. He looks away from her, stowing the shirts in the chest of drawers.

'The trouble is,' she says, 'that Clem and I can't really make a move without all his parishioners looking on. It's just not the usual scenario. He lives in the vicarage in a very small village. I don't see how we'd ever get started, to be honest. What about Jakey, for instance? How do you make that first move with a small boy around?'

He thinks about it and then looks up at her. 'Got an idea. Why don't we make a plan to see both of them? You and me. Clem and Jakey. Just a casual meeting somewhere. The Chough? Can you take kids there?'

Tilly makes a face. 'You can, but I work there, remember. That's what I mean. Everybody would know. I'm not ready for that. I've only met him a couple of times.'

'No, OK. What about inviting them for fish and chips at Rick Stein's? You know? You say something like, "Harry and I are going over to Padstow for fish and chips. Do you and Jakey want to come?" Keep it casual. And we go anyway and see what happens.'

She stares at him. 'I don't know,' she says uncertainly.

'Oh, come on, Tills,' he says impatiently. 'Don't

173

ask, don't get. It's worth a try, isn't it? If we all go it won't be so scary.'

She nods, still cautious. 'OK then.'

'Fab.' He grins at her. 'Phone him. Make a date.'

'It would have to be a Saturday. Not weekdays because of school, and obviously not Sunday. Only Saturdays are changeover day at the pub and I don't finish till half past twelve.'

'So I come with you to the Chough and drink coffee in the bar and read the papers until you finish and then we scat on to Padstow. We can be there for one o'clock. Make the date, Tills. Do it.'

'OK, I will.' She beams at him, suddenly confident. 'Thanks, Hal.'

'Cool,' he says nonchalantly.

The door from the sitting-room opens and Dom comes up the stairs. Tilly waves to Harry and slips away through the connecting door on the landing to Mr Potts' bedroom. Harry gets up and continues to unpack. Dom pauses at the open door.

'Got everything you want?'

'Yes, thanks.'

'Sleep well, then.'

He disappears towards his own room and Harry closes the door. He sits down on the bottom of the bed, leans forward and takes a book at random from the bookshelf. *The Picts and the Martyrs.* He opens it at the first chapter, 'Visitors Expected', and begins to read.

· · ·

Billa and Ed are clearing up. The rack of lamb was a great success: tender and pink inside, charred and caramelized outside. The candles have been extinguished, the dishwasher is rumbling, and Billa and Ed take their coffee and go to sit beside the remains of the fire in the hall.

'Great fun,' Ed says contentedly. 'He's looking well, isn't he?'

'Very well,' says Billa. Suddenly she feels melancholy. The evening with Harry and Tilly, full of laughter and fun and silly jokes, has called up the shades of her babies; those might-have-beens whom she will never know. The keen, familiar sense of loss twists her heart, and she puts an arm around Bear's neck as he leans companionably against her knees. Would they have been pretty girls like Tilly? Good-looking boys like Harry? Would they now be bringing their own children to stay? Well-meaning friends sometimes tell her that she's well out of it; that children cause heartbreak and disappointment. She's trained herself to nod, to agree, battling with the longing to scream at them; to try to make them understand what it feels like to have carried her babies, even for such a short time, only for them to disappear for ever.

Ed is watching her with compassion; he recognizes these black moments when they come.

She manages a smile. 'It's such luck that he's got

175

a place at Camborne,' she says, making an effort to recapture the earlier mood. 'We shall see him often, like we did when he was at Oxford, and it's great for Dom. We need young people to jolly us up.' She yawns suddenly, hugely. 'Gosh, I'm tired. You deal with Bear, Ed, will you? I'm going to bed.'

CHAPTER FIFTEEN

The next morning Ed sits in his car at the edge of Colliford Lake, hoping to find inspiration for the next chapter of his book. He raises his binoculars to scan the choppy water for the sight of a bird, looking across to the opposite shores of the lake in search of movement, for some sign of life. Above the marshy banks, where stunted willow and furze shiver in the chill north-westerly wind, one white horse stands in a small field. It looks towards Ed, still as a statue in the sunshine, its mane flickering and blowing.

Ed wonders whether to get out and take a photograph of the lake and the horse—he likes to take as many photographs as he can whilst each book is in progress—but he knows that the tripod will be at risk in this strong wind and, after all, there are no birds. Yet the horse appeals to him. He knows that technically the horse is called a grey, though its coat is white as milk, and he wonders why it is all alone in its scrubby little field.

Even as he watches, a boy appears out of the sharp black shadows of the thorn hedge. He is carrying a head collar looped over his arm and he keeps one hand in his pocket. He approaches the horse confidently and it raises its head in welcome and trots to meet him. Ed sees it nuzzle the boy's shoulder—he can imagine the whicker of warm breath—and the boy takes his hand from his pocket and offers the horse a treat. As it drops its heavy head to the boy's palm he slips the collar on quickly and then turns away, leading the horse across the field. At the gate they pause; both boy and horse turn as if to look back at him. Watching them through his powerful binoculars, Ed catches his breath. They seem to be staring directly at him, challenging him. The boy's face is friendly, open, as if he is encouraging Ed in some endeavour; the horse's eye is intelligent, his ears pricked forward. Then they turn, the boy unfastens the gate, pushes it open, and they go through it and disappear from sight behind the hedgeline.

Ed continues to stare after them for a moment and then lowers the binoculars. He thinks about the horse and the boy, and a story begins to form about them; a magical story that children might love. Almost immediately he shies away from it. What does he know of children? So many times he's had this odd longing to write and illustrate a book for children but each time he's rejected it. He's had no children of his own—Gillian's two were teenagers when he first knew them—and he has no experi-ence of what they like.

'But you were a child once,' a colleague said, years ago, when he'd confided his thoughts to her. 'You read books and loved them. Why shouldn't your own experience be enough?'

He thinks about it, sitting there by the lake, staring at the field where the horse and the boy had been.

'I've never been a one for taking chances,' he said to Billa last night. Might the time have come to take a chance; to write the book he's dreamed about, to illustrate it, and risk the humiliation of it being a complete failure?

Suddenly he sees the horse galloping along the skyline, the boy perched on his back. Ed raises his binoculars again. Though they are at some distance he can see the free movement of the horse, the ripple of muscle, the rhythmic pounding of its hoofs. Its mane is flying, and the boy clings to its neck, laughing. He raises an arm, as if he is saluting, and Ed takes one hand from his binoculars and waves back, smiling in return, though he knows they cannot see him. He watches them out of sight and then puts the binoculars on the seat beside him, still smiling, feeling a fool.

He wishes now that he'd taken the photograph of the horse and the boy, but he knows that he will remember them. A different kind of inspiration has been vouchsafed him, one that he feels he must commit to, and he is filled with exhilaration and terror. It is as if he has—with a smile and a wave—made a promise.

He starts the engine and drives slowly back, past the dark waters of Dozmary Pool towards Bolventor and the road home.

At Peneglos, a solitary surfer rides switchback on the muscular shoulders of tall glass-green waves which tower up to crash and race along the beach. The screeching gulls run before the tide, sometimes ankle-deep in swirling water, taking off to fly and float in the wild salty air. Once Hercules would have chased them, barking excitedly, dashing into the sea; now he is content to plod at Alec's heels, but occasionally his ears twitch and his gait quickens as he remembers days long past when he was young.

Alec strides out, hunched against the wind, heading back towards the sea wall and the village. He tries to remember the things he needs from the shop and takes off his glove to scrabble in his pocket for the list. No list. He's left it on the table or on his desk, but never mind. He's not going to take himself to task for that, though he can imagine Rose's reaction; hear her voice in his ear. 'Silly old buffer,' she says—but her words are whirled away in a gust of wind. He attaches Hercules' lead to the hook provided on the wall and steps gratefully into the shelter of the small shop.

Old Mrs Sawle greets him. Her son and his wife run the shop now, but Mrs Sawle was there first and she doesn't ever let them forget it. She despises modern trends, mocks faddy holiday-makers who demand organic milk, bottled water, and reject good Cornish butter in favour of tasteless spreads.

'Tedn't nat'ral,' she mutters, withered old lips curled in disdain, and Billy Sawle nudges her and says, 'Times've changed, Mother. Don't 'ee be so rude now.'

Rose loved Mrs Sawle. 'She's Prudie Paynter to the life,' she'd say after a session at the shop. ' "Tedn't right, tedn't fair, tedn't hooman, tedn't nat'ral." What a dear old Sawle she is.'

Now, Mrs Sawle looks up as the bell jangles and nods to him from her corner behind the counter where she sits hunched and wrapped in woollies, squat as an over-dressed toad.

'Mornin', Sir Alec. Blowy ould day, ennit?'

He agrees, they discuss the health of Hercules, tied up outside—Mrs Sawle loves dogs—and then he prowls the shelves, trying to jog his memory.

'Newspaper,' he mutters to himself. 'Butter. Coffee. Must get coffee.'

He can't help a snort of amusement as he remembers Dom's reaction a few days earlier to the fact that he'd run out of coffee.

'I'm so sorry,' Alec said. 'But I've got these for emergencies. Actually, I've become rather

180

addicted to them.' He showed Dom the sachet of instant coffee, dried milk and various other ingredients. 'I call them my chemicals in a cup.'

He handed Dom the mug of frothy cappuccino and watched as he took a sip. Dom swallowed the mixture, raised his eyebrows and nodded.

'I can see why,' he said drily. 'Quite a jolt to it, isn't there?'

Now, as he collects the required items, pays Mrs Sawle for them and puts them into the old carrier bag he keeps in his coat pocket, Alec thinks about Dom. Throughout the hour or so that they spent together he had the feeling that Dom was slightly distracted. He told Alec about his grandson, who was taking up a place at the Camborne School of Mines, his daughters and their families in South Africa, and then they'd talked of the countries they'd lived in and their people and customs.

Two well-travelled old boys, both widowers, both with children living far away. Lots to talk about, yet, at the end of it, Alec knew there was still something on Dom's mind. It puzzled him. He guessed that Dom wasn't a man who gave away his secrets easily—and, after all, he had Billa and Ed to talk to—yet Alec was certain that something was bothering him.

As he climbs the hill, Hercules panting along behind him, he passes the vicarage and looks for Clem. The garden is tidy and well tended; there is a trampoline on the small lawn, and a football

181

lying by the wall, but there is no sign of Clem. He's very fond of Clem. He wishes the dear fellow would make some move towards Tilly; he longs for them to get together though he can see why they both hesitate.

'Life's too short,' he mutters, breathing fast as he fumbles for his key, fitting it into the lock. 'Shouldn't waste it by dithering.'

Shutting the door behind him, he pauses for a moment, listening to the silence, waiting, out of habit, for Rose's shout of greeting. Terrible loneliness engulfs him; the finality of his separation from her and the loss of companionship. He feels the tears gathering, burning behind his eyes, and tries to summon up his courage; to brace himself.

'For goodness' sake, don't start,' calls Rose sharply from the study. 'You were always a sentimental old fool. Tears at the least little thing.'

It's true: love, goodness, misery, all these things can move him to tears. He thinks of the deprivation he has seen: the Fellaheen of Cairo; the grinding poverty in the slums of Calcutta. How helpless he'd felt in the face of such vulnerability and weakness. He'd strived to improve things in his own small patch but his efforts were puny, pointless. Old, familiar sensations of despair and anger grip him and he struggles against them.

'Put the kettle on,' advises Rose, who seems now to be in the kitchen. 'Make some decent coffee. Get a grip. And give that poor dog a drink and a biscuit.'

Alec looks down at Hercules, panting beside him on the doormat. As usual, Rose is right.

'Come on, old chap,' he says. 'Best paw forward. Let's get to it.'

CHAPTER SIXTEEN

When they set off for the Chough on Saturday morning, Harry can feel that Tilly is tense with a mixture of anxiety and excitement. Clem's text was very positive, very upbeat: *Great idea. We'd love it.*

'Cool,' said Harry when she told him. 'It'll be great.'

Now he sits beside her, watching her drive her little car through the twisty lanes. She's a good driver: quick, neat, assured, and he feels quite at ease with her, envious of her having a car.

'Will you have a car, Hal?' she asks, reading his thoughts. 'When you come back to start at CSM in September? It's a pity you can't stay now you're here.'

'Mum wanted me to have a gap year after Oxford,' he says. 'I think she and Dad hoped I might change my mind about studying in England again. I just wanted to get on with it but I agreed because I know that this whole mining thing is a big deal for them. They'd rather I stay in Jo'burg and join the clan. I want them to see that this is not just a spur-of-the moment thing so I agreed to take a year out to think about it.'

'And have you?'

'Nope. Don't need to. I've been doing some work for a big international charity Mum runs, and visiting some of the rellies who are detailed off to make law and banking sound like great career moves. So I'm off to Geneva after next weekend to stay with some cousins for Easter. We're going skiing.'

Tilly lifts an eyebrow. 'More bankers?'

He nods. 'But I shan't change my mind,' he says serenely. 'I shall be back in September.'

'Will you get a car then?'

He shrugs. 'My dad doesn't give handouts. He believes you need to earn money to appreciate it. I'd like one. Who wouldn't? I'll get a holiday job if I can. Save up. I've got a bit of birthday money stacked up.'

'Dom would help you buy an old banger. It would mean you could dash up from Camborne to see him more often.'

'Probably, but I don't want Mum and Dad to think he's doing me favours. He's got other grand-children. It's difficult, you know, when you're doing something the family doesn't approve of. We're a very tight-knit clan, fingers in lots of pies, hundreds of connections and we all stick together.

I'm stepping out of line and I want to show them I can do this under my own steam.'

'I'm impressed,' says Tilly. 'Well, I can always scoot down to Camborne to pick you up. You can pay for the petrol.'

'You'll still be around?'

She glances at him, disconcerted. 'Why not?'

'Oh,' he shrugs. 'Just wondering. You said Sarah is moving soon and I don't know what your plans might be.'

He notes with interest the colour rising in her cheeks and wonders if she's thinking about Clem.

'I can carry on even if she goes,' she says. 'Though I'm not sure I'd want to.'

'Running the business from Mr Potts' bed-room?'

She laughs. 'Why not? As long as Dom doesn't chuck me out.'

'He won't do that. He loves having you there. You know he does.'

Tilly pulls into the Chough's car park and they get out.

'It's an awfully long time to sit about, Hal,' she says anxiously. 'I hope you'll be OK.'

'I'll be fine,' he assures her. 'I've got a book and I've got some texting to catch up on. It'll be great to chill out.'

She nods. 'OK. See you later.'

She disappears through a back door and Harry goes round to the bar. To his surprise and delight a fire is already crackling in the wood-burner and a man is sitting at a table reading a newspaper. The landlord appears from the room behind the bar and grins at him.

'Tilly says you're up for some coffee,' he says. 'Anything special? Filter? Cafetière?'

'Cafetière, please,' says Harry. 'Thanks.'

'Newspapers on the rack behind you,' the landlord says, and disappears.

Harry glances round, catches the eye of the man sitting beside the fire and does a double take.

'Hi,' he says. 'Didn't we meet before? Weren't you delivering something to Mellinpons over near St Tudy?'

The man is staring at him with an odd expression, a mix of amusement and disbelief.

'Yes,' he says. 'Yes, we did. My company is carrying out market research in the area. Solar power, wind farms, energy, that kind of thing. I'm staying here for a bit. Are you going to join me or are you a "newspaper in silence with your coffee" kind of man?'

Harry laughs. 'I don't really do silence. But I don't want to disturb you.'

'Christian Marr.' He casts aside the newspaper and holds out his hand. 'Most people call me Chris.'

Harry takes his hand. 'Harry de Klerk.'

Chris raises his eyebrows. 'South African? You don't look it.'

'I know. I live in Jo'burg but the Cornish part of my family comes from round here,' says Harry, sitting down at the table. 'I'm staying with my grandfather, Dominic Blake. I don't suppose you know him? Or the St Enedocs?'

Chris shakes his head. 'Doesn't mean anything to me. So are you on holiday?'

They sit down together, companionably. Harry is pleased to have someone to talk to, with whom to share the next two hours. He likes the look of Chris: there is a continental touch to his tanned skin, and his black high-necked cashmere jersey and narrow jeans. The expensive-looking leather satchel hangs from the arm of his chair and he has a cosmopolitan air. He looks more like a musician or an artist than a market researcher.

Harry's coffee arrives, and a plate of chocolate brownies.

'On the house,' says the landlord with a wink. 'Enjoy.'

When Tilly puts her head round the door and smiles at Harry, Tris raises his hand to her. She comes further into the bar.

'Good morning, Mr Marr,' she says. 'The flat's all done. Come on, Hal. We're going to have to hurry.'

Tris and Harry stand up and shake hands, and Tilly and Harry go out together.

Tris sits down again and begins to laugh quietly

to himself. He simply can't help it. Chance has given him the opportunity to sit here, talking to Dom's grandson, Billa and Ed's great-nephew, finding out more about them in two hours than he's been able to discover in nearly two weeks. He's stayed in pubs and B and Bs in a ten-mile radius of the old butter factory, resisting the temptation to move into the flat at the Chough until two days ago because he feared that it was too risky to be actually staying so close. And now he's been given it all on a plate; the boy was so open, so artless, so trusting. How easy it's been to get information from him. Now he knows that Billa is a widow with no children and that Ed is divorced and also childless. Dom is widowed, and his children, with their children, live in South Africa. Tilly is the daughter of an old colleague and the boy, Harry, will be leaving soon. In short, there are no tough younger members of the family to come hurrying to question and confront him when he finally turns up at the old butter factory with the will Elinor made all those years ago.

Tris begins to laugh again. He's taken the chance and it's paid off.

'Good joke?' asks the landlord as he collects the coffee things.

Tris nods but doesn't enlarge. He orders a gin and tonic and asks to see the lunch menu. As he studies it, he broods. Harry is the thorn in the flesh; the fly in the ointment. Tris knows that he'll have to continue to lie low until after next week-end and this might be tricky now he's moved to the Chough. Apart from that, the coast is clear. All he has to do is wait for Harry to go.

Later, much later, Tilly sits at the dressing table in Mr Potts' bedroom and thinks about the meeting with Clem and Jakey. Downstairs, Dom and Harry are playing Scrabble; arguing over every word, disputing each double or triple score letter, as they have always done since Harry was six years old.

Slowly, Tilly begins to brush her hair with long sweeps of the brush, staring at herself in the glass, thinking about Clem. It was disconcerting to see him in his jeans, Jakey in tow, like any young dad on a day out with his son. Jakey looks just like him and was very well-behaved, fun, quite at his ease with three adults. He and Harry imme-diately hit it off and after the fish and chips they'd gone ahead, wandering round the harbour, leaving Tilly with Clem.

Tilly puts down the brush, thinking about it. Jakey's presence changed things. Up at the convent she and Clem approached each other as equals; two young people, attracted to each other. Today, Clem was a young father, a widower, with an important past relationship. Perhaps if she, too, were divorced, or just out of a long-standing relationship, with a child of her own, they'd be on more equal terms: but she isn't. She's had boyfriends, one slightly serious relationship, but she is still looking for the big one: the right man, romance, special holidays together. How does that work with a widower who has a child already?

She and Clem strolled together, still very aware of each other—all the right vibes—but as she watched Jakey dancing ahead at Harry's side she was filled with fear. She remembered Sarah's pejorative words and feared they might be true. Her confidence slowly ebbed from her and it was a relief to catch up with Jakey and Harry, who were talking about Newquay Zoo. Clem had promised to take Jakey to see the *Madagascar* experience and he was longing to see it.

'It sounds brilliant,' Tilly said, smiling at his eagerness. 'I love the film.'

'Well, why don't we all go?' suggested Harry. 'What about this afternoon?'

Jakey, silenced by such an amazing opportunity, stared up beseechingly at Clem.

'Well, why not?' he answered, slightly taken aback by such a sudden proposition. 'It's my day off so we could go, if you'd like it?'

He glanced at Tilly—who was just as surprised as Clem at Harry's suggestion, but grateful, too. It prolonged the afternoon and gave her the chance to try to sort out her feelings. Jakey jumped about, punching the air, utterly delighted at the prospect of such a treat. They left Tilly's car in the car park and all went in Clem's car, Jakey and Harry in the back, old friends now, joshing and laughing together. Clem and Tilly sat together, talking much less easily, still painfully conscious of the other. They'd been in time to watch the penguins being fed and Harry and Jakey agreed that the penguins were their favourite characters in the film. On the way back to Padstow one or the other would say: 'Smile and wave. Smile and wave,' and they'd shout with laughter and do high-fives.

'It was really weird,' she said to Harry later as they drove home together. 'It wasn't like going out with a boyfriend at all. I think Jakey's an absolute darling but whatever we do it'll be like having a chaperon with us, won't it? Clem gets one day off a week, Saturdays, so he can spend time with Jakey, which is perfectly right. But when would Clem and I get time together? How would it work? And even if it did, then there's that second wife thing people talk about when the first one has died so young. Like she'll always be perfect and enshrined in blissful memories because she didn't get the chance to grow boringly familiar or irritable or picky or jealous.'

Harry was silent, which somehow made her even more defensive.

'You can see what I mean, can't you, Hal?'

'Yes,' he said, after a moment. 'I can. But you really like Clem, don't you?'

'Yes,' she said, almost irritably. 'Yes, I really like Clem.'

'And it's clear that he really likes you. It's just that it's, like, a terrible waste, that's all.'

'But you see my point?' she insisted. 'OK, I admit that I could easily fall in love with Clem but I'd want to be romantic and happy and silly with him. How do you do that with a seven-year-old watching? I don't want a sensible, motherly role. I'm not ready for that, Hal. I want children but after I've had fun first. I'm not ready to move from complete single freedom into being a stepmother.'

'Then it all comes down to whether you do actually fall in love with Clem, I suppose,' Harry said thoughtfully. 'You'd have to love him enough to want to make some kind of compromise work. Clem knows that, which makes it tricky for him.'

'What d'you mean?' She glanced sideways quickly at Harry.

He shrugged. 'I like Clem. He's reserved but he's got a great sense of humour and it's clear he really fancies you. He'd be much more proactive if he wasn't bringing so much baggage with him. It must be really difficult for him, too. Would you rather we hadn't arranged to go over for tea tomorrow?'

She shook her head. 'No. And anyway, Jakey really wants you to see his toys or whatever. You certainly made a hit, and it's easier with you there, Hal.'

'Well, I shan't be for much longer so you'd better make the most of it, Tills,' he said.

Now, she wonders how it will be, meeting Clem at the vicarage tomorrow; seeing him in his home. It will be so difficult to act casually. The door at the foot of the stair opens and Harry calls up to her.

'Supper's ready, come and get it,' and Tilly goes out and downstairs to join them, determined to put her anxieties aside for the evening.

CHAPTER SEVENTEEN

W hen they arrive at the vicarage for tea, however, Clem isn't there. Jakey is bouncing on the trampoline, watched by a woman with that familiar silvery-gilt fair hair, those narrow dark blue eyes that sometimes look brown. She turns quickly as Tilly and Harry come in through the gate and Jakey shouts a welcome and bounces even higher. The woman waves, coming to meet them.

'Clem's a bit late,' she says. 'I've just brought Jakey back so we're waiting for him.' She holds out her hand. 'I'm Dossie. Clem's mum.'

Tilly and Harry introduce themselves whilst Jakey shouts louder, bounces higher still and does clever tumbling tricks, showing off.

'You've made a huge hit,' says Dossie to Harry. 'He tells me that you live in South Africa and you've seen elephants and tigers and lions in the wild.'

'Courtesy of Kruger National Park,' says Harry, grinning. 'Hi, mate,' he calls to Jakey, and goes to admire his acrobatics, leaving Tilly with Dossie.

Tilly feels ludicrously shy; for once she can think of nothing much to say, but Dossie is quite natural.

'Rather a dreary little place, isn't it?' she murmurs, indicating the bungalow. 'The sixties were such a terrible time for building. You can see why Clem can't wait to get back to the Lodge. He and Jakey nearly froze to death this last winter. Appalling metal windows that don't fit, and wait till you see the lino in the kitchen.'

Tilly is surprised and amused. 'It's not very pretty,' she agrees cautiously.

Dossie snorts expressively. 'Never mind. It won't be for long. Would you like a cup of tea or shall we wait for Clem? He had a baptism, and I expect somebody's pounced on him. One of the drawbacks of the job. Everyone wants a piece of you.'

When Dossie smiles she looks like Clem, and Tilly smiles back at her.

'Let's wait for Clem . . . Or will he have had enough tea, do you think?'

'He'll be awash with it,' says Dossie cheerfully. 'Let's get the kettle on. Or I could leave Jakey with you and go on home.'

Tilly hesitates, confused. She doesn't know whether Dossie would rather go and whether

Jakey would make a fuss if she did. How late might Clem be?

'Well, let me show you where everything is,' says Dossie, seeing her hesitation. 'And we'll take it from there. The kitchen's dire, I warn you.'

'Where do you live?' asks Tilly, following her into the bungalow.

'We're at St Endellion. My parents and I run a B and B. We've been there for centuries but it's a nice old place. It's about twenty minutes away so we have Jakey at half-terms and holidays, and when Clem needs a break.'

Tilly thinks about this as she stares round the small kitchen: so Clem has a support group close at hand and Jakey has a grandmother and great-grandparents.

'There's a cake in this tin,' Dossie is saying, as she fills the kettle. 'I cut a couple of slices off for Mo and Pa, but there should be enough. Clem tells me you're in IT and doing clever things for Chi-Meur.'

'Well, not quite yet but I'm working on it. And there is certainly lots of material to work on. It's a fantastic place, isn't it?'

Tilly looks for cups or mugs and Dossie swings open the door of a Formica cupboard above the working surface, indicating the piles of crockery.

'Chi-Meur is gorgeous. Everyone wants to make a success of it and there's so much support.' Dossie finds teabags and brings milk from the fridge. 'Have you met the Sisters yet? Oh, that sounds like Clem.'

There are voices in the garden and shouts of greeting from Jakey. Tilly turns almost apprehensively, wondering if Clem will mind her rootling in his cupboard, and sees him standing in the doorway watching them. His wary expression is so utterly that of a young male wondering if his mother has put her foot in it with someone that matters to him that Tilly nearly bursts out laughing. It is clear to Tilly that Dossie is thinking exactly the same; she is looking at her son with amusement.

'Hi,' he says. 'Sorry I'm late.'

'We thought we might start without you,' Dossie says. 'But now you're here I can get back to Mo and Pa. I've booked Wednesday out for Jakey. It is Wednesday, isn't it?'

'Yes. Thanks,' Clem says. 'He's having tea with a friend tomorrow, and Sarah's offered to have him for Tuesday straight from school. If you could do Wednesday it'll be great. I'm OK Thursday and Friday.'

'Fine,' she says. 'I'll see him on the way out.' She smiles at Tilly and passes Clem in the doorway, reaching up to give him a quick kiss on the cheek. ''Bye, Tilly. Respect the cake.'

'Oh, I shall,' Tilly assures her, suddenly wishing that Dossie wasn't going.

After her initial reaction, her amusement at his

wary expression, Tilly is struck now with the difference between the Clem in his jeans, eating fish and chips, and this tall young man in his clerical collar. He looks austere, remote—and she is seized with another attack of shyness.

'It must be difficult,' she says at random, 'trying to juggle your work and Jakey.'

He nods, coming right into the kitchen, putting his small case on a chair. Tilly turns to make tea, deciding to take the initiative, feeling extremely surprised at herself standing here in Clem's kitchen with mugs and spoons and teabags as if it's all quite usual.

'I'm lucky to have Dossie and Mo and Pa so close,' he says. 'I couldn't manage without them. Sarah helps after school sometimes, and so do some of the other mothers, but holidays and Sundays would be impossible.'

He leans with his back to the sink, watching her.

'Dossie's made a cake,' she says, 'but we wondered if you might have overdosed on tea.'

He grins, and at once the austere, remote Clem vanishes. She beams back at him, suddenly at ease.

'I'm on a permanent caffeine high,' he admits, 'but I'd like a cup of tea. And some cake. Thanks.'

Neither of them remark on the fact that she's making herself at home and Clem opens a drawer and produces a cake slice and some forks.

'Does Jakey drink tea?' she asks.

'I try to keep him on milk,' he says, 'but the Sisters got him into bad ways, I'm afraid.'

She laughs. 'Sister Emily?'

'The same,' he agrees ruefully. 'Her experience of small boys was limited and he rather got the taste for tea and coffee early on. If we're lucky he won't think about it and he'll just drink his milk. He tends to show off in front of company and he's developed a huge crush on Harry.'

'So where do we have tea?'

He opens a door into a big room, which doubles as a sitting-room and dining-room. A rather beautiful old merchant's chest stands against one of the walls, which have been freshly painted, and there is a sliding door opening into the garden. Tilly puts the cake and some plates on the pretty, drop-leaf table; Clem follows, carrying the mugs of tea and Jakey's milk on a tray.

'I'll call them in,' he says. He looks slightly embarrassed, as if he is suddenly aware of his role as host, and Tilly realizes just how much she likes him.

'Go on, then,' she says, 'and I'll cut the cake. Harry will be starving. He always is.'

Alone, Tilly stares around the room. She wonders if it is Dossie who has tried to introduce the feminine touches: an Indian cotton throw draped across the sofa; the bowl of dwarf daffodils on the bookshelf. A plush, striped rabbit, with long ears and legs, reclines on a cushion in the corner of an armchair and some toy racing cars are ranged on the low square glass-topped table beside it. Tilly feels as if she is spying, as if she has some unfair advantage, and then the others come into the hall and she turns quickly to cut the cake.

When Tilly and Harry leave, Clem feels oddly flat.

'I like Harry,' says Jakey.

He climbs into the armchair, picks up Stripey Bunny and lolls against the cushion. He looks suddenly weary. After tea the four of them walked down to the beach where Jakey and Harry played a very long and energetic game of football.

'I have to say,' Clem murmured to Tilly, watching them, 'that, if I could afford a nanny, this time round I'd have a bloke. It's exhausting, keeping up with a seven-year-old.'

He'd spoken briefly of those early years in London, after Madeleine had died, and how he'd given up his training for the priesthood and gone back to his former job in IT so as to earn enough money to pay for a nanny for Jakey and build up a reserve so when the opportunity arose he could sell the flat and take his chance to get out.

'It looks like it's paying off,' Tilly said, not looking at him, but watching Jakey and Harry racing together on the beach.

He wanted to say to her that he could see that a relationship with a priest must be fraught with difficulties—that when he was chaplain at the retreat house it would be a rather different scene—but he didn't know where to start.

'I hope so,' he said at last. 'I shall be priested in June and then I shall go back to the Lodge, to Chi-Meur, and take my chance on how it works out as their chaplain.'

'It sounds as if it might be . . . well, very challenging. In a good way,' Tilly added quickly.

'And more privacy,' he pointed out. He wanted her to see that; it was important that she realized that it wouldn't be such a goldfish-bowl environment.

Now, he looks at Jakey.

'Bedtime,' he says, with that sinking feeling that he's got a fight on his hands.

Jakey clutches Stripey Bunny tighter. 'I want to watch *Kung Fu Panda*,' he says. 'No, *Madagascar*. Harry's seen lions *and* giraffes *and* hippopotamuses in the wild.'

He drops Stripey Bunny and scrambles to find the DVD, and Clem watches helplessly, wondering how Tilly would fit into this scene, knowing that it will take a very long period of adjustment, assuming she's prepared to try it. And why should she? She's such a gorgeous girl; she must be besieged on all sides by young, single males. Jakey flourishes the DVD.

'Please, Daddy. Just some of it. Pleeeeze.'

He'd like to say: 'What do you think of Tilly?

200

Do you like her?' but he knows that Tilly hasn't really registered on Jakey's radar.

'OK.' He is too tired, too dispirited, to argue. 'Fifteen minutes, but then that's it and I don't want any arguing, Jakes. OK? Promise?'

Jakey nods solemnly. He can see that Daddy's just a little bit on edge and that it wouldn't be a good idea to push his luck. He puts the DVD in, and presses buttons, fetches Stripey Bunny and they sit on the sofa to watch *Madagascar* companionably together.

'Harry's uncle has a dog called Bear,' he tells Clem. He leans against him, resisting the temptation to put his thumb in; he's a big boy now. 'He says we can go and see him. He's absolutely huge. Nearly as big as a bear. His grandfather has a dog as well called Bessie. I want to see them.'

Clem thinks about this. It might be a good idea to see Tilly on her own patch; maybe it would give her confidence. Perhaps he might have more of a chance with her . . . His spirits rise a little.

'OK,' he says, putting his arm round Jakey. 'We'll do that.'

'Cool,' says Jakey contentedly.

'Please don't go away, Hal,' Tilly pleads with Harry as they drive home. 'I think I might just have a faint chance if you stay. Jakey utterly adores you.'

'He's a great kid,' says Harry. 'Don't be such a coward, Tills.'

'But I am a coward,' she cries. 'It's a huge thing. They've had seven years together, just the two of them. How on earth can I bust in on that?'

'You don't bust in on it. You take it very slowly so that Jakey gradually becomes used to you and then realizes that he likes having you around. He spends quite a lot of time with Clem's family, by the sound of it, so you'll have plenty of chances to be on your own with Clem. Stop panicking. You really like him, don't you? Clem, I mean. Surely it's worth a try?'

'I do like him,' she answers. 'I really do, but this is really freaking me out.'

'Well, the next step is to get them over here. Jakey wants to see Bear and Bessie. We'll make a plan with Billa and Ed.'

Tilly looks sideways at him, marvelling that one so young can have such a calming effect. She wonders if Dom was like this at twenty-one.

'OK,' she says, 'but they'll tease me rotten about it. You know that, don't you?'

'Don't be wet. You can hack a bit of leg-pulling. Shall we get Sir Alec over as well? Make it a bit of a party so it doesn't look like you're inviting Clem home to meet the rellies stuff. He can bring Hercules and make Jakey's day. Three dogs at one go.'

'You are completely brilliant, Hal,' Tilly says fervently. 'That is a fantastic idea. So when?'

'Soon,' says Harry confidently. 'I've kind of set it up. Text Clem and suggest it.'

'Yes,' she says, her spirits rising. 'OK, Hal, I will.'

CHAPTER EIGHTEEN

At the Chough, Tris is packing an overnight bag. He's run out of his cocaine capsules and he's planning a few nights away to collect some from his contact, the Weedhound, in Bristol. He is quite happy to leave the patch for a few days; he's confident now that nothing will happen in his absence to change his plan of campaign. The postcards have been sent; Dom and Billa and Ed will be wondering and waiting. Of course, he'd hoped by now to have made his move but he's going to have to wait until the boy, Harry, has gone, which will not be until after the weekend. The problem is, the one thing he doesn't have is time. And now he'll need the extra medication.

It is irritating that his two attempts to spy out the land have been foiled: first by the huge dog and second by Harry. He'd checked so carefully on each of those days; watching them all coming out of the old butter factory and then actually seeing them happily ensconced at the Chough for lunch.

It should have been perfect. The next attempt was more of a risk. From his vantage point he'd seen Billa drive away, watched Dom and Ed and the dogs going down to the woodland, and then he'd driven round the valley and parked under the ash tree. He guessed that a door might be left unlocked—that was how they lived in this remote area—but anyway, he knew how to pick a lock. It wouldn't have been a problem. And then Harry arrived and the moment was lost.

Tris shakes his head, remembering the shock of looking at what seemed to be the ghost of the young Dom. The trouble is, he likes Harry. The fact that the boy is so like Dom adds zest to the liking. If the situation had been different, long ago, Tris might have liked Dom, but he saw straight away how it was going to be. 'If you're not one up you're one down.' He couldn't have taken the chance, back then, but somehow it's different with Harry. And he knows why. It's because Harry reminds him of Léon. Oh, not in looks, of course. Harry is a St Enedoc, a black Cornishman, and Léon is like Tante Berthe, with a mop of thick fair hair and blue eyes. Nevertheless, both boys share the casual grace of youth: the optimism and courage.

As he finishes packing his bag, Tris wonders how Léon and Harry might get on, were they to meet. Despite their genetics, neither Léon nor his father, Jean-Paul, spoke a word of English. That was rule number one, once he and Andrew were back in France. Tris sits on the edge of the bed, thinking about the boarding house in Toulon where Andrew took him after their flight from England. He remembers how Andrew turned up at the school following a phone call telling the headmaster that Tris must be ready to accompany his father abroad. Nobody told him much but clearly his father made it sound urgent: even Matron was kind, which really worried him. But he was used to flight, to change, to precious possessions being abruptly abandoned, and he went along with it docilely enough. He'd learned not to make friends—it was too painful.

Tante Berthe was different, though. He knew at once that it was going to hurt when the time came to leave Tante Berthe. She wasn't his aunt, of course, but the fiction was useful for a while, until she became pregnant with Tris's half-brother. The stream of lodgers that came and went at that rather shabby boarding house in Rue Félix Pyat didn't care. The tall, narrow house with its red-tiled roof and blue-painted shutters was first-rate cover. Tris didn't quite understand the muttered words 'extradition' or 'Interpol', though he began to guess the reason for his father's newly shorn head, his job down at the docks, and the instruction that English was never to be spoken.

The baby, Jean-Paul, was good cover, too, until something happened and there was another change, another flight abroad. But this time, Tris refused to go. For the first time for fourteen years he had a family and he couldn't bear the prospect of being ripped away from them.

'Leave him,' Tante Berthe said to Andrew. 'Leave him and get out while you can. He's nearly a man now. He will look after me and little Jean-Paul.'

And he tried to do just that—he really tried—and it had worked for a few years. The trouble was that taking risks was hard wired into his blood; he couldn't resist. He began to live too near the edge until things went wrong and he, too, was forced to flee. But he never lost touch with Jean-Paul. Jean-Paul is dead now—an accident at the docks—and Tante Berthe is long gone, too. Andrew simply vanished, probably to perish in prison in some distant country. But there is Jean-Paul's son, Léon, still living with his mother in four small rooms on the top floor of the narrow, shabby house in Rue Félix Pyat. Léon has a job at the new smart marina where once the docks were, and he tries to take care of his mother, who suffers from depression and drinks too much.

Tris thinks of Harry, with his wealthy family back in South Africa, and of his inheritance here in Cornwall. He stands up, takes his bag and the satchel. He failed Tante Berthe, and he didn't make much of a fist of being a half-brother to Jean-Paul, but he's damned well going to do something for Léon before he dies.

Ed sits at his desk thinking about the boy and the white horse. Ever since the morning at Colliford Lake he's been turning the scene over in his mind, trying to find his way through to a story. Images have presented themselves: the horse up on its hind legs, its front hoofs parrying a huge serpent with a beaklike head; the boy on the horse's back, dressed sometimes as a princeling, wielding a short sword.

At last he decides to make some sketches of his thoughts in the hope that these will lead him on to the story. He knows that he should be working on his book but he is distracted, and so he puts a Dinah Washington CD in the player and takes out his sketchbook. He draws quickly, capturing the magical qualities of the white horse and the fizzing energy of the boy; he sketches Morgawr, the monstrous, hump-backed serpent with its beak-like head, rearing up from the sea, watched by a group of wicked spriggans—wizened, puny old men with huge heads—who guard the cliff-tops and the cairns where treasure might be buried. He draws the Wrath of Portreath, the giant who lived in a cave called Ralph's Cupboard and terrorized sailors. These are the stuff of Cornish myth and legend, and he fears that he is simply plagiarizing the long-forgotten fairy tales of his childhood, but he continues to draw: a swaggering weasel, a goose with a basket strapped on its back, an immense toad with a jewelled collar. All at once he remembers his father telling him stories of the Knockers, those underground spirits who inhabit the mines and could lead the miners on to rich seams. Ugly creatures with big noses, slit mouths and a delight in making terrifying faces, they might turn malicious if a miner didn't leave a morsel from his pasty, luring him to dangerous areas of the mine. Ed begins to draw a little group of them, thumbing noses, crossing their eyes, bending double to grimace from between spindly legs. Yet he still cannot see any connection between these mythical creatures and the boy and the horse.

Dinah Washington is singing 'Mad About the Boy' when Billa opens the door and asks if he'd like some coffee. He gets up at once, glad to be distracted, and goes downstairs where Bear greets him, wagging his tail and pushing against Ed's knees with his heavy head. Ed thinks of putting Bear into the book with the boy and the white horse, and then gives it up in despair.

'Tilly has a request,' Billa is saying, putting the coffee on the carved chest. 'She'd like to invite Clem and his little boy over to meet us. Well, actually, she wants them to meet Bear and Bessie. I think we're rather a long way down the list.'

'Clem's the curate?' Ed brings himself more fully into reality.

'He is. And his little boy is called Jakey. She'd

like to invite them to tea. I don't see a problem, do you?'

Ed shrugs, shakes his head. 'Why should there be? Is she really serious about him?'

'I think she'd like to be if she could get past him being a man of the cloth with a seven-year-old son.'

'It's quite an undertaking. A man with a child.'

'You married a woman with two children,' Billa reminds him. 'It didn't put you off.'

'The girls were teenagers with lives of their own. And Gillian hadn't taken Holy Orders. You've met Clem. What do you think?'

'I like him. He's very straightforward. Very good manners and a quick sense of humour. Alec rates him and he's known him for quite a little while.'

'Well, I should imagine he's a good judge of character. Perhaps Tilly just needs time to adjust.'

'It'll be good for her to see Clem here amongst her own family, as it were. I always think of her as one of the family and she seems to feel the same. She wants to invite Alec, too. And Hercules.'

'That's quite a good idea,' says Ed. 'Takes the pressure off, doesn't it?'

He gets up and piles some logs on to the fire. Outside, the wind flings handfuls of chill rain against the windows and down the wide chimney to hiss and sizzle on hot ash. Puddles form on the slate paths where the rain plips and plops, tap-dancing its way to the stream.

'Fine, then,' says Billa. 'I think Thursday after-noon is being pencilled in.'

'I expect I shall be here,' says Ed, sitting down again. He's just had an idea about the three dogs and the boy and the horse. 'I don't suppose it will matter much, will it, if I'm not?'

'It will matter to me,' Billa tells him firmly. 'I want you to meet Clem and then tell me what you think about him. Tilly matters to us. I want your input.'

Ed is always surprised and pleased to know that his opinion is valued. 'OK,' he says amiably. 'I'll be here.'

Billa looks at him with exasperated affection. 'Make sure you are,' she says. 'This is important to Tilly. You can show Jakey the frogspawn. He can help you take some of it out of the lake. He'll like that.'

Ed seizes gratefully on this distraction from writing. He must make sure the plastic containers are clean and he'll need to clear a space on the shelves in the summerhouse and find the fishing net. He is filled with relief: the boy and the horse can be banished for a while.

CHAPTER NINETEEN

When Tilly arrives to check in and catch up on new punters, Sarah is hoovering. She pushes the vacuum cleaner into the cupboard under the stairs, indicates that George is asleep upstairs, and they go into the kitchen.

'Dave's dropped a bit of a bombshell,' she says, filling the kettle. 'Someone's offered him a rented house in Yelverton. We could have it for two years. Seems like an offer we can't refuse.'

'Oh, no.' Tilly is startled. 'I mean, I know it's the right thing, and what you wanted, but it's still a bit of a shock, isn't it?'

'It is,' Sarah admits. 'It's like something that was always going to happen, but not just yet.'

She's been surprised by her own reaction; she doesn't want to leave this little cottage or Peneglos. She's settled in, Ben is happy at school, and she knows so many people after all the holidays she's spent here. And apart from that, her business is beginning to thrive.

'I thought you'd be pleased,' Dave said, disappointed by her lack of enthusiasm. 'We both agreed we need to be nearer to the dockyard. It's what we always planned. It's crazy when the ship's in, to have that daily commute.'

'I know,' she said quickly. 'I know it is. It's just

I suppose I'm really settled here. Well, it's my home in a way, isn't it?'

'Well, it's up to you,' he said rather coolly. 'But it's a one in a thousand offer so you'll need to make your mind up quickly.'

And then George started to scream and she said she couldn't talk now but she promised to phone back later.

'I don't know what to do,' she says now, to Tilly. 'Well, I do. There isn't an option, to be realistic. It's very difficult finding rented property on the edge of the moor there. It's where I wanted to be, it'll be great for the boys, and easy for Dave to do the dockyard commute, but I hadn't realized I'd find it so difficult to leave Peneglos.'

'It's only to be expected,' protests Tilly. 'It's not only that you've got Ben at school and U-Connect going really well. This has been your family's bolt hole for years. It's home from home for you, which is really important with Dave away so much.'

Sarah is grateful for Tilly's sympathy but feel she needs to resist it, lest it weakens her. She's still feeling over-emotional and stressed. Mainly it's to do with lack of sleep, which is another reason why she knows that it's sensible to live where Dave can be home quicker and spend more time with them. Soon the ship will be in for a month and the commute will really begin to take its toll then. Her mother was outspoken on the subject—'Of course you must grab it, darling. You can still use the cottage for leaves, if you want it. It was only going to be temporary, wasn't it?'—which didn't make Sarah feel any better.

'What's the house like?' asks Tilly. 'Did Dave tell you?'

'It's a Victorian terrace house on the edge of the village. They're lovely houses and it would be crazy to let it go.'

There is a little silence.

'You'll carry on with U-Connect?' asks Tilly.

Sarah nods. 'We always agreed that it doesn't really matter where we are. What about you? Will you continue here?'

Tilly hesitates. 'I'll certainly wrap up any of the clients we've started but I'm not sure I would want to go it alone.'

Sarah feels a pang of disappointment, almost loss. U-Connect is her baby, her brainchild. She can't bear to think of it being abandoned.

'You could get someone to work with you,' she says.

'It's not that. You know I was never sure that I wanted to be totally committed. It was your project, and it's been great to get it up and running, but I like to be part of a team. Perhaps I'll apply for a job at the retreat house, helping out, just until I get another job. It's lucky that U-Connect depends on new clients all the time but I shall hang in with the old ones until they're sorted. Don't worry. I shan't let anyone down.'

'I know,' says Sarah. 'It's OK. I know it wasn't absolutely your thing. Anyway, what's new with you?'

'Oh,' says Tilly casually, 'well, not much. Harry and I met up with Clem and Jakey on Saturday for fish and chips at Padstow and then we all went to Newquay Zoo. It was really good. All of it, I mean, not just the zoo.'

Sarah stares at her almost indignantly; how had Tilly managed to achieve all that so unexpectedly?

'And then,' Tilly goes on hurriedly, rather as if she might lose her nerve, 'Clem invited us to tea on Sunday. Really, it was because Jakey really took to Hal and wanted to show him his toys and stuff like that.'

She makes it sound as if she's apologizing for something, as if she knows that Sarah rather considers Clem to be her property—which upsets Sarah even more. It's as if everyone around her will be going on happily without her, not even missing her.

'I shall really miss you,' Tilly says, just as if she's reading her thoughts. 'But I'm sure you'll settle in really quickly and get U-Connect up and running from Yelverton. And you can always come here for holidays, can't you?'

'You sound just like my mother,' Sarah snaps, and then feels guilty. It's not Tilly's fault. 'Take no notice of me,' she says with an effort. 'Let's look at the client list. We've got a couple of new punters we can deal with quite quickly. Lucky we pulled the advert for a week or it would be a bit embarrassing. I shan't put it in again. We'll go through the list and see what you can manage. Like you said, there will be a few that will be ongoing for a while but we can deal with that.'

'When will you be going?' asks Tilly.

'Oh, at the end of the month, I imagine, when Dave starts his leave. I didn't ask him. We didn't get that far.'

'It'll be fun,' ventures Tilly. 'You and Dave doing the move together and settling in. It was where the other let was, wasn't it? The one that fell through. It was where you wanted to be. Lots of other naval people around and Dartmoor on the doorstep.'

'Yes,' says Sarah politely, bleakly. 'It'll be fun. Shall we get on with this client list?'

Tilly gets into her car and sits for a moment, her lips pursed in a silent whistle.

'Phew,' she mutters. 'That was a tricky one.'

Poor Sarah; her face looked white and brittle, as if it might shatter, and she was so tense. Tilly is filled both with sadness that Sarah is going and remorse that this end of the business will shut down just when it was getting going. Of course it's been fun: driving all over the county, dropping in to see Sarah to arrange appointments, and to debrief after a session with a client, but this is because Sarah is a very old friend. It's difficult to imagine doing it with anybody else; to have the responsibility of making it viable commercially when your heart isn't really in it. It's better to be part of a team, working on your own special part of the project whilst liaising with other members of the group so as to make the whole mesh together like clockwork. Actually, the retreat house is a good example of just that kind of project, though she can't imagine where the suggestion that she might ask for a job came from; it just popped out of her mouth.

She thinks of Clem as she straps on her seat belt, wondering how he'd react to this suggestion, fearing that he might think she was pursuing him. She wonders why she can't simply drive down to the vicarage, knock on the door and see if he is there. Why shouldn't she? She tries to imagine the scene, but shakes her head. She'd feel too awkward, embarrassed. He might be in the middle of composing his sermon for next Sunday, or a parishioner might be there. Tilly shivers with the horror of it. But suddenly she knows exactly where she will go. She drives away from the cottage and down the steep, narrow hill, pulls on to the hard-standing behind Sir Alec's car, switches off the engine and gets out.

When he opens the door his face lights up with genuine pleasure and she is so grateful that she feels she could hug him. She does hug him, and he hugs her back with the enthusiasm of a man who knows all about proper hugging. She follows him in, stoops to greet Hercules, stands up and comes face to face with Sister Emily who is sitting at Sir Alec's kitchen table.

A green cotton handkerchief is tied gypsy fashion over her fine white hair and she is wearing a navy-blue jersey over narrow, cord jeans. Tilly, who has only seen her in her grey habit, is taken aback.

'Oh,' she cries, confused. 'I am so sorry. I don't want to interrupt.'

'But you're not,' says Sister Emily. 'This is delightful. I have a whole day off so I've come to see my good friend. I've put that nun away in the cupboard just for today.'

Sir Alec smiles at the expression on Tilly's face. 'I expect you've been with Sarah,' he says, 'but could you manage another cup of coffee?'

Tilly sits down at the table. Suddenly she feels full of light-hearted happiness. 'Only if it's Fairtrade,' she says wickedly. 'None of your chemicals in a cup, today, Sir Alec.'

Sister Emily laughs aloud, appreciating the joke. 'And there is *cake*,' she says gleefully.

'Only from the village shop,' says Sir Alec, 'but it's made locally and it's good cake.'

He makes more coffee, cuts her a slice of cake, and Tilly strokes Hercules, who has come to sit beside her at the head of the table.

'Hercules presides,' says Sister Emily. 'We think it is *we* who are in charge here, but really it is Hercules.'

'He isn't allowed cake, though,' warns Sir Alec.

He fetches a dog biscuit from the larder and gives it to Hercules, who crunches gratefully while they watch him.

'We're having a dogs' tea party on Thursday,' Tilly tells Sister Emily. 'My godfather, who I'm staying with, has a golden retriever called Bessie and his brother and sister, who live nearby, have a Newfoundland called Bear. Hercules is coming to the party and so are Clem and Jakey. The party is for Jakey, really. He wants to see Bear.'

She manages to say the names quite casually— 'Clem and Jakey'—but Sister Emily's eyes are keen and Tilly feels the traitorous blood rising in her cheeks.

'I'm looking forward to it,' says Sir Alec, sitting down. 'I think Jakey will be very impressed by Bear.'

'A Newfoundland,' muses Sister Emily. 'I don't think I know the breed.'

'They're huge,' says Tilly. 'Twice as big as Hercules, with really thick coats.' She glances at Sister Emily, assessing this new information that nuns have days off, watching her tackling her slice of cake with evident relish. 'You could come, too,' she suggests tentatively.

'Well, there's an offer you can't refuse, Em,'

says Sir Alec—and Tilly receives another little shock at hearing Sister Emily addressed so casually. 'I'll pick you up.'

'I'd love it,' she answers rather wistfully, 'but I don't think I deserve another day off quite so soon. Jakey will tell us all about it when we see him, I'm sure of that.'

'Do you see him quite often?' asks Tilly.

'Oh, yes. He comes to visit Janna, who looks after us. The community lives separately from the retreat house, you see. We are in the Coach House and Janna keeps an eye on us. She looks after Jakey sometimes when Clem has duties over in the house. We love to see Jakey. He keeps us young.'

She watches Tilly, and her gaze is far-seeing, almost questioning.

'I was just saying to Sarah,' Tilly says recklessly, unnerved by that steady appraisal, 'that I might apply for a job at the retreat house.'

There is a silence; they both stare at her.

'But I thought that this job you're doing with Sarah was going very well,' says Sir Alec.

'It is, but Sarah will be moving soon. You know that she's always planned to move back nearer to the dockyard? Well, Dave's been offered a house that they don't think they can turn down. Sarah's very torn, of course, but it's the right thing to do for all of them. And I don't want to go on with U-Connect on my own while I try to find a job I really love. There's a lot of travelling about, for one thing. Really, I prefer to work as part of a team. It was Sarah's thing, and it's been fun doing it with her, but I shall have to think of something else.'

'I hope you're not going to abandon me yet,' says Sir Alec, alarmed. 'We've only got to the letter M on my database.'

Tilly laughs at him. 'Of course I shan't. I shall carry on with our existing clients, but we simply won't be taking on any new ones around here.'

'And are you serious,' asks Sister Emily, leaning forward a little, 'about applying for a job at the retreat house?'

Tilly feels a whole mixture of things: anxiety, embarrassment, annoyance at having allowed herself to speak without thinking. Yet still the happiness that she experienced when she first came into the kitchen is buoying her up and carrying her forward.

'Yes,' she says, 'except that I don't really know anything about what you do. And I'd need some kind of salary and you probably can't afford it.'

Sister Emily takes a deep breath and sits back again. 'What lovely joy,' she says lightly.

Tilly looks at her anxiously and Sir Alec smiles to himself.

'And what do you see as Tilly's role?' he asks, since Tilly seems unable to speak.

'Everything,' says Sister Emily expansively. 'Anything. Tilly is capable of drawing us all together. Fitting the pieces of the jigsaw into one pattern so that we all work as a whole.'

This is so exactly what Tilly was thinking earlier that she remains silent. Sister Emily smiles at her.

'This is your *gift,*' she says, in that high clear voice that sounds so sure, so certain. 'It is your *talent*. What a privilege if you would put it to work for us.'

Tilly stares at her, alarmed yet impressed. Nobody has ever considered that she has a talent, let alone one that might be considered by others as a privilege.

'Well, there you are, Tilly,' says Sir Alec, seeing her confusion. 'Looks like you've got a job.'

'But is there such a job?' asks Tilly. 'I mean, how do I apply? And I thought that your funds were still . . . you know?'

'We are doing very well,' says Sister Emily confidently. 'We've had some very generous donations and a very sizeable bequest. I'm sure something could be managed. We would feed you, of course, and,' she adds eagerly, 'you could have a *room.*'

'A room?'

'The Priest's Flat,' cries Sister Emily, her eyes gleaming with excitement. 'Years ago we had a resident priest but times changed and the flat is used by guests. Just a big bed-sitting-room *but* it has its own bathroom and lavatory.'

She sighs with pleasure at such a prospect,

clearly feeling that this will be impossible for Tilly to resist. Tilly thinks about Mr Potts' bedroom, her brain reeling with these suggestions and ideas, and feels that she is being swept inexorably along on Sister Emily's enthusiasm.

'I don't know,' she says uncertainly. 'I'd need to find out a bit more.'

Sister Emily beams at her. 'Come and see us,' she says. 'I shall talk to the others when I get back. You will come, won't you?'

Tilly nods. 'I'm coming to see you tomorrow morning, anyway. About the website.'

'Excellent,' cries Sister Emily. 'Somebody shall show you the flat.'

'Yes,' says Tilly. 'Thank you. Gosh, is that the time? I must be getting on. Thank you for the coffee, Sir Alec. I'll see you on Thursday. Goodbye, Sister Emily.'

At the door, Sir Alec grasps Tilly's elbow. 'I call it the S. E. E.,' he murmurs in her ear.

She stares at him blankly. 'Sorry?'

'The Sister Emily Effect,' he whispers. 'Powerful stuff. But she's usually got the root of the matter in her. Good luck tomorrow morning. And you can tell me all about it on Thursday.'

CHAPTER TWENTY

D om is in the potager, checking the willow fencing that edges the beds, planning what he will sow and plant for the coming summer. In his mind's eye he sees patterns and shapes taking form in the empty beds; a riot of colour painted over the cold, bare earth. Actually, he doesn't need the potager now. With Mr Potts' garden added, he has room to separate the vegetables and flowers—and Ed has offered him land that he can use—but he loves Granny's potager and keeps it in the spirit that she created it, faithful to his memories of her and of his childhood. Sunflowers will look out from between the runner beans climbing their hazel wigwams, and there will be red and green lettuce, maroon amaranth, sweet-corn, opium poppies, pumpkins, gourds, and chard with ruby and yellow stems. There will be sweet peas scrambling amongst the mangetout, and many-scented herbs growing at the foot of the encircling stone wall, which carries a miniature rockery of phlox and campanula and dianthus.

His own girls loved the potager, though Griet could never see the point of grubbing in the earth when she could buy vegetables and fruit all year round from a supermarket. Kneeling there, the sun like a blessing on his back, Dom thinks of the years they spent here, as a family; his teaching job at the Camborne School of Mines; the girls at the local schools. Here he began to see that Griet, far from her own home, was finding it difficult to adapt. Without the support system of her huge family and their social commitments she grew edgy. The girls became her whole world, but even they were not enough.

Dom commuted to Camborne each day. He bought a Daimler 4.2, which guzzled petrol but drove like a dream, and hoped that Griet would begin to love her new home. It was clear that she needed projects, goals. The first project was the house itself. One or two things had been done to turn it from two cottages into one but now Griet took it in hand. She approached it carefully, thoughtfully, and, with the help of a local builder who was a carpenter and a craftsman, the cottages were slowly reshaped, opened up. Dom approved. The essential character remained whilst convenience, light, and the benefits of modern life were brought into the original structure.

These were happy times. Griet rose each day, took the girls to school and then she and Andy began work. Rubbing down, painting walls, polishing and waxing floorboards fell to her lot but she loved it. Once the conversion was complete, however, Griet had to look elsewhere for outlets for her considerable energy. As the girls grew older, her talent for planning parties and outings was no longer required; the girls were capable of doing it for themselves. The locals found her rather bossy and overbearing—though they respected her skills for organization and fund-raising—and she grew discontented. The trips back to South Africa became more frequent and lasted a little longer each time and, as her parents grew frail, she began the campaign of moving back to Johannesburg.

Dom gets to his feet, wanders along the paths that wind through the potager and into the little orchard. Only West-country apples grow here: *Malus* Cornish Gilliflower, Tom Putt, Cornish Aromatic, Devonshire Quarrenden. He touches the trees lightly, greeting them as old friends. A blackbird hedge-hops into the orchard, flying low between the rough, grey tree trunks, flipping over the far hedge. In the ash tree on the lane a great tit sings its two notes insistently, demanding to be heard. Dom stands, listening, trying to remember when it was that he'd discovered the difference between solitude and loneliness. As a boy, as a young man, he'd learned to listen in the silence to the chaos that was inside himself, beginning to face his own frailties, until slowly, very slowly, he'd come to terms with some of them. Gradually he discovered that this made him a little more tolerant of the shortcomings of others but this solitude of the heart, the contentment that can only be found in silence, was unknown to Griet. Without friends, telephones, radios, books, she

225

was lonely. She needed immediate relief from her loneliness and so she sought companionship, requiring noise and busyness to satisfy her craving.

With the two girls at university, one at Bristol, the other at Exeter, she grew lonelier, and when Dom was given the option to extend his contract he refused it. He took early retirement, found a tenant for the cottage and returned with Griet to Johannesburg. He knew it was the only way to save his marriage.

'But you'll come back,' Ed said. 'You're a St Enedoc, like us. You'll come home one day.'

Billa said nothing, but her expression struck at Dom's heart. The closeness between them all had deepened during these last ten years. He'd witnessed the rare cracks in Billa's stoicism after she lost her babies, and he recognized the emptiness that existed within her own marriage to Philip, but he suspected that these two—his brother and sister—had the same inner reserves he'd discovered in himself. Their understanding of solitude, the real peace it offered, sustained them during the bad times.

Yet Dom retained that childhood sense of responsibility towards them; he had a strength from which they drew courage. He reminded himself that, genetically, he came from a very strong line in the courage stakes. After all, his grandfather had been a Cornish tinner, his grandmother was tough and durable, their daughter—his mother—brave and loving. And everything Billa and Ed had told him about his father indicated that he'd been fun to be with; such a happy, positive man that his death nearly destroyed them.

Dom guessed that when he arrived, so soon after their father's death, Billa and Ed subconsciously adopted him as part elder brother, part father, and this relationship—so crucial during those months of mourning and the years that followed—had never changed. He'd seen the photographs, he knew how like their father he was, and he could imagine how much older and more confident he must have seemed to the seven-year-old Ed and nine-year-old Billa. He gladly inhabited the role they cast him in and, in return, their love was a balm to his own wounds; their instant acceptance and need of him went a long way to healing him. Yet, at some deep, unresolved level, he'd still hated the man who had begotten him and then denied him—'So you're the bastard!'—and when Ed pleaded with him to change his name by deed poll, to become a St Enedoc, he rejected it out of hand.

'You're as much a St Enedoc as we are,' Ed cried passionately. 'Don't be stubborn, Dom.'

But he refused, laughing at Ed's disappointment, pretending that he was very happy with the situation as it was. Later, when he was a father himself, Dom began to see why his father behaved as he had: loyalty to Elinor and Ed and Billa, perhaps? Embarrassment? Horror at the confusion and shame the truth would cause?

Slowly the hatred dissolved. It was a comfort to Dom to know that his father hadn't known the truth until he was already married with a daughter and another child on the way. He hadn't deliberately abandoned Dom's mother. Now he could feel a twinge of pity for the young man who was caught out for his act of passion, spent seven years at war and died when he was thirty-five. Yet the pain remained.

Dom saw, too, how Ed's natural detachment, his reluctance to total commitment, was affecting his marriage.

'He shouldn't have married,' he said ruefully to Billa. 'He hasn't got the temperament for it.'

'Has anyone?' she retorted.

'We're all damaged,' he answered sadly. 'Everyone has baggage, inadequacies, private dreams waiting to be smashed. Survival is a miracle.'

She nodded, and he knew she was longing to ask about him and Griet. 'What's it like for you?' she wanted to ask. 'How do *you* manage?' But she remained silent. On their weekends at the old butter factory, Billa and Ed saw a great deal of Griet but Dom knew they'd never become real friends. She was too strongly defined to become part of their small group; just as he could never completely mesh with her enormous family.

In Jo'burg he pined for the fresh blast of cold

salty air blowing across the north Cornish coast, or the soft touch of warm mizzling rain; he longed for the sight of early primroses, gleaming in a wet hedgerow, or a new moon rising, thin as a blade, above the sharp granite tors. And so, after Griet died and with his daughters married and settled happily within their extended family, he gave notice to his tenant and came home.

Now, as he passes through the garden, he thinks of his children and longs to see them, to put his arms around them. And as he thinks it he sees Harry, crouching by Bessie, who is stretched out by the back door in the sunshine. Dom's eyes fill with unexpected tears and he bends to kick off his boots lest Harry should see his emotion.

'So there you are,' says Harry, getting to his feet. 'I was wondering where you'd got to. I hope you've remembered that we're all going to a tea party and that Bessie is one of the guests of honour.'

'How could I forget?' asks Dom. 'I'm going to meet Tilly's curate at last.'

'Well, no funny remarks,' says Harry severely. 'Our Tills is in a real old dither. She's gone on ahead.' A pause. 'You're not going in those filthy jeans, are you?'

Dom pulls a face that indicates he has been suitably reprimanded. 'Clearly not,' he says. 'I'll go and change while you brush Bessie. If she's a guest of honour you'd better get rid of some of those tangles. How long have I got?'

Harry consults his watch. 'Twenty minutes max. I said we'll be there before the others arrive.'

'Poor Clem,' says Dom. 'I should think he'll feel like Daniel in the lions' den.'

'You're not a lion, are you, Bessie?' says Harry, encouraging her to her feet. 'Tilly says she's going to let the dogs decide. If they approve of Clem then she might consider him in a more serious light. It's up to Bessie and Bear now.'

'Pretty sound thinking,' says Dom. 'She could do a lot worse. I'll be with you in ten minutes.'

CHAPTER TWENTY-ONE

C lem sits in silence beside Alec, unaware of the beauty of the unfolding springtime beyond the car window, thinking of the ordeal ahead. He'd accepted gladly when Alec offered him and Jakey a lift.

'Not much point taking two cars,' Alec said. 'Can't get Hercules into your little bug so how about coming with me?'

Clem suspects that the older man knows just how nervous he's feeling and is trying to remove some of the pressure. It will be much easier to arrive with Alec and Hercules; dogs always relieve tension and encourage friendliness. Even so, he is still very nervous.

'Charming people, the St Enedocs,' Alec is

saying now. 'Interesting fellow, Dom. Worked all over the world . . .'

He talks gently on about Dom, allowing Clem to remain silent. In the back, perched on his seat, Jakey is tense with excitement and high expectation. By twisting in his seat he can just touch Hercules' head where it rests on the back of the seat behind him. Jakey twiddles the satiny soft yellow ear and tries to imagine how big Bear is and wonders whether he will be frightened of such an enormous animal.

'He's huge, mate,' Harry said. 'Really huge. And his paws are this big.'

He demonstrated, with his hands stretched wide, just how big Bear's paws were and Jakey's eyes grew round with awe. He loves it that Harry calls him 'mate' and he's tried it once or twice, just casually, on his friends at school.

'Just you wait 'til you see him, mate,' he murmurs to Stripey Bunny.

Stripey Bunny isn't going to the tea party, just in case Bear eats him in mistake for a real rabbit, but he is allowed to come along in the car and see Bear from the window. Jakey holds Stripey Bunny up to look at Hercules, who sniffs at him but isn't much interested.

Clem glances round at Jakey and winks at him. The important thing is that nothing rocks the boat for Jakey. Another spasm of fear twists Clem's gut. It seems impossible to imagine a different way of life: a life in which Tilly could be included. He and Jakey have been a little unit for so long now that Clem wonders how another person might be absorbed into it. He gives a deep, despairing sigh and Alec glances sideways at him.

'Things have a habit of working out,' he says encouragingly. 'Given time, most problems can be overcome.'

Clem doesn't pretend not to understand him. They've already touched on the matter once or twice and Clem knows that Alec approves of Tilly, whilst acknowledging the difficulties. He doesn't want to talk about it now, though, in front of Jakey, so he just nods, smiles, accepting Alec's encouragement.

'That's Dom's cottage,' says Alec, as they pass a stone and slate cottage that was clearly once two cottages, 'and here we are.'

He drives over the little bridge whilst Clem looks appreciatively at the old mill house and Jakey sits up straighter, peering from the window for his first sight of Bear. Harry emerges first, and Jakey beams at him, and behind him is the largest dog Jakey has ever seen. It does indeed look like a brown bear. His smile fades into a gaze of fascinated awe and for once he doesn't struggle to undo the seat belt and try to be first out of the car. He sits staring whilst his father gets out, shakes hands with Harry, makes introductions, and then bends down—not very far down—to stroke Bear.

Bear's tail is wagging, his tongue lolls out, and still Jakey sits watching until his father opens the car door and says, 'Come on, Jakes. Come and say hello,' and the little boy scrambles down and approaches warily. Bear is almost as tall as he is. He stretches out a cautious hand and Bear suddenly swipes a tongue round Jakey's face so that he ducks and then laughs, and suddenly everything is fine.

'Hi, mate,' Harry says, and Jakey says, 'Hi, mate,' back to him and it's cool, and he touches Bear again, less tentatively, and strokes the soft coat and feels brave and really happy.

Billa and Tilly, watching from the doorway, smile at the scene.

'He's a sweetie, isn't he?' says Tilly, anxious that Billa should like Jakey. Sometimes Billa is a bit odd around children, rather cautious and diffident, and Tilly wants this to be a happy moment.

Billa's heart has already gone out to Jakey. She's seen that initial fear, the sudden startle back when Bear's tongue swipes Jakey's cheek, then his relief and delight that sweeps the fear clean out of him and leaves a rush of high spirits. She sees the way he's responding to Harry with an attempt at a grown-up swagger whilst instinctively, childishly, he reaches for Harry's hand and begins to talk earnestly to him.

'He is,' she answers. 'And he obviously adores Harry. Ah, here comes Clem.'

Clem comes to meet them just as Ed and Dom come out of the kitchen, and more introductions are made. Bessie now makes her entrance and soon Jakey is in the centre of the three dogs, jumping and clowning and showing off for Harry's benefit.

'Dogs' tea party,' says Dom, shaking Clem's hand, liking the look of him. 'I hope you like dog biscuits.'

'As long as I don't have to eat them in the dog-house,' responds Clem valiantly, trying not to look overwhelmed, and they all laugh appreciatively at his little joke.

Tilly beams at him, approving of him. She's been wondering if she'll be embarrassed in front of all of them and find that she's being offhand with Clem because of it. Luckily this doesn't seem to be the case. It's as if there's no focal point here; it's not about her and Clem. Everyone is talking, moving about the kitchen, quite at ease. The dogs come rushing in and Jakey is allowed to give each of them a biscuit, snatching his hand away rather quickly when Bear takes his and then laughing with relief again.

Ed suggests that Jakey might like to see the tadpolarium while tea is being prepared and the two of them, with Harry and the dogs, all disappear outside.

'I don't know about a dogs' tea party,' says Billa. 'More like a circus.'

Dom is telling Clem the history of the butter

factory, taking him up to the galleried landing to show him where the churns were brought in from the back of the house to be emptied into the vats below, and Alec sits down at the slate table. Billa has made egg and cress sandwiches, sausage rolls, and two kinds of cake.

He looks at them appreciatively. Tilly grins at him.

'None of your shop cake and chemicals in a cup here,' she says.

He grins back at her, longing to ask how she got on at the retreat house yesterday but resisting the temptation. He wonders if Clem knows anything about it. He hasn't mentioned it to him—he's not been a diplomat for nothing—but his curiosity is almost overwhelming.

'There will be eight of us,' says Billa. 'I think it's only fair that if Jakey has to sit up for tea then we all join him, don't you? We need two more chairs, Tilly. There's one in my study and one in the hall. No, don't get up, Alec. Tilly can manage.'

Tilly is almost relieved to have a few moments alone. She feels nervous about being on her own with Clem, of telling him about yesterday when she went to Chi-Meur, and how Mother Magda came to her in the office and said that she was so thrilled to hear that Tilly might be joining the team.

'We need someone to manage us. To make a coherent whole out of all the individual tasks that we are undertaking. There is a sum of money, fifteen thousand pounds each year, set aside for this position and Sister Emily tells me that you might require accommodation and full board, which would make the offer more attractive. That would be splendid. Perhaps, when you've finished, I could show you the Priest's Flat?'

Later, almost in a dream, she'd climbed the beautiful wooden staircase behind Mother Magda, turned down a corridor and followed her through a door into a kind of hall or passageway from which stairs twisted down again. At the bottom of the stairs was another door, which opened into a small vestibule with its own door to the outside.

'You see, you are quite private here,' said Mother Magda, opening the door to the left and motioning Tilly forward.

The room was big; a corner room with two windows looking south and another looking west. An armchair and small table were placed at one of the windows beside a bookcase, and a square table with two chairs stood beneath another. The bed was in a corner against the wall with a cabinet next to it. There was an old-fashioned wardrobe, a white-painted chest of drawers and a small washbasin. It was at least three times the size of Mr Potts' bedroom and, with its mullioned windows and uneven floor, was full of charm.

She thought: I love it.

'And here,' announced Mother Magda proudly, 'is your own bathroom.'

Tilly followed her across the narrow passage and into another big room. It had a huge bath with a shower fixed above it, a lavatory, and a basin. A built-in airing cupboard took up one wall and the sash window looked over the uneven roof-scape of the old manor house. Mother Magda was watching her with hopeful eyes.

Tilly smiled at her. 'The thing is,' she said, 'that I still don't quite know what the exact job description is and if I could manage it.'

'Oh, my dear, neither does any of us,' said Mother Magda ruefully. 'That's rather the point, isn't it? We are led forward and we hope and pray that we're travelling in the right direction.'

'Yes,' agreed Tilly rather doubtfully. 'I can see that it would be like that for you. It rather does go with your job, I imagine. Trust and faith are part of the spec.'

'Exactly. And with yours, too, if you join us.'

Mother Magda looked anxious and Tilly could see that she was a worrier; her brow creased, her thin frame tensed as if ready for disaster, but her dark blue eyes were beautiful.

'Sister Emily wanted to show you the flat,' she said, 'but I was rather worried that she would be over-keen and that you might feel we were pressuring you. She feels very strongly that you are exactly the right person for us. She is a very . . . enthusiastic person.'

'I know. I think she's brilliant,' said Tilly.

'Yes,' agreed Mother Magda. 'Yes, indeed. She is a very special person . . .'

She hesitated. She'd spoken very affectionately but with a certain weariness; as a parent might speak about a wayward, self-willed but beloved child. Tilly could imagine the unspoken end to the sentence '. . . but sometimes I would like to smack her very hard,' and she grinned with such sudden sympathy and understanding that Mother Magda smiled back at her. All the anxiety lines and tension vanished into that wide, delighted smile, the blue eyes shone, and for that moment they were in complete accord.

"If you are happy, then, I should like your permission to bring the subject up at Chapter on Friday morning,' she said hopefully.

'I would be very happy,' Tilly said. 'And then, perhaps, we could talk again.'

Now, remembering, Tilly picks up the chair, wondering if she is quite crazy. She hasn't mentioned the interview to anyone yet but she wonders if Clem might already know. Surely, though, if he'd known he would have said something, given some hint? She wonders how to start the conversation and how he will react. At this moment Jakey, Harry and the dogs surge back into the kitchen, followed by Ed. Clem and Dom reappear, still talking about the history of the house, and Harry is dispatched to fetch the chair from the hall.

As they sit down around the table, Jakey watches in amazement as first Bear and then Bessie climb on to the old sagging sofa and settle down. Hercules stands beside them, sniffing at them, before settling down on the floor beside them. Jakey crouches down, he strokes Bear's head but Bear is too exhausted by his afternoon's activities to acknowledge him. He stretches out comfortably and begins to snore gently. Jakey pats Bessie, who gives him a brief lick, whilst Hercules thumps his tail on the floor.

Jakey remains crouched beside them. 'I wish *we* had a dog,' he says in the aggrieved tone of someone whose request has been denied many times.

'So do I,' says Tilly, much in the same tone, and Jakey looks at her quickly. For the first time he really sees Tilly as a person, rather than just another grown-up, and his interest quickens.

'Won't they let you have one either?' he asks sympathetically, as one martyr to another.

Tilly shakes her head, making a little face of commiseration at him.

'Certainly not while you're staying in Mr Potts' bedroom,' says Dom firmly, and Tilly nods at Jakey, as if to say, 'You see what I mean?'

'When you find your own place,' Dom goes on, selecting a sandwich, 'then you can get your own dog.'

'Well, as it happens,' Tilly says indignantly, 'I

might have found my own place. I applied for a job yesterday at the retreat house and it's got accommodation to go with it.'

The silence is absolute, and Tilly blushes a bright pink. She feels a complete fool; she can't imagine what has made her speak out in front of everyone. She doesn't dare look at Clem. But Jakey, watching her, feels an instinctive sympathy for her. It is as if Tilly is another child who has said something silly in front of the grown-ups and he wants to comfort her, to show solidarity. He gets up and goes to her and stands beside her.

'Are you really going to live at Chi-Meur?' he asks. 'We're going back to the Lodge soon. Couldn't you have a dog there? Daddy says we could have a dog if someone would look after it while I'm at school and he's at work. Oh.' His eyes widen and begin to shine. 'If you were there you could look after the dog for us.' A better idea seizes his imagination. 'We could share it.' He turns to Clem. 'We could, couldn't we, Daddy?'

Clem, staring at him, thinks: this could be the connection. This could be the thing that could bring the three of us together. Walks with the dog on the cliffs, down to the beach . . .

'Well,' he says, 'it's certainly a thought. Remember, though, we can't go back to the Lodge until the summer. But if Tilly thinks she could help out . . .'

'I'd have to live in at the house for my job,' says

Tilly quickly. 'But I'm sure we could manage a dog between us.'

She glances anxiously at Clem, who is watching her with that secret amused look, and she blushes again.

'But,' she adds, facing him down, 'I might not get the job. My application has to go before the Chapter meeting.'

'Oh, I think you'll get it,' he says. 'I am invited to Chapter. Sister Emily and I will be rooting for you.'

Alec leans forward. 'And remember what I told you about the S. E. E.,' he murmurs in her ear.

'We'll have a dog,' crows Jakey to Harry.

'And don't forget, mate,' says Harry, 'that I shall be back in the summer to go to college. I'll bring Bessie over to see you all when I come home for weekends.'

At these last few words Dom catches Billa's eye and they smile at each other. Alec sees the look of happiness that passes between them. Ed sits contentedly sipping his tea. His eyes, though fixed on Jakey, have a faraway look as if he is in another world, making his own story, about another boy, perhaps. Tilly is laughing and Clem raises his teacup to her. Jakey is already discussing the merits of particular dog breeds with Harry.

Alec sits back in his chair. He feels very much at home, as if, in these latter days, he has found another family, quite different from his own:

disparate, unusual, but united by threads of the many different kinds of love. Now, Tilly is explaining about the job, which Clem seems to know more about than she does, and there is a general sense of optimism and wellbeing. Billa asks questions about the accommodation and Clem is explaining why the salary is not very high, given the responsibility of the job.

'But if it's all found,' Dom says, 'if accommodation and food is free, then you can add quite a bit to that.'

'The important thing,' says Ed, who has been roused from his reverie, 'is that Tilly is happy and working with people she likes.'

'Hear, hear,' says Alec.

'And she'll be able to sneak out,' says Harry enviously, 'and go surfing.'

'And we'll have a dog,' says Jakey firmly, lest this crucial fact should be forgotten in the excitement.

'What sort of dog shall we have, Jakey?' asks Tilly recklessly, wondering exactly how a dog will fit in with her new duties and hoping the nuns are animal-lovers. 'A Newfoundland like Bear? Or a golden retriever like Bessie? Or a Labrador like Hercules?'

Jakey eats a second sausage roll as he reflects on the subject.

'*Not* a Newfoundland,' says Clem firmly. 'Much too big.'

Instantly Jakey looks at Tilly, sensing she will be his ally. Tilly winks at him, shrugs.

'They are a bit big,' she says. 'Very boisterous when they're young. He might pull you over.'

Jakey nods judicially, letting everyone see that it's his decision. 'OK,' he says.

'It will require much thought,' says Dom. 'You might find a very nice rescue dog. Try the Cinnamon Trust. That's where I found Bessie.'

'I've got *The Observer's Book of Dogs* in my study,' says Ed to Jakey. 'Would you like to see it?'

Jakey is off his chair in an instant; he runs round the table and grabs Tilly's hand.

'Come on,' he says, and he and Tilly and Ed go out together.

' "May I get down, please?",' mutters Clem under his breath, anxious that Jakey has not asked permission to leave the table but deciding not to make an issue of it.

'Typical Ed,' says Billa, cutting cake. 'Books first, food second. Sorry, Clem. Not a good example for Jakey.'

'It doesn't matter now and again,' says Clem. He sees that Dom is looking at him rather quizzically and wonders what Tilly's godfather is making of him. 'I'm sure Tilly will be happy at Chi-Meur,' he says reassuringly. 'The Sisters are very flexible and things tend to happen organically. I think she'll enjoy it.'

'I wasn't fearing for Tilly,' says Dom. 'I was

243

just wondering if they know what they're taking on. I warn you that Tilly gets very enthusiastic about her work.'

'Just what we need,' says Clem cheerfully. 'I'll tell them that at Chapter tomorrow.'

'You do that,' says Dom affably, 'and I look forward to seeing the experiment unfold. But perhaps I won't invite anyone else to stay in Mr Potts' bedroom. Not just yet.'

CHAPTER TWENTY-TWO

Sarah hangs the washing out in the small paved courtyard behind the cottage. From where she stands, looking down the valley, she can see the village gardens where magnolias and camellias are in flower: cloudy shapes of cream and pink. The cottages huddle together, like old friends gossiping in the shelter of the small, steep fields where sheep are grazing, and she can hear the lambs' high thin cries as they jostle and butt at their mothers' flanks, nuzzling for milk.

She stands for a moment, the laundry basket at her feet, enjoying the sunshine and feeling calmer. Now that she and Dave have agreed to take on the house in Yelverton, and the move is going forward, a sense of peace has enveloped her. Dave is delighted that she and the boys will be so much nearer to the dockyard; that his journey will be so much shorter and easier. He's talked of all the things they will do together and what fun it will be to go to the parties and social events connected with the ship that up until now have been simply impossible.

Sarah agrees with all this and says that she can't wait to see the house. It's odd that, knowing Tilly has got the job at Chi-Meur and that Clem and Jakey will be moving back into the Lodge in a few months' time, things are different. Without the promotion of U-Connect to occupy her mind or the prospects of Tilly's regular visits—not to mention Clem dropping in—it feels right to be moving on. After all, U-Connect can be set up anywhere; that is the beauty of it. But, somehow, she can't quite imagine doing it without Tilly. She's managing to be quite upbeat with Tilly, now; much more positive about her new prospects at the retreat house. It seems churlish to be other-wise when Tilly is so excited about it all.

'I've got some really good marketing ideas,' she told Sarah, when she'd come in to discuss the final intake of new punters. 'I can see how we can target two separate groups. The couples or single people who come on what Sister Emily calls Holy Holidays and the others who come in a group on led retreats. We can have a different approach for each of them, make it much more focused. I've been googling other retreat houses, looking at their websites and the things that they're doing. For instance, Epiphany House in Cornwall produces a lovely House Programme of events for the year. Things like that make such a difference.'

It becomes clear that Clem is going to be closely involved in these new plans and Sarah has managed to steer clear of any pointed remarks about their proximity once Tilly moves into the Priest's Flat and Clem is back in the Lodge. In fact, Tilly hasn't spoken of any personal aspect of the relationship apart from casually mentioning a dogs' tea party with the St Enedocs and Sir Alec Bancroft, to which Clem and Jakey were invited. She seems more concerned by the fact that Harry will be leaving them very soon and how much she'll miss him.

Sarah's attention is caught by a bluetit who is examining the nest box that Sarah's mother fixed to a holly tree on the boundary hedge years ago. He pecks at the rough wooden edging around the hole for a moment before disappearing inside. Presently his cross little face can be seen peering out and then he flies away. Sarah wonders if he's pleased with it or whether he considers it too dingy; too small. Maybe he'll return with his mate and they'll discuss the merits of raising their family in it.

Rather like me and Dave going to Yelverton, she thinks.

The thought amuses her and she picks up the laundry basket and goes back indoors. It is dark inside after the brightness of the garden and she decides that it will be rather nice to live in big, light rooms with tall windows and high ceilings. She sits at the table in the kitchen and picks up the details of the Victorian house in Yelverton, which the owners have sent to her. She looks again at the room measurements and considers which bedroom will be right for Ben; she checks the little study that she can use for her next experiment with U-Connect. It raises her spirits to be planning like this and she wishes that Dave was with her, sharing his natural enthusiasm for any new project.

The owners are another naval couple, submariners moving to Faslane for two years, and they are leaving the house furnished. Sarah is quite pleased that she and Dave won't have the expense of new furniture but slightly disappointed that once again they will be living with other people's choice.

'Much better to wait until we can afford to buy our own place,' Dave says.

And he's right, of course, and at least the move will be very straightforward. Their personal belongings won't take much packing and Dave has already decided that he'll hire a small van and move the whole lot in one journey.

Sarah pulls her laptop towards her and switches it on. It's time to do some work before George wakes and wants his bottle.

Harry, too, is planning his departure. It's not too painful because he knows he'll be back soon and, anyway, they've all been here before. When he was reading Geology at Oxford everyone got used to him appearing at short notice and then dashing away again. The really good thing about Dom and Billa and Ed is that they don't fuss about him; they don't attempt to pin him down. They always welcome him, and any friends he likes to bring along, and this makes him very much more inclined to want to see them. His friends love the whole scene and consider Harry to be very lucky to have such a bolt hole. Indeed, some of his university friends still occasionally visit Dom, staying in Mr Potts' bedroom, having a weekend surfing or walking and going to the pub.

As he gathers his belongings, brings out his bags, Harry feels rather pleased with himself. It seems that Tilly will be sorted out after all. The dogs' tea party was a great idea and things have moved on pretty quickly. She's got the job at the retreat house and seems to be much more relaxed with Clem: they look all set to get it together.

'Thanks, Hal,' she said, hugging him before she drove off to work. 'You've been fab. Don't break a leg on the slopes and come home soon. Wait till you see my new quarters. I'll be settled in by the time you're back. Stay in touch.'

'I'll text,' he promises. 'And we'll be Skyping.

I shall want to know how you and Clem are shaping up. And little Jakey.'

As for Jakey . . . Harry smiles to himself. He's rather touched by Jakey's hero-worship.

On Saturday afternoon, Tilly drove him over to say goodbye to Jakey. A small party had been organized. They were going to have tea, watch *Madagascar* and then have a pizza supper. Jakey was so proud to be host, to organize it all. During tea he and Harry had tried to outdo each other on quotes from the film and Jakey soon discovered, to his joy, that Harry really did know it just as well as he did. At intervals one or the other would say 'Smile and wave. Smile and wave,' and they'd do a high-five and laugh together.

'I wish you weren't going,' Jakey said at the end, looking suddenly very sad.

'But I'll be back before you know it, mate,' Harry said. 'Don't forget I'm going to teach you to surf this summer.'

Jakey perked up a little. 'And you said you'd send me some postcards,' he reminded Harry.

'For sure I will. From Geneva, and when I get back to Jo'burg.'

'You could start them, "Hi, mate",' suggested Jakey rather wistfully, thinking of showing them to his friends at school and bragging about his friendship with this dazzling young man.

'I wouldn't start them any other way,' Harry assured him. 'Oh, and I've got you this.'

He took out a photograph that Billa had taken at the dogs' tea party and printed off on her computer. She'd laminated it so that it wouldn't get dirty or tear, and Jakey reached eagerly for it and studied it. He was in the centre of the photograph next to Harry and they were surrounded by the three dogs. Bear sat next to Jakey, their heads at nearly the same level, Jakey's arm around Bear's huge furry neck. Bessie stood beside Harry and Hercules lay in front of the group.

Jakey's face was transformed with joy. It was everything he could desire. There he was with the god-like Harry, the enormous Bear and the two other dogs. He couldn't wait to show it to his friends.

'Can I keep this and take it to school?' he asked eagerly.

'Sure,' said Harry. 'It's yours. I've got my own copy to show to the family back home.'

Jakey drew a deep contented breath. When the time came, he and Clem walked to the car with Tilly and Harry and watched them get in. Harry let the window down and winked at Jakey, whose mouth began to turn down at the corners.

'No tears, mate,' he said. 'Remember our secret. "Smile and wave. Smile and wave."'

Now, Harry wanders downstairs with his bags and dumps them in the hall. Dom is listening to *You and Yours* on Radio 4 whilst preparing an early lunch before taking Harry to the train. They eat companionably, talking about the relatives with whom Harry will be staying in Geneva and the skiing, and then the journey back to South Africa. Harry is grateful that Dom makes no fuss; Harry might be taking the train for a day out at Penzance, such is the older man's pragmatism.

Later, as they drive though the lanes towards the A39, Dom pulls in to make room for another car coming in the opposite direction. The lane is narrow and Dom is too busy manoeuvring to take stock of the driver. Harry recognizes him, though, and raises a hand.

'Friend of yours?' asks Dom, pulling away.

'It's the chap who's staying at the Chough,' says Harry. 'Christian Marr. He's an energy consultant.'

Dom frowns, as if the name has rung some kind of bell in his mind, but Harry begins to talk about Tilly and Clem and the moment passes.

Through his rear-view mirror Tris watches the car drive away and laughs softly: it's like an omen. He's returning just as the boy is leaving. The timing is perfect. He is quite certain that Dom hasn't seen him—even though he'd be unlikely to recognize him after all these years—but it doesn't matter too much if he has, because Tris is going to make his move at last. First, he plans to get Billa and Ed alone. He suspects that they'll be much more vulnerable, more open to his explanations about the past, without Dom around, but sooner or later he'll have to face up to all three of them. Tris is excited. Weedhound has come up with some very special cocaine capsules and just for the moment they're blocking out all the symptoms of the tuberculosis that is eating his lungs away. He's on a high and ready to go.

He checks back into the Chough and is welcomed by the landlord. His little suite of rooms is clean and fresh and he unpacks, still chuckling to himself now he's decided to make his move. Of course, he might be wrong, and the boy and Dom are just out for a drive, but he doesn't think so. He'd seen the bags on the back seat. Something tells him quite certainly that Harry is on his way and if Dom is driving him to the station he'll be gone for a couple of hours; perfect.

Tris sits on the end of the bed and takes his mobile out of his pocket. He scrolls down to Billa's number, taken from her mobile, and dials. She answers quite quickly.

'Hi,' he says. 'Hi, Billa. So how are you after all this time? It's me. It's Tris. Hope you got my postcards. I've just arrived and I thought I'd pop over to see you and Ed. I'm not far away. See you very soon. 'Bye.'

He switches off and begins to laugh again. She was too shocked even to speak, apart from saying 'Hello'. He picks up his satchel, checks for his car keys and goes out.

CHAPTER TWENTY-THREE

B illa sits silent, still holding her phone.
  'Who was it?' asks Ed.

They've only just finished lunch and are still at the table which as usual is strewn with books, papers; also a dark red vase of daffodils and a small camera.

'It's Tris,' says Billa. 'He's here. He's on his way.'

Ed gapes at her. 'What?'

What with the dogs' tea party, the good news about Tilly's job and Harry's imminent departure there hasn't been time to think of Tris. Now, suddenly, they are back in the nightmare world of fear and speculation. What does he want?

'We could go out,' suggests Ed. 'Just get in the car and go. Where was he speaking from?'

Billa shakes her head in answer to both questions. There is no point in running away and she has no idea where he is.

'We can't let him think he's frightened us,' she says. 'And all he said was that he'd see us very soon. Damn. And Dom will be driving Harry to Bodmin Parkway by now. We're just going to have to face him. Help me clear this lot away, Ed.'

They get up and start to clear the table, each getting in the other's way, terrors rattling like marbles in their heads. Ed fills the dishwasher, clattering and clashing the plates in his nervousness, and Billa drops a handful of knives on the floor. She swears beneath her breath and Bear climbs off the sofa and comes to see what she's dropped. She is comforted by his huge presence and drops down on one knee so as to put an arm around his neck and hug him as she gathers up the knives.

'We've got to try to be prepared,' Ed is saying. 'We mustn't let ourselves be stampeded by whatever he says or does. We know he'll try to wrong-foot us, probably threaten us, and we simply mustn't let him.'

Billa looks up at him. She feels the familiar sensations of affection for him and the need to protect him. Yet he looks quite strong; quite tough now that the moment is at hand. Billa remembers how Ed at twelve defended their father's study, stood up for his memory, and she nods and tries to smile at him.

'You're absolutely right,' she says. 'Whatever he says, we won't be fazed. Or at least we won't let him see if we are. We'll just pretend we think he's looking us up for old times' sake. Play him at his own game. After all, you won when it came to the study. Never forget that.'

Ed nods back. Now that it's happening, he feels that same anger rising. Yet when Tris taps smartly on the kitchen door and opens it, just as if he is a member of the family, his gut churns again. And the real shock to both of them is that he looks so much like Andrew. They stare at him as if he is a ghost come from the past to mock them.

Tris grins at them; that old wicked grin that dares and provokes. He hangs his leather satchel on a chair.

'Well, well,' he says. 'Just like old times. So what's new?'

Bear, who has been drinking at his bowl, comes forward to inspect the visitor and Tris steps back a little, making a comical face and raising both hands in mock defence.

'Whoa,' he says. 'Now this chap's new. What the hell is he? A bear?'

'That's exactly what he is,' says Ed. 'Bear, this is Tris. You have my permission to kill him if he tries any nonsense.'

'Hey,' says Tris, laughing protestingly. 'Well, now, there's a welcome. And it's nice to see you, too, Ed. And you, Billa.'

Billa is completely nonplussed. The fact that Tris is so like Andrew has completely knocked her off balance; she simply doesn't know how to react. She remembers the postcard of Bitser and wants to scream at him and turn him out of the house. At the same time some deeply ingrained tradition of hospitality makes her try to smile back at him.

'We've just finished lunch and we're going to have some coffee,' she says. 'Would you like some?'

'Thanks. Yes, I would. It's really weird being back here, you know. Nothing's changed. It's like walking into a timewarp. Of course, I never got to say goodbye to you guys, did I?'

Billa pushes the kettle on to the hotplate and Ed sits down again. He is determined to remain calm, unmoved by this sudden time shift, but there is a sense of unreality here. He looks into those light frosty eyes and his spine stiffens in readiness for the attack.

'You certainly disappeared very suddenly,' he agrees. 'We never quite knew what happened.'

Tris grins at him. 'But I guess you didn't care much, eh? Too glad to see the back of me. Good riddance to bad rubbish. Wasn't that the phrase back then?'

There is a little silence and he laughs out loud, as if he has scored a point. Billa puts the jug of coffee on the table with some mugs.

'Milk?' she asks him. 'Sugar?'

He shakes his head. 'Black's just fine, thanks.'

Billa pours three mugs of coffee and sits down. 'Yes, we were glad to see the back of you,' she says coolly. 'But it's always puzzled us. What happened?'

Tris sits back in his chair; he visibly relaxes and the smile fades from his eyes.

'It's quite a story,' he says rather grimly. 'How long have you got?'

Billa and Ed stare at him warily; once again they

are confused by conflicting emotions. They don't want to trust him but there's some expression of veracity in his face now that unsettles them.

'Long enough for a story,' says Ed, picking up his mug.

Tris shrugs. 'OK. I'll keep it short. I was born in France. My mother was French. My father killed her when I was four years old. I don't know if it was an accident. He hit her, she might have fallen and cracked her head open, or he might have battered her to death. I'll never know the truth about that. I heard cries one night and I got out of bed and went downstairs. My father was going out of the front door so I went into the drawing-room and found Maman lying on the floor. There was blood in her hair and she didn't move, she wouldn't answer me, and then my father came back with some old sacks and I hid behind the curtain while he bundled the body up and took it out into the grounds.'

He pauses to sip his coffee. Ed and Billa sit in horrified silence. Instinctively they know that Tris is telling the truth.

'I raced back to bed,' Tris goes on, 'and then he came up to say that there had been an accident and Maman was dead and that we must go away at once. He said that if we stayed I would be taken away from him and he might go to prison. He said that I must never, ever, tell anyone about Maman. He didn't know that I had seen her, of course. After that we moved from place to place but each time I thought we might settle down, have a home again, we'd have to lift and shift. That's what happened here. My father was tipped off that Interpol had tracked him down and that he would be extradited back to France to stand trial. I think that there were other things apart from murder that they were after him for, but he couldn't wait around to find out.'

He looks at them, raises his eyebrows. 'Does that answer the question?'

Neither of them can think of anything to say that doesn't sound lame and ineffectual. Both of them feel certain that he's being totally honest. He watches them almost sympathetically, as if he knows how they must feel.

'Sorry,' he says. 'Only you did ask and there's no point to any more lying. I got so tired of the lying.'

'But you were only four,' says Billa. 'How did you manage at four to stay silent about what you'd seen?'

Tris looks amused. 'Fear,' he says briefly. 'It's a powerful incentive. My father was all I had. I couldn't face losing him, too. He told people that Maman had died in a car accident and hoped that I was too little to make much sense about it if I talked. People might simply think I was muddled, confused, of course. But I didn't talk. I just remembered her lying there with the blood in her hair.'

'I'm sorry,' says Billa quietly. 'It's tragic. Awful. What happened after you left here? Where did you go?'

'We went to Toulon, to someone my father knew very well indeed, where he could lie very low. I was happy there with Tante Berthe, happier than I had been since Maman died.'

'And they didn't catch your father?'

'Not for a while. He went on the run again when I was fourteen but this time he went alone. I stayed with Tante Berthe and my baby half-brother.'

'Baby half-brother?'

Tris shrugs, makes a humorous face. 'So I guess she wasn't my aunt after all. But I loved her and I loved my baby brother and nothing was going to separate me from him. Father went alone. Then when I was twenty we heard rumours that he was caught up in something else and we never heard from him again.'

After a moment Ed shakes his head. 'There's nothing to say, is there? What can we possibly say that isn't trite? And this isn't meant to be rude, but why have you come back? You can't have been happy here.'

'No, not particularly. By the time we got here I knew it would be just another place where I'd settle a bit, get fond of people and then have it ripped away. I was too damaged, I guess, to want to play the game any more. I wanted to hit back. I started as I meant to go on. But your mother was very kind to me. I've never forgotten that.'

'So why send the postcards?' asks Billa, puzzled. 'Why remind us of what you did?'

Tris takes a deep breath. 'I thought it was only fair,' he said at last. 'It was faintly possible you might have forgotten, and I wanted it to be all open and fair. You could simply chuck me off your land or we could have some closure. I wanted you to have time to think about it.'

'Yes, but why now?' asks Billa, muddled by conflicting sensations of residual irritation, sympathy and even compassion.

Tris fetches another sigh, drinks some more coffee. 'Well, this is the embarrassing bit. The trouble is that the big fella upstairs has called time. I haven't much longer to live. I've got advanced TB, allied with years of substance abuse, and I've been trying just to sort a few things out and get some stuff off my conscience. But I didn't want to blackmail anyone just to get the sympathy vote. So I sent the postcards so you'd remember what I was really like and then hope we could just sit round the table like we are now and try to sort it out.'

'I thought TB was curable these days,' says Billa.

'Yeah, well, if you take the triple therapy drugs in the right combination it can be. If you don't, and I didn't, it becomes resistant to the treatment. And it's a very complicated treatment. One pill out of sync and you've had it. It's very easy to get it wrong, especially if you're getting stoned at regular intervals.'

Once again Billa and Ed sense that Tris is telling the truth. They are utterly confounded.

Tris pushes his mug away and stands up. 'Look,' he says. 'I'm going now. I'm staying at the Chough. I've booked in for a week. If you want to see me again I'll leave you my card.'

'Well, hang on,' begins Ed uncomfortably. 'Wait a minute. You don't have to rush off.'

'Yes, I do,' says Tris firmly. 'You both need time to think about this. I'd love to come back and have a look around the old place and have a cup of tea. But if you can't hack it I shall quite understand. There's my card. Thanks for the coffee.'

He smiles at them both, gives a little nod as if to say 'That's it. No nonsense,' picks up his coat and satchel and goes out quickly, closing the door quietly behind him.

There is silence. Billa and Ed look at one another.

'So how do you read that?' asks Ed after a moment.

Billa shakes her head. 'It's . . . bizarre. But I felt that it was all true. Did you?'

'Yes, I did.'

Billa takes a breath. 'So what now?'

'Well, it's a kind of olive branch, isn't it? And what harm can inviting him back and having a cup of tea do?'

'Poor Tris,' says Billa suddenly. 'How utterly

appalling. No wonder he was such a ghastly little tick. What a terrible life he's had. I thought it was rather touching that he still calls his mother "Maman". How do you get over something like that?'

'You probably don't,' says Ed. 'But it explains why Andrew left so suddenly.'

'I can't wait to tell Dom,' says Billa. 'Gosh. I feel as if I've been hit on the head.' She pours them both some more coffee. 'But we'll invite him back, won't we? Just like he says, as closure. Perhaps we all need it.'

Tris climbs into his car, drives a short way and then pulls into a farm gateway and stops. He's laughing so much he can barely see to drive. He wheezes helplessly, his hands pressed against his chest, gleefully reliving the scene. And the beauty of it is: it's all true. Everything he told them was the truth. As he sat there at that big old slate table, feeling their hostility, testing the depths of their wariness, he suddenly saw that the one way to disarm them totally was by telling the truth. Tris laughs till he cries. He is confident that there will be another invitation. The St Enedocs are such foolishly decent people; good manners and right feeling will overcome their natural suspicion and their instinctive dislike, and will guarantee that he gains entrée—and after that . . .

Tris gets out his handkerchief and mops his

eyes. He knows he's in danger of overdoing it, and that he's being a bit too free with the magical stuff his contact in Bristol has given him, but he can't resist. He feels so good, so strong. There's nothing in the world so sure to get the adrenalin pumping as taking this kind of risk. He'd even given them a clue by using Billa's mobile number. How did they think he'd got that?

Tris starts the engine again and pulls away. He makes a bet with himself that he'll get a phone call in the next twenty-four hours giving him an invitation to go back to the old butter factory. He stretches an arm sideways and pats the satchel.

'Then it'll just be you and me, baby,' he murmurs.

CHAPTER TWENTY-FOUR

A re you OK?' Tilly asks Dom at breakfast. He was out last evening when she got home and it occurs to her that he's been rather distracted this morning, though she's been pre-occupied with her own thoughts, too. Yesterday, after she'd dropped in to see Sarah, she'd seized her courage in both hands and driven down to the vicarage. Clem wasn't there but Dossie and Jakey were. They welcomed her so warmly that she was still glowing with the memory of it.

Jakey had invited a school friend and, once they'd had tea and were settled in Jakey's bedroom with various games and toys, Dossie and Tilly were able to have a quiet moment to themselves. They sat together on the sofa, Dossie turned towards Tilly, one leg tucked beneath her. She looked youthful in her jeans and an oversize jersey, and she was so like Clem that Tilly was aware of a great affection for her.

'Congratulations on getting the job,' Dossie said. 'You'll love it. I promise you, it will be like nothing you've ever done before.'

'I believe you,' said Tilly, thinking of her interview with the Sisters and Father Pascal. 'But I'm very excited about it. I'm sure we can do so much more on the marketing front and organization in general. And I love the Priest's Flat.'

'Janna will be thrilled,' said Dossie contentedly. 'Have you seen her quarters in the Coach House?'

Tilly nodded. 'She invited me over to see where she is after my interview with them all. She seems very happy there.'

'She used to live in a caravan in the orchard, which she loved, but she was persuaded to move in when the Sisters transferred over to the Coach House and the retreat house was opened. They're so lucky to have her.'

'But it seemed to me that it works both ways and she feels lucky to have them.'

'Absolutely right,' agreed Dossie. 'Janna came to Chi-Meur looking for a family and she's found one. But it'll be lovely for her to have you not so far away, too. You can both have a moment together when you're feeling fed up with community life.'

Tilly laughed. 'I can see that we might need to let off steam from time to time.'

'And what's this,' asked Dossie, looking mischievous, 'about you and Jakey sharing a dog?'

Tilly knew the colour was rising in her cheeks. 'It was a bit crazy,' she admitted. 'He and I were both saying how much we'd like to have a dog and Jakey thought that if he and Clem were at the Lodge and I was up at the house we might manage it between us. I'm feeling a bit guilty about that one. I honestly don't know how it could work, though Clem agreed that it might be managed.'

'Well, I've been thinking about it, too,' said Dossie. 'Between us all, it could be a possibility. Mo and Pa's old Lab died last year and they miss him terribly. I'm wondering if we could help out when it gets really difficult. It would have to be a very adaptable dog, though, and definitely not a puppy.'

Tilly shook her head. 'Definitely not a puppy. Maybe a rescue dog. At least we've got time to think about it. Nothing can happen until Clem is priested and moves back to the Lodge. Jakey knows that, doesn't he?'

'Mmm,' said Dossie. 'But he won't forget about it. We need to have a plan of action.'

'That sounds good, but where do we start?'

'I've got an idea,' said Dossie. 'Give me a

265

chance to make a phone call. I just wanted to be really sure you were up for it, or whether it was just Jakey.'

'I think it would be great,' Tilly said. 'But it's got to be practical.'

'Exactly,' said Dossie. She stretched and sat up. 'Come on. The sun's come out. Let's take the boys down on the beach for half an hour before it gets dark.'

'I'm fine, Tilly,' Dom says now. 'Really. An old friend from the past has resurfaced and last evening Ed and Billa and I were exchanging notes about him.'

'Oh, that's nice,' says Tilly. She gets up from the table and takes her porridge bowl and coffee mug through to the kitchen. 'I'm off to Bodmin this morning and then to Wadebridge. See you later.'

She comes back into the parlour, bends to kiss his cheek and grab her bag, pauses to stroke Bessie and hurries out. Dom watches her go. He's still in shock at what Billa and Ed have told him and their reaction to Tris's story. He wants to believe them when they say that Tris is telling the truth; that even the reason for the postcards is plausible. He remembers his own reaction when his postcard arrived; how he'd wondered then what had made Tris the destructive child that he was. Nevertheless, Dom remains cautious. He is not quite so ready to be convinced that Tris is a reformed character.

They have all agreed that Tilly must be kept out of it. She's completely absorbed in the prospect of her new job and all that goes with it and now, with Harry gone, she might just as well move into the Priest's Flat and take up her new position. There's nothing to stop her except her own sense of guilt at leaving Dom alone. She knows he'll be missing Harry and she doesn't want him to be lonely. Also she thinks she should wait for Sarah to move at the end of the month so that they can properly wind up U-Connect.

However, with Tris not far away, Dom almost wishes that Tilly was at Chi-Meur. He can't quite accept that this is simply an opportunity for Tris to kiss and make up. He'd said as much to Ed and Billa.

'But he's dying,' Ed told him. 'He's been told he hasn't long to live. How terrible it is. I suppose that facing his own mortality has made him see things in quite a different light.'

'And the way he spoke about his brother—his half-brother, Jean-Paul—' Billa said, 'it was actually rather moving. And the way he still calls his mother "Maman". What a ghastly thing to happen to a four-year-old. No wonder he was so damaged.'

'Can we believe that Andrew was the sort of person who might kill his wife, though?' Dom asked, thinking back, trying to remember.

'He always had a bit of an edge,' Billa said.

'Perhaps that's why Mother was drawn to him. And it does answer a lot of questions. Like why he left so suddenly and why we never heard from him again. Of course, it might have been an accident.'

'I think we should ask Tris back,' Ed said. 'He was very genuine about not outstaying his welcome and giving us time to think it all through.'

'Did he mention me?' Dom asked.

Billa shook her head. 'He wasn't here very long. But we'd like you to be here when we invite him back. I'd like to get it over with rather than us all sitting about brooding. What about tomorrow? Ed's away in the morning and I've got someone coming to discuss a charity event. What about tea? He said he'd booked in until the weekend but I think I'd rather get on with it. I feel rather sorry for him but I don't particularly want him hanging around.'

They watched her while she picked up the card and dialled the mobile number. There was no answer but she left a message: 'Hi, Tris. Billa here. If you'd like to come to tea tomorrow we'll be around. Half-three? See you then.'

'And there was nothing that made you suspect anything?' Dom asked when she'd finished. 'Nothing at all?'

Billa put down her phone and frowned. Dom raised his eyebrows but she shook her head.

'Just then something came and went,' she said.

'But I can't think what it was. No, I think he was genuine, Dom, I really do.'

Now, Dom gets up from the table and begins to clear the remaining breakfast things. He opens the back door to let Bessie out into the garden and switches on the radio. There is a knock on the front door, then a short, sharp peal of the bell. Dom goes out into the hall and opens the door.

'Hi, Dom,' says Tris. 'Sorry not to phone first but I couldn't find your number.'

Despite Billa's warning, Dom is completely unprepared to see Andrew's double standing at his door. All the old antagonism floods into his brain, sends the adrenalin racing through his veins, and he makes no attempt to step back to allow him in.

'Tris,' he says unsmilingly. 'It's been a long time. Thanks for the postcard.'

Tris laughs: he looks faintly shamefaced.

'I might be carrying an olive branch,' he says, 'but I didn't want you to forget that I haven't always been a dove.'

Dom shakes his head. 'No chance of that.'

'No, well.' Tris pulls down the corners of his mouth. 'The truth is, I've got a document here I'd like you to read. I decided not to show it to Billa and Ed until I had your opinion of it.' He pulls forward the satchel slung over his shoulder, holds it up. 'Have you got a minute?'

Dom stands quite still: all his instincts tell him that this document is what it's all about. His curiosity is aroused. Then he stands back and gestures that Tris should come in. He does so, looking around him curiously.

'I've never been in here,' he says. 'Where do I go? In here? Oh, and here's another dog. Not as big as that great brute at Mellinpons, thank goodness. I don't really do dogs but he looks nice. Hi there, old fellow. Let me give you a pat. There. Now we're friends.'

'It's a she. Bessie.' Dom switches off the radio. 'So what is it you want to show me?'

Tris smiles. It's an open friendly smile that very slightly mocks Dom's curtness, and Dom feels a little ashamed of his brusqueness and indicates that they should go through to the parlour. They sit down and Tris opens the satchel. He does it with great candour as if to show Dom that there is nothing inside except a large brown envelope, a flat leather wallet and several small bottles that slip out on to the table.

'My medication,' explains Tris, putting them away. 'Just in case I get an attack. I've got a bit of a problem.'

'Billa told me,' says Dom briefly, refusing to be sidetracked into sympathy. 'And a drug habit, too, so she said. How would we know which bottle to use in an emergency? Or do you inject?'

Tris bursts out laughing. 'Don't be too kind to me,' he says. 'I might cry. Now here it is.'

He opens the flap on the envelope, slides out the

document and pushes it across the table to Dom. Even from a distance Dom can see that it is a formal will—though not drawn up by the family's lawyer—and his heart sinks. He picks it up and studies it very carefully. In short, it states that Elinor Caroline St Enedoc bequeaths all her property, shares and belongings to her children Edmund Henry and Wilhelmina Jane, and to Andrew Richard Carr the sum of ten thousand pounds. If he should predecease her then the sum reverts to her children. It is signed, dated and witnessed.

Tris watches him across the table.

'But he didn't predecease her,' he says. 'I've checked.'

Dom reads it again and then pushes it back towards Tris.

'Rather late in the day, isn't it?' he asks. 'Why now? According to Ed and Billa you won't have much time to spend it, assuming that it were to stand up in a court of law after all this time.'

Those cool frosty eyes survey Dom carefully, then they grow softer; he looks away.

'It's for Léon,' he says.

Dom frowns. 'Léon? Is that your half-brother?'

Tris shakes his head. 'My brother's name was Jean-Paul. Léon is his son. My nephew. He's just twenty.'

Dom stares at Tris. Like Billa and Ed, he is aware of a complete authenticity in Tris's state-

271

ment. He has no doubt at all that he is speaking the truth. There is a look in his eyes that tells Dom that Tris loves Léon very much.

'I'm sure that Billa and Ed have already told you the story,' Tris says. 'When my father and I left here we went to Toulon. Tante Berthe took us in and then she had my father's child. Jean-Paul. I loved him so much. It was my first chance at having a family again and when my father had to move on I stayed with them. With Tante Berthe and Jean-Paul. I wanted to look after them as I grew up but I didn't make much of a fist of it. In the end I had to leave and Jean-Paul got a job down at the docks. He was killed when he was in his early twenties. An accident with some machinery. Léon wasn't much more than a baby. Aunt Berthe died soon afterwards but Léon is still there with his mother in the old house in Rue Félix Pyat. They have four rooms on the top floor. He tries to look after her—she's rather sickly—and he has quite a good job at the marina but it's pretty tough going. Ten thousand pounds isn't much in the scheme of things but it would be one hell of a lot to Léon.'

'And you have nothing of your own to leave him?'

'This is mine. It was left to me, like your father left you this cottage and Ed and Billa Mellinpons. There's no shame in that. Elinor left my father ten thousand pounds and he left everything to me. It's legally mine.'

'So why didn't you show the will to Billa and Ed?'

'It wasn't the only reason I came back and I didn't want to talk about it on that first visit. Anyway, I wanted you to see it first. I know it's a legal document, I've had it checked, though the time lapse might prove awkward. But I wanted you to tell me what the chances are of me getting the cash.' He laughs. 'Come on, Dom. Get real. If anyone is going to block this it's going to be you. We might as well get that over with straight away. Billa and Ed would probably do the decent thing and pay up but I suspect that you still have great influence with them and you won't be quite so ready to let bygones be bygones.'

'No,' Dom answers honestly. 'I shan't. Leopards, in my experience, don't change their spots.'

Tris shakes his head rather sadly. 'I was a little kid, Dom. I saw my mother dead on the floor when I was four and after that I never knew a moment's security. How do you think it felt coming amongst confident people with houses and families and dogs and all the stuff that had been torn away from me? I'd lived with two other families before I came here and I'd learned some pretty tough lessons, I can tell you. "If you're not one up, you're one down" became my mantra. Get in first before some other bastard does you down.' He pauses at the use of the word and gives a little chuckle. 'Sorry,' he says. 'Not a very tactful use of the word.'

Dom laughs. Oddly, the fact that Tris has used the word makes him more open towards him; it adds to his authenticity.

'Not very,' he agrees.

'I suppose,' says Tris, after a minute, 'I struck at you where I was at my weakest. I'd lost my mother so I attacked yours. I'm not a psychologist but there might be a connection there. I was ten years old and I hated you all.'

Such honesty is refreshing. Dom allows himself to relax, just a little. He indicates the will. 'What do you intend to do?'

Tris shrugs. 'I can take it to a lawyer. Like I said, I wanted your reaction. Would I get the money anyway?'

Dom hesitates. Between them all they could probably raise the money, but why should they? Elinor made the will as a gesture to Andrew because she loved him, but two years later he'd abandoned her. And he'd never been the man she imagined him to be. Dom has no doubt that when all these facts are arranged before a court that no money will be forthcoming. On the other hand it was Elinor's intention, her wish . . . and there is Léon in Toulon, attempting to support his sickly mother, trying to survive. Unexpectedly Dom thinks about Harry, about the same age as Léon but much better equipped to deal with life.

Tris is watching him. He takes the document and puts it back in his satchel. 'It didn't matter much before,' he says. 'To be honest, I never thought it would run. But now I've had the death sentence passed—and there's Léon. Anyway. Think about it. I'm here for a few days. It's waited all these years, a few more days won't make any difference. Like I said, it wasn't the only reason for coming back.'

He stands up and Dom stands, too.

'Shall I tell Billa and Ed?'

Tris shrugs again. 'I leave it to you. I certainly shan't mention it to them until we've had another talk about it. Are you coming to tea this afternoon?'

Dom thinks about it; shakes his head.

'I don't think so. We'll meet again when I've had the chance to think it all through. Twenty-four hours, perhaps.'

'Good,' says Tris. He takes a card from his back pocket and lays it on the table. 'There's my mobile number.'

He goes out and Dom closes the door behind him. He is disturbed by the interview, confused. He needs time to think. He goes through to the back door, puts on his boots and with Bessie running ahead he sets off towards the woods.

Tris gets into his car and sits quite still. This time he has no inclination to laugh. Dom is a very different proposition from Ed and Billa but he thinks he's hit the right note. Tris heaves a huge breath and closes his eyes. The interview has left him exhausted. He thanks all the gods at once for Harry. Those hours in the pub with him were indeed a gift from the gods. During that time Tris was able to pinpoint the St Enedocs' weakest spots: Billa's lack of children: Ed's creative and emotional instincts: Dom's love for Harry himself. Artlessly, the boy had laid all these facts out before the attentive, fascinated Tris.

Tris opens the satchel, takes out a bottle and pops a pill. He wonders if Dom has picked up on his love for Léon. Oh, it's genuine enough—there's nothing he wouldn't do for Léon—but has Dom connected, sympathized far enough to convince Ed and Billa that they should cough up? He'll have to wait and see. Meanwhile he's invited to tea at Mellinpons and he can begin his next move of the real game. The interview with Dom, just like the will, is simply a sideshow. He'd told the truth when he said it wasn't the only reason for coming back.

Tris starts the engine, turns the car and heads off down the lane.

CHAPTER TWENTY-FIVE

Clem comes out of the front door just as Sir Alec is passing the vicarage gate. He's walking slowly, with Hercules plodding at his heels, and carrying a bag of shopping. Clem calls to him and goes to meet him. The older man is looking tired and he's limping a little and Clem feels anxious.

'Are you OK?' he asks. 'You look a bit "dot and go one", as Pa would say.'

Sir Alec grimaces. 'Turned my ankle. Just slipped off the bottom stair and gave it a twist. Nothing serious. We've managed to hobble along the beach together and Mrs Sawle did offer to deliver the shopping later on when the shop shuts at lunchtime but I needed a few things.' He looks at Clem hopefully. 'Time for some coffee?'

Clem shakes his head regretfully. 'Nice idea, but I've got a meeting with the rector. I've got time to carry that home for you, though.'

He takes the bag from Sir Alec's unresisting hand and they walk together up the steep hill.

'Things seem to be working out,' observes Sir Alec, pausing for a moment, taking a breather. 'I hear that Tilly's got the job. That's a really good start, isn't it?'

Clem stands beside him, waiting, turning to look back out to sea. He's beginning to dare to believe that things are indeed working out.

'It's good news, isn't it?' He hesitates, unwilling to be too optimistic. 'The Sisters are very pleased.'

Sir Alec chuckles and sets off again. 'Sister Emily must be dancing for joy.'

'She is,' agrees Clem, thinking about Sister Emily's delight. 'She was in very good form when

I saw her yesterday. She told me that she's given up self-pity for Lent but she's finding it more difficult than she realized.'

'The last thing I'd associate with Sister Emily is self-pity,' says Sir Alec. 'But I suppose we're all at it, one way or another. Rooting about in the injustices and resentments of the past, clinging to a sense of grievance. Why is it so difficult to let it all go and move on?'

Clem thinks about it. 'Perhaps it adds to our sense of self-righteousness,' he suggests, 'if we feel wounded and hard done by. We need grand gestures of apology and abasement to soothe our egos.'

'Even so,' says Sir Alec, as they reach his front door, 'that doesn't seem to chime with Sister Emily's character. Now if she'd given up that glass of wine she so enjoys on Feast Days, I'd have said it was a far greater sacrifice.'

Clem laughs as he watches Sir Alec delving for his key. 'I don't think they celebrate Feast Days in quite the same way during Lent. I'll have to ask her.'

He helps take the shopping inside, hurries back down the hill and gets into the car, thinking about the way he had rooted about in the injustices of the past after Madeleine died. His anger and resentment had caused him to turn his back on his vocation, to deny it for three years, until the day he'd seen the advertisement for a gardener and handyman at Chi-Meur and decided to take a chance; to take the first step on the road home. It was a signpost.

Father Pascal used the same word when Clem, still resentful and angry, questioned his future, which, despite the healing influence of the Sisters and Janna, and Father Pascal himself, still seemed obscure.

'The generosity of strangers and the love of friends are signposts on the road to God,' the old priest said. 'The promises of God, who is on the road ahead of you.'

'I thought I'd already started on that road,' Clem answered wearily, 'and then it blew up in front of me.'

'But you found Chi-Meur,' Father Pascal told him. 'You are on the road again. Perhaps even a little further on. But the initiative is with God.'

Now, as Clem drives out of the village he feels fully in tune with the spring that is unfolding all around him. The cold, sealed earth is stirring and breaking with new life and Clem is filled with hope and energy. His own emotions, so long frozen in, are beginning to emerge just like the uncurling leaves, and it is a very painful process. Because of Jakey he still knows how to love, and to be tender; because of Dossie, and Mo and Pa, he still knows how to be affectionate and caring, but the commit-ment to a long-term emotional and physical relationship fills him with terror.

There will be time for us to get to know each other, he reassures himself. Jakey will need time. We all will.

He was very impressed with Tilly at her interview: she was focused, eager, and very aware of what the retreat house needed to continue its progress. Clearly she'd done her homework, researched other retreat houses and weighed up Chi-Meur's strengths and weaknesses. Everyone was delighted with her and he was foolishly proud and had to stop himself from grinning madly. Just once Sister Emily's eyes had met his own and he knew that they were privately sharing a high-five, though neither of them even smiled.

Afterwards, Sister Emily had whisked Tilly away to have another look at the Priest's Flat and to meet Janna again, and it was much later before he was able to congratulate her on her presentation and tell her how well she'd done. He was getting used now to that little blush that stained her cheeks and the way she pressed her lips together to prevent herself from beaming.

'I can't wait to start,' she said. 'I've got to give notice at the pub, of course—that's not a problem—and I need to keep up with U-Connect's clients until the last ones are sorted.'

'Perhaps you could do both,' he suggested. 'Would that be possible?'

'Nearly,' she said cautiously. 'I've got some new people to put on to Skype, and there's Sir Alec's

280

database, of course. We've got a long way to go there.'

'Well, you certainly can't abandon him. I'm sure it could be sorted out. Let me know if you need any help.'

She beamed at him then, full of excitement at the prospect opening up before her, and he wanted to seize her in his arms and kiss her.

'I will,' she promised. 'Elizabeth is great. She's been designated my assistant and our first job is to sort out the office. She's been doing a terrific job but I think she's very relieved that I'm taking over. Everyone's really kind.'

'Good,' he said lightly, sticking his hands into his pockets lest he should reach out for her. 'I thought Sister Emily was going to break into a jig.'

'I utterly love her,' Tilly said fervently, and then they'd looked at each other for a long, telling moment until she blushed again and said that she and Sister Emily were having coffee with Janna and she must go.

Remembering, Clem smiles, then thinks of the rector and puts his foot down on the accelerator.

Alec takes his shopping into the kitchen and begins to unload it. The walk to the beach and back has caused his ankle to throb and he sits down gratefully, bending to touch it gingerly, feeling it ache beneath the elastic bandage.

'Shouldn't slop around in slippers,' he can hear

Rose saying. 'Silly old fool. That's the way to get carted off to hospital, and then what?'

He sighs, acknowledging this to be his greatest nightmare, and stands up again to unpack the groceries.

'We'll have some coffee, old chap,' he murmurs to Hercules, 'and a choc bic. Well, I shall. Not good for you, I'm afraid. Got to keep your weight down. You could hardly get up the hill today, poor fellow.'

Something happening to Hercules is Alec's second biggest nightmare. He cannot imagine life without Hercules.

At the word 'bic', Hercules' tail bangs to and fro against the cupboard doors and he pants hopefully.

'Hang on,' his master says. 'Give me a chance. Got to put this stuff in the fridge.'

He unloads the bag, folds it and puts it back in his pocket.

'If I hadn't got a dog to talk to, what would I do?' he asks Hercules. 'Tell me that. Talk to myself, I suppose. Not the same thing at all.'

He takes down a box of dog biscuits, gives one to Hercules, fills the kettle and then sits down again. He longs for Rose to come in, bustling around getting things sorted, making the coffee; or for Tilly to be across the hall in his study working on his database. The kettle boils and switches itself off but he doesn't move. When the telephone rings, however, he gets up quickly, curses the stab of pain in his ankle and hobbles to the phone.

'Bancroft.'

It's Dom asking how he is, suggesting they meet up.

'I'd like that,' says Alec. 'The trouble is I'm a bit crocked at the moment. Ankle's a bit iffy. Not sure driving is a good idea.'

But Dom doesn't mind that. He's ready to drive over to Peneglos whenever it suits.

'Come to lunch,' says Alec eagerly. 'I've just bought fresh rolls from the shop and there's some nice cheese. Won't be much of a feast but I'll rustle something up. Can you manage it?'

Dom is very happy with the idea, says he'll bring some home-made soup, and Alec replaces the receiver with a sigh of relief and pleasure. Now he has something to look forward to and his spirits rise.

A little later, at the old butter factory, Billa paces the kitchen, watching the clock. She's invited Tris for half past three and it's nearly a quarter past. She and Ed have had a very simple lunch; neither of them felt very hungry.

'Funny, isn't it?' Ed says. 'I don't feel quite the same about him now. The trouble is that I've disliked him for so long that it feels a bit odd.'

'To be honest, I hadn't thought about him for years,' Billa says. 'And then it all came rushing back as fresh as ever when we got the postcard. Awful, really, that you can hang on to such a destructive emotion for such a long time. When I think about him seeing his mother dead it's gut-wrenching. No wonder he was so appalling.'

'And it must be terrible to know you haven't long to live,' says Ed. 'Poor fellow.'

Now Billa paces again. She's disappointed that Dom won't be coming to tea but he's explained why.

'It gave me a shock to see him like that on the doorstep,' he said on the phone earlier. 'I know you warned me but it's quite different when it actually happens, isn't it? I just want time to think about things. I'm sure I'll see him again before he goes.'

Billa can understand that Dom needs time to take stock. They've all suffered at Tris's hands, and welcoming the prodigal son home isn't as easy as it seems. Bear slumbers on the sofa, stretched full length, totally at ease, and Billa envies him his relaxed detachment. She pauses beside him and strokes his soft coat. His eye half-opens and his tail gives a feeble thump before he settles again to sleep.

But now she hears the sound of an engine and she hurries to the window to see Tris's car drive over the little bridge and park beside the garage. He gets out, looking as relaxed and at ease as Bear, and Billa studies him safe in the knowledge that he can't see her. As he leans in to get the satchel he had with him last time she sees in his quick movements, the lean energy, what must

284

have attracted her mother to Andrew. Just for a moment she remembers Andrew lounging in her mother's bed, his strong hand grasping her delicate wrist like a handcuff, his eyes lazily smiling at Billa, stiff and tense in the doorway. She remembers her mother's besottedness and, as Tris swings the satchel over his shoulder and turns to look at the house, she is attracted by his magnetism, that same sexy edginess that once made a fool of Elinor St Enedoc.

Billa goes quickly to the door and opens it.

'Hi,' she says. 'Come on in.' And then she turns and hurries into the hall, calling to Ed. 'Come on down, Ed. Tris is here.'

For some reason she doesn't want to be alone with him and she is shocked and confused by her reaction. She goes back into the kitchen to find Tris standing in the doorway, looking rather puzzled at finding the kitchen empty.

'Sorry,' she says. 'Just giving Ed a shout. He's in his study.'

Tris smiles reminiscently. 'Ah,' he says. 'The study. The inner sanctum. I wasn't allowed in there, was I?'

'Well, it was our father's room,' she says, almost apologetically, still thrown off balance by her attraction to him. 'Ed felt very strongly about it. He still does.'

'So I still don't get to see it, then,' says Tris teasingly. 'Oh, well, I guess I can live with that.'

285

'Of course you can see it,' says Billa almost indignantly, as if Ed has already denied it. 'Things were a bit different back then. Ed and I were gutted when our father died.'

Even to her own ears she sounds as if she is offering an explanation for their behaviour and, in an attempt to reignite her animosity, she has to remind herself that it was Tris who was the first to strike a blow. Immediately she imagines the defenceless four-year-old, crouched beside his mother's body, and she is seized with pity for him. She glances at him and sees those frosty, clear grey eyes fixed on her as though he is seeing right into her mind, and when he smiles at her she feels very uncomfortable and oddly shaky.

'Tea,' she says, pushing the kettle on to the hotplate, and her voice is false with a determined jollity like some school mistress caricature from a 1930s film.

'I'd love some,' he says quite naturally. 'Thanks, I really appreciate this, Billa. I'm glad to be able to come back.'

'Would you like to look around?' she asks, and her voice sounds normal again. 'Just to see if you remember anything?'

'I'd love it,' he says. 'I remember this kitchen very well. This big slate table is amazing. And I remember some kind of strange fireplace in the hall and the ceiling way up high. Is that right?'

'Absolutely right. Come and see.'

She leads the way into the hall, passing Bear, who remains comatose and makes no attempt to greet Tris.

'Hi, old fellow,' Tris says to him, but doesn't touch him. He follows Billa into the hall and looks around and up into the high vaulting of the ceiling. 'Wow,' he says softly. 'This really is something, isn't it?'

Just then Ed comes out of his study and stands looking down at them from the gallery.

'Tris was just saying that he was never allowed in your study,' Billa says to him. 'Could you show him around while I make the tea?'

'Sure,' says Ed, very comfortable, quite at ease. 'Come on up, Tris. How much of this do you remember?'

This is just so weird, Billa thinks as she goes back into the kitchen. He's gone from monster to welcomed guest overnight. How does that work?

She hums as she makes the tea and puts some small cakes on to a plate. Billa never hums and she knows that she's doing it to distract her mind away from the fact that she finds Tris attractive and that this is making her think of her mother in a different light. She feels as if the past is in some way repeating itself, she sees her mother and Andrew together, and she is both drawn to and repulsed by these images at the same time.

Ed and Tris come in together talking animatedly and she turns, determined to be cool.

'I like the man-bag,' she says lightly. 'Very pretty. I wouldn't mind one like that.'

'Oh, this.' Tris smiles, slipping it from his shoulder and hanging it on the chair. 'I carry my medication in it. I rarely wear a jacket and the bottles are uncomfortable in a trouser pocket. I've got my prescription in there too, in a wallet, and instructions in case I get taken ill. I collapsed recently and that's when I learned that it was very sensible to have it at hand. Everything I need is in there, just in case.'

Billa is wrong-footed by this reply, embarrassed by her flippancy, but Tris reaches out quickly and touches her wrist. He encircles it, making a handcuff with his fingers, and then lets it go just as quickly so that Ed doesn't even notice.

But Bear, roused from slumber, notices, and he growls quietly as he climbs down from his sofa and pads across the kitchen to stand beside Billa. She strokes his head absentmindedly while the kettle boils, her back to Tris and Ed, who are now discussing the work Ed has been doing in the woods along the river.

'You'll see a real change down there,' Ed is saying. 'We'll take a stroll after tea.'

'Great,' Tris says. 'I'd really like that. I was very happy there in the woods just up on the edge of the moor. Sometimes when I was here for an exeat and you were both at school I'd go up there with Bitser. I felt free. You know? Felt it just might work out after all. I got caught in a storm up there once and Bitser wouldn't come back with me. He was digging after a rabbit, I guess, and I grabbed him and he bit me. Took a chunk out of my hand.' He looks at Billa. 'At least now I can say sorry.'

She stares at him, shocked, and he lifts his shoulders and his hands in a Gallic shrug.

'I know. Much too late. But I wanted you to know.'

Then the kettle boils, Billa makes the tea and they sit down together at the table.

CHAPTER TWENTY-SIX

At seven o'clock, with the sun just rising, the woodland along the river is a mysterious place. Walking with Bessie in the early light, Dom is distracted from his thoughts of Tris by the clamour of birds: the clarion ring of their voices echoing amongst the bare, empty branches, the flutter and clap of their wings, and the continuum of rushing water. The pale gleam of a rabbit's scut bobs on the path ahead and Bessie chases after it, dry dead leaves and clods of earth thrown up behind her scudding paws. Beneath the trees, where the land rises towards the moors, daffodils glimmer between rocky boulders. Later there will be bluebells, and in April the azaleas will blossom; purple and white and red, and the wild yellow luteum with its heavenly scent.

Dom surveys the work he and Ed have put in over the years with satisfaction. They must have planted thousands of bulbs. The snowdrops are fading now but there are hellebores growing beside the path and tiny cyclamen. He walks on, his mind focused again on his conversation yesterday with Sir Alec. At last he told him about Andrew and Elinor, about how Tris had returned with the will, and Ed and Billa's reactions.

Alec asked a few very pertinent questions and then remained silent for a while.

'Would you,' Dom asked at last, 'if you were in our shoes, part with the money? I know that Billa and Ed will be influenced by Tris's history, you see. They are already sorry for him and regretting their own reactions to him all those years ago. Ed is moved by the fact that Tris is dying, and Billa by the fact that he saw his mother dead when he was four. And I believed him when he told me about his half-brother and his nephew. When Billa and Ed find out about the will they will feel, rightly or wrongly, that some reparation is required.'

'And they *are* facts?'

Dom hesitated. 'It's odd,' he said slowly, 'but I believe him and so do they. He's a chancer, he has a drug habit, I should say he's completely untrustworthy but yes, I believe him. Is that crazy?'

'No, not all,' answered Alec at once. 'It is possible to detect that someone is telling the truth just as it is possible to know without doubt that someone is lying.'

'But would you part with the money? Billa and Ed have always regarded me as an elder brother and, even at this late stage in all our lives, I might be able to influence them.'

'What is your real anxiety?'

'Tris says that he's dying and that the money is for his nephew, Léon. I suppose you could say that, if we feel that the will stands, then we have no right to decide what Tris should do with his legacy, but part of me feels very strongly about ten thousand pounds disappearing into a drug dealer's pocket. I'd like to know if there is someone called Léon living with his mother in the Rue Félix Pyat in Toulon.'

'But you said that you believe in the existence of the boy?'

'Yes, I do, and I'm wondering if Léon should get the money direct.'

Alec raised his brows, gave a little whistle. 'Bypass Tris? Cut him out?'

'He says he wants the money for Léon. That he's dying and he has no use for it. So let's put him to the test.'

'How?'

'Ah, well, that's where you come in. Is it possible that you still have some connections who could make a few enquiries?'

'Oh-o, I see how your mind is working. Check the boy out and if he's this hard-working fellow who looks after his mother then you can tell Tris that you'll pass the money straight to him?'

'That's the idea. And if Tris balks, then we can all think again. The will won't stand up in a court of law. Clearly Andrew persuaded Elinor to use his own lawyer rather than the family firm, which is why Billa and Ed didn't know about it. It all happened so long ago and it could be proved, I imagine, that Andrew was an adventurer. I'd also want to be very sure when Andrew died. We only have Tris's word that it was after Elinor's death. I feel that one should respect the wishes of the dead but Elinor might have changed that will once she knew Andrew was never coming back, and if she hadn't begun to suffer from those bouts of terrible depression. Perhaps she thought that ten thousand pounds was neither here nor there; perhaps she just forgot about it. The point is that I think we might consider coughing up if there's a worthy cause on the end of it. Then honour will be satisfied.'

'That sounds very fair,' said Alec, 'and very generous. I can still pull strings. Give me twenty-four hours.'

Dom walks on, wondering what Sir Alec's sources will discover. The sun rises behind the trees, casting sharp black shadows like bars across the path. With a flash of blue, a jay dashes between the bare branches above Dom's head and his raucous cry is mocking, derisory. Dom watches him, feeling a sudden sense of disquiet, wondering if there is something he's missed and whether he should warn Billa and Ed about the will. He'd rather tell them face to face and he wants, now, to wait for Sir Alec so as to have all the facts. Twenty-four hours, he'd said. Nothing could happen in twenty-four hours. Clearly Tris kept his word and hasn't mentioned the will to Billa and Ed but Dom still feels uneasy. Perhaps, after all, it was foolish to take time to think about it. He'll phone Billa and suggest he goes in for a drink this evening. By then he might have heard something from Sir Alec. Bessie comes wagging up to him, pleased with herself, wanting her breakfast, and they go on together.

Ed finishes his breakfast and pushes his plate aside. He knows that Billa wants to talk about Tris, to go over yesterday's visit again, but he simply can't concentrate. His mind is full of images, of scenes that flash upon his mind's eye, of the legends of the Cornish Knockers deep in the tin mines, and the giant that wades out into the mountainous seas to grab passing sailing ships and tow helpless sailors to their deaths. He sees the boy and the white horse, the princeling with his flashing sword, and another boy, smaller and more vulnerable, who travels with three large dogs that protect him. The story is beginning to weave and flow in his mind and from time to time he makes lightning sketches on the pad beside him on the table.

'Dom suggests we invite Tris to coffee tomorrow,' Billa says to him. 'He promises he'll come, too. I think that's a good idea, don't you? All of us together. But Dom says he'd like to pop round this evening for a drink. I've said that's fine. I'll be back from Wadebridge about six.'

Ed nods obligingly. He'll agree with anything as long as he can get up to his study and do some work. Billa recognizes the signs and shrugs resignedly. Ed sees the shrug and is seized with guilt.

'That'll be good,' he says. 'To see Dom, I mean. And Tris. It's good that we all have some kind of closure.'

Billa nods. 'I keep feeling a bit guilty. We weren't terribly nice to Mother, were we? We made no allowances for her being lonely after Daddy died.'

'We weren't old enough to understand that,' points out Ed reasonably. 'We couldn't imagine that she'd need a substitute. We thought she should be content with us. After all, it never occurred to us to need another father.'

'The point was that we had Dom,' Billa says. 'He came just when we needed him. She had nobody. I was pretty beastly to her over Andrew.'

Ed watches her. Tris's arrival has changed her, softened her, and he is faintly worried by it.

'We were children,' he says consolingly. 'Children are naturally selfish. There were lots of reasons for the way we behaved. It's no good looking at past mistakes in isolation. We have to remember the whole context or we get a completely biased view of it. Don't beat yourself up.'

She smiles at him gratefully. 'I won't,' she says. 'I just wish I'd been a bit nicer to her before she died. That awful depression did for her. Sitting about in her dressing gown and those terrible bouts of weeping. I really believe that she thought Andrew had left her for another woman, you know. She really loved him but I think it was in a very physical way that drove her mad.'

Ed doesn't quite know how to react to this; it's not really his kind of conversation.

'Mmm,' he says non-committally. 'You could be right.'

Billa gets up from the table. 'Go and do some work,' she says. 'I'll phone Tris about tomorrow and I'll bring you up some coffee later on. Don't forget we're having an early lunch.'

'OK,' he says, relieved. 'Great.'

He gathers up his papers, hurries away upstairs into his study and closes the door behind him. He stands still for a moment and the room seems to gather and settle round him, welcoming him. Ed takes a deep, happy breath and sits down at his desk.

'I think we've got everyone in the diary now,' Sarah says. 'Are you sure you're going to manage with the few that need more time?'

'Quite sure,' says Tilly confidently. 'They're going to be very flexible up at Chi-Meur and because I'm living in I can always work early or late. I'm doing extra at the pub for these next few days and then that's that. Don't worry, I shan't let anyone disappear through the net. Sir Alec will need quite a bit more time. I'm going on to spend an hour with him when we've finished here.'

George begins to grizzle and Tilly whisks him out of his chair and begins to dance with him, blowing raspberries into his neck until he starts to giggle. She can see that Sarah is wanting to make some retort about spoiling him, but just managing to restrain herself, and Tilly feels a great surge of affection for her. She's having these moments quite a lot lately, with Dom, with Billa and Ed, with Sir Alec. She is so happy she is almost effervescing with it, but she knows that Sarah will be slightly embarrassed by such an overflowing of joy so she resists the urge to give Sarah a hug and contents herself with kissing George's smooth, satiny cheek.

'So when are you moving in?' Sarah is asking, still checking the database and making notes.

'Monday week. I shall have got through lots of our work by then and I'll have finished at the pub. You must come up and see the Priest's Flat. There's a huge bank of lilac trees growing just under the windows. Sister Emily says the scent is paradisical when they flower.'

' "Paradisical",' Sarah snorts. 'Very nun-like. And you won't keep calling it the Priest's Flat, will you? People will think it's a bit weird.'

Tilly shrugs. 'I can't help that. Everyone calls it that. I can't just move in and change it; it's not my flat. Anyway, I rather like it.'

'You'll be taking Holy Orders next,' says Sarah waspishly. 'How will your street cred do when you tell your friends you're going to be living in a convent?'

'Actually, they think it's rather cool, and Mum and Dad are pleased now they're over the shock of it. They think I'll be really safe now. Even better than Mr Potts' bedroom.'

Tilly sits down with George on her lap. She is sad that Sarah is going, she's going to miss her, but she wishes that Sarah was more upbeat about her own move.

'Let's see those house details again,' Tilly says. 'It looks really nice. I bet you can't wait for Dave to come home and get going. After all, this was *your* home, wasn't it? Your family home. It's going to be really great moving into this house with Dave and the boys.'

Sarah gets up from the computer and fetches the house details' folder. She sits down again with it between them. Tilly shifts George to one side, and together they begin to reread the spec.

It's quite a relief, a bit later, for Tilly to leave Sarah's cottage and drive down to Sir Alec's house. He greets her warmly but she sees that he is limping and he looks rather drawn and tired.

'Couldn't get out this morning,' he admits. 'Would be the right ankle, wouldn't it? Driving's tricky and I couldn't face the long haul down to the beach. Poor Hercules is housebound.'

'I'll take him out,' Tilly says at once. 'I'd love it. I'll give him a walk when we've finished the session,' and an hour later she and Hercules set off together down the hill towards the beach. Half-way down she hears an engine behind her, the approach of a big vehicle, and turning she sees the school bus coming. She hauls Hercules well into the side until it's passed and then sees an excited face at the back window, a hand fluttering. It's Jakey. When she and Hercules reach the vicarage he's waiting for them, his school bag dumped by the front door.

'Shall I come with you?' he asks. 'Are you going down to the beach?'

'Yes,' she says. 'Poor Sir Alec has twisted his ankle. But you need to ask if you're allowed to come. Is Dossie waiting for you? Or Daddy?'

'It's Daddy,' he answers, running to the front door and opening it with a shout of greeting.

Tilly's heart does a little hop, and when Clem appears at the door she gives what she hopes is a nonchalant wave. Jakey is explaining the situation, words tripping and tumbling in his eagerness, and Clem says, 'Hang on a minute,' disappears and then comes back out, dragging on a jacket and putting keys in his jeans pocket. He's wearing his clerical collar but he pulls the jacket collar up so it's not too obvious, and anyway Tilly doesn't mind. She quite likes the way he's prepared to stand up and be counted.

'Not too long,' he cautions Jakey, and he smiles at Tilly and they all go together down the village street and out on to the beach.

It's very wild and windy. Their words are snatched from their mouths and tossed about like the gulls in the great cloudy spaces above them.

'Dossie's been on the phone,' Clem says, as they stroll behind Jakey and Hercules. 'She's got this friend who breeds black Labs. Because of the economic pinch they're planning to find a home for their oldest breeding bitch. She's about five, very gentle and sweet, and Dossie thinks that if we're going to have a dog she might be a good choice.'

Tilly's heart glows at his words, 'if we're going to have a dog'. There's something satisfyingly permanent about them.

'Sounds good to me,' she says. 'I'd love to see her.'

'That's what Dossie thought. She says that she could take you over to meet them before we mention anything to Jakey.'

She nods. 'Great. Shall you phone Dossie? Or shall you give me her number?'

'Both,' Clem says decisively.

Jakey is scaring the seagulls wading at the water's edge. He runs, just dodging the in-sweep of the tide, his arms outstretched like aeroplane wings, and Hercules runs with him, barking.

Tilly and Clem laugh.

'It's going to be good,' Clem says suddenly, confidently, and Tilly, overwhelmed with happiness, can't resist slipping a hand inside his elbow. He presses it against his side and they stride out together, heads bent against the wind.

Tris drives cautiously along the lanes between the Chough and the old butter factory, keeping a wary eye open for Dom or Billa. He's taking a risk, a huge risk, but every instinct is telling him to make his move. When she invited him for coffee for the following morning Billa told him that she would be out this afternoon and he guesses that Dom, in that case, won't be visiting. He and Ed might be working down in the woods but that will suit his purpose just as well. Anyway, Tris has his story well prepared in case he is taken by surprise. He is fizzing with an adrenalin rush, with energy and excitement. He can barely breathe.

He drives in over the bridge, picks up his satchel and gets out, closing the car door as quietly as he can. Billa's car is gone and there is no sign of Ed. Gently, gently, Tris presses down the handle on the kitchen door and walks in. Bear is nowhere to be seen and Tris advances silently across the kitchen towards the open door into the hall. He can see Bear now, stretched on the slates by the front door, and Tris reaches into his pocket for the treats he has brought specially for this eventuality. As Bear raises his head, Tris bends to put the tasty snack beside him. Bear hesitates, still recumbent, growls half-heartedly, and then begins to sniff. He hauls himself up a little and begins to eat the first treat.

Quickly, quickly, Tris runs up the stairs and pauses outside the study door. He listens for a moment, waits for a heartbeat and then opens the door. Sitting at his desk, his laptop open in front of him, Ed gazes at him in astonishment. Cursing to himself, Tris closes the door behind him and advances into the room, his hands upraised in apology.

'I am just so sorry about this,' he says. 'Nobody heard me knock and that old Bear is fast asleep in the hall. But listen, Ed. I've had a call. An emergency back in Toulon and I've got to go. I didn't have your phone number so I thought I'd

301

just dash round and say goodbye. I guess that Billa is out.'

'Yes, yes, she is.' Ed is on his feet now, still looking rather dazed. 'I'm sorry to hear this. Nothing too bad, I hope.'

'Well, it's Léon's mother. She's been taken very ill and Léon is at his wits' end.' Tris pauses, drags a gasping breath, doubles over and sits down rather suddenly in the little armchair. 'Sorry, Ed. Sorry. Shouldn't have run up the stairs like that.' He leans forward, head in hands, massaging his brow with his fingers, still gasping for breath.

'Are you OK?' Ed is really concerned now, coming out from behind his desk, bending down to look at Tris.

Tris breathes quickly, glancing up from between his fingers. Actually he does feel rather ill—shouldn't have popped that pill on the way over—but it adds authenticity to the next part of his plan. He leans back in the chair and presses his hands now against his ribcage. Then he slips the satchel from his shoulder, opens it carefully so that Ed can't see inside it, and begins to rummage in it.

'Damn,' he says. 'Damn, damn, damn. I remember now. My tablets, Ed. They're in the car. Had to take one coming over. Do you think you could . . . ?' He groans. 'Sorry.'

'No, no,' says Ed, clearly alarmed. 'Will you be OK?'

302

Tris nods. His breathing is laboured and ragged. 'On the front seat. Not locked.'

Ed hurries out. Tris sits up, listens for a moment and then he's on his feet and crossing the room to the cabinet containing the John Smart miniatures. Yesterday he managed to try the lid, just lifted it an inch or so to make sure it wasn't locked, and now he removes from his satchel a small Perspex tray made specially to transport the precious little miniatures without damaging them. He stands it on the desk and opens it, lifts the lid of the cabinet and swiftly takes out the six ivory ovals and sets them carefully into their appointed places in his tray. He closes it and slides it gently into the satchel, shuts the lid to the cabinet and he's back in his chair when Ed returns, out of breath, with the tablets.

'Do you need water?' he asks anxiously, giving Tris the bottle, but Tris shakes his head, takes out a capsule and swallows it down. He sits without speaking, his eyes closed, giving himself time to recover. He feels he might explode with excitement.

Presently he opens his eyes again and almost smiles at Ed's worried expression: what a sweet, gullible guy he is. Tris has to subdue a spurt of laughter.

'Thanks,' he says gratefully. 'That's much better. I'm really sorry about that.'

'Don't be sorry,' says Ed predictably. 'I'm sorry that you have to be like this.'

Tris sighs: not in a self-pitying way but in a 'Well, that's life' kind of way. He shrugs. 'I think I'd better be on my way,' he says. 'It's a shame not to have seen Billa or Dom again. But say good-bye for me, will you? None of you knows just what it's meant to me to be able to come back. There's been closure here for me. I really mean that.'

He's getting up, walking to the door—but not too quickly, still playing it carefully—and managing to look regretful and grateful all at the same time. Ed, clearly uncomfortable, concerned, follows him down the stairs, offering him tea, a glass of water, whilst Tris edges as quickly as he can through the kitchen and out to the car.

'If I can get back in the next twenty minutes I'll be fine,' he assures Ed. 'The tablet will get me that far, don't worry. Thanks, Ed.'

He holds out his hand and Ed takes it, shakes it firmly.

'But you'll stay in touch, Tris,' he says. 'Now we've got this far. We'll want to know how you are.'

'For sure,' says Tris, sliding into the driving seat and placing the satchel carefully beside him. 'And thanks again, Ed. It means a lot.'

He starts the car, raises his hand and drives back across the little bridge. Tensed against the possibility of meeting either Billa or Dom in the lane, he hunches over the steering wheel, still subduing the desire to burst out laughing. He reaches out to pat the satchel: at least two hundred thousand pounds worth of miniatures just riding along on the passenger seat. He'd get that much on the open market but it isn't an option. He doesn't mind. He's got his private collector lined up, all ready to do a very good deal.

'Thanks, Dad,' mutters Tris, as he negotiates the twisting lanes.

He thinks of the sheaf of photographs his father left in the envelope with Elinor's will; photographs of valuable items that he'd seen in the old butter factory: the miniatures, two paintings, a few pieces of furniture and some first editions. Clearly his father intended to use these photographs to get some idea of the value of these items, just in case, but his time at Mellinpons had run out. Over the years Tris occasionally studied those black-and-white photographs, watched the market rise and fluctuate, filed them away for future reference; and then six months ago he was at an auction where a John Smart miniature had sold for forty-three thousand pounds and he pricked up his ears. He knew that Ed would never have parted with his miniatures. Then, when he was told that his time was nearly up, he decided on this one last throw of the dice. The will had always been a sideshow; a ruse to enable access to the old butter factory, if necessary, for talks and discussions whilst he waited for just such an opportunity that he's been given today. And what fun it has been.

The plotting and planning, choosing the postcards, watching and waiting, those two aborted tries at straight burglary, and then this moment of victory.

'For Léon,' he mutters, the laughter spurting out at last. It hurts to laugh, though; a fist seems to be squeezing his lungs and he feels sick.

He's glad to pull into the Chough car park and slump for a moment, leaning over the steering wheel. He wishes now that he'd followed his instinct, packed his case and checked out before he went to the old butter factory. But caution had stayed his hand, warned him that he might not get away with it this time, that he'd look a fool if he needed to come back. If he'd trusted his instincts, by now he could be on his way to Bristol and on a plane out. Instead he must take this extra time to explain the emergency, pack up and pay. He doesn't want anyone suspecting, raising any kind of alarm. He gets out of the car, taking the satchel with him, and goes into the pub.

There are a couple in the bar, chatting to the landlord, but he can't see them very clearly. The bar seems to be darker than usual. The door opens and the girl, Tilly, comes in behind him.

She smiles at him. 'Hi, Mr Marr,' she says, and then her expression changes and she looks alarmed. 'Are you OK?' she asks.

And he isn't OK. The hand is squeezing harder, crushing his ribs so that he can't get a breath, and he grasps at the bar with one hand and grips the satchel tightly with the other. He is slipping, sliding, crumpling on the floor, and all the while he is cursing to himself: 'Not now. Not yet.' He seems to lose consciousness for a few seconds and now, as he recovers, there is a woman kneeling beside him; her long fair hair falls forward, brushing his face. Her lips move as though she is calling his name but he cannot hear her. He is weak, helpless. 'Maman,' he cries, and this time it is he who is lying on the floor whilst she bends over him, touching his hair. But his voice makes no sound, and it is growing darker, and someone pulls her away from him so that he can no longer see her.

CHAPTER TWENTY-SEVEN

Tilly kneels beside Christian Marr, calling his name, trying to edge the satchel from his arms so as to make him more comfortable. One of the customers at the bar comes hurrying over, talking about the recovery position, pushing Tilly to one side and firmly removing the satchel, which he lays on the floor. Tilly picks it up, out of the way, as the man heaves Mr Marr on to his side. The landlord is dialling 999, calling for an ambulance.

'Dash up and pack a bag for him,' he calls to Tilly. 'Pyjamas and stuff. Wait. Here's the pass key.'

Tilly grabs the key, runs out and up the stairs.

She realizes she's still holding the satchel, hesitates, and then hurries on. She opens the bedroom door and goes in, laying the satchel on the bed. There are two grips lying inside the hanging cupboard and she takes the smaller one, seizes pyjamas from the bed and dashes into the bathroom. She takes up a sponge bag and puts in a toothbrush and toothpaste, sees an electric razor, picks up a bottle of after-shave.

Back in the bedroom, she opens the drawers of the chest and takes out boxer shorts, two pairs of socks and some handkerchiefs. She hesitates over a jersey, wondering whether he will need it and whether he has any friends locally who ought to know what's happening. She looks at the satchel. She's never seen Mr Marr wearing a jacket so perhaps he keeps his private things in the satchel. She hesitates to open it and then decides that there can be no harm in it.

She undoes the buckle, lifts back the flap and looks inside. There's a solid, white object: something quite big that takes up most of the room. Carefully, Tilly draws it out. A brown envelope is pulled out with it, and several pill bottles roll on to the bed. These might be medication and Tilly puts them into the grip. She peers into the satchel and sees a wallet. This could contain information about relatives so she opens it. At the back, with some twenty- and ten-pound notes, is a photograph. A blond young man smiles out at her, eyes creased against the bright sunshine. He's casually dressed and behind him is a line of boats as if he has posed for the photograph in a harbour or at a marina. There is a prescription but no other information. She lays the wallet down and looks at the big envelope. Cautiously she opens it, slides out a stiff document and stares at Elinor St Enedoc's last will and testament. Perplexed, she reads it through twice. She lays it on the bed, still puzzling over it, and then she draws the Perspex tray towards her and opens the lid. To her absolute shock, she recognizes Ed's miniatures. He has told her the history of them, pointed out the family likeness he was so proud of when he was a little boy.

Tilly makes a lightning decision. She closes the lid, puts the miniatures back into the satchel along with the big brown envelope, and slides it under the bed. She picks up the wallet and the grip and hurries out, locking the door behind her.

She goes into the bar where a little group have now formed around Mr Marr, who seems to be unconscious. She shows the grip to the landlord and gives him the wallet.

'I'm just going out for a moment,' she says to him in a low voice. 'I feel a bit shaky.'

He nods understandingly. 'Paramedics on their way,' he says. 'But I don't like the look of him at all.'

'There's medication in the grip and a prescription in the wallet,' Tilly tells him, and with another look at the unconscious man she slips out to the back of the pub. Sitting in her car she takes out her mobile and phones Dom, but there is no reply. She remembers that he was going to see Ed and Billa so she phones the old butter factory. Billa answers.

'Listen,' Tilly says. 'I'm at the pub. This is going to sound really weird. There's a man staying here who's just collapsed. He's called Christian Marr. Billa, he's got your John Smart miniatures in his satchel. I'm sure it's them but before I make a fool of myself, could you go and check?'

There is a silence.

'What did you call him?' asks Billa.

'Christian Marr. Look, could you just go and check? He's being carted off to hospital any time now.'

'Wait,' says Billa sharply, and Tilly can hear the sound of voices in the background.

'Tilly.' It's Dom's voice and she heaves a breath of relief. 'Ed's gone to check. Did you say this man's collapsed?'

'Yes. I'd just followed him into the pub and he kind of keeled over. He was clutching his satchel. He's always got it with him. I went to pack a case ready for the ambulance to come and I looked in the satchel, just to make certain there was nothing he might need in it, and there were the miniatures in a proper little tray with a lid. Like it had been made for them. And, Dom, this is bizarre: there was a will made by Elinor St Enedoc.'

'I know about that,' says Dom. There is the sound of an urgent voice in the background and Dom says, 'Listen, Tilly, Ed says the miniatures have gone. You're at the pub? Well, stay put. I'm coming straight over. Don't part with the satchel.'

'It's still in his room, under the bed. I'm in my car. Round the back.'

'I'll be there as soon as I can.'

Tilly switches off her phone and sits holding it with her hands clenched between her knees. She's trembling. She thinks about Christian Marr, who Harry said was an energy consultant, and of the miniatures and the will in the satchel. Slowly, slowly, the minutes pass. There's the wail of a siren, the paramedics arrive and hurry into the pub. Then Dom's old Volvo slides around the corner of the wall and parks beside her.

He climbs out of the Volvo, leans back in and brings out a rucksack. Tilly leaps out of her car and dashes round to him.

'What's going on?' she asks. She feels trembly and weak, and so relieved to see him that she puts her arms round him. 'Who is he, Dom?'

He holds her tightly for a moment and then lets her go. His voice is quite calm. 'His real name is Tristan Carr. His father married Elinor fifty years ago and then left her a few years later. Tristan came to see us yesterday. He came again

311

today unexpectedly, appeared to have some sort of heart attack and took the miniatures when Ed went to get his medication from the car. Now we must be quick, Tilly. Where's the satchel?'

Tilly leads him in through the back entrance and up the stairs. She unlocks the bedroom door and they go in.

'I put it under the bed until I'd spoken to you,' she says. 'I couldn't imagine Ed giving them away but I didn't want to make a prat of myself.'

She pulls the satchel out from under the bed and gives it to Dom. He turns back the flap and looks inside, then he draws out the Perspex case. He opens the lid and shows the miniatures to Tilly.

'I don't want you to be a part of anything you're unhappy with,' he says. 'You agree that they are Ed's miniatures?' She nods solemnly. 'We're not going to make a fuss about this. Tris is dying and he is Ed and Billa's stepbrother so we shall simply return them to Ed. You don't have a problem with that?'

'No. They're definitely Ed's.'

'OK then.' He puts the Perspex case into the rucksack and opens the envelope. There is Elinor's will, and the photographs, which he looks at carefully. 'He must have had these for years. Black-and-white. Andrew must have taken them as insurance against a rainy day. Are you happy if we take these, too? This could be construed as theft.'

'Don't be a twit,' she says. 'We're all in this together, whatever it is.'

He puts the envelope into the rucksack and throws the satchel back on the bed.

'There was nothing else?'

She shakes her head. 'Just a wallet with some money and a prescription in it. Oh, and a photograph of a boy with some boats. Like he was in a harbour somewhere.'

'Ah,' says Dom, 'that must have been Léon. OK. Now I'm going to ask you to take the miniatures and the envelope and drive straight to Billa and Ed. I'll see you later.'

'Where are you going?' she asks, taking the rucksack carefully, still feeling rather trembly.

'I'm going downstairs to see how Tris is. I shall follow the ambulance to the hospital. Sure you'll be OK?'

She nods and they go out and lock the door. Dom takes the keys from her and she hesitates.

'Go on, Tills,' he says. 'I'll tell them you feel a bit shocked and you've gone home.'

He disappears through the door that leads to the bar and she goes out and gets into the car. She wedges the rucksack very carefully on the passenger seat, drags on her seat belt and starts the engine. As she drives out of the car park she can hear again the distant wail of the ambulance siren.

• • •

'He completely betrayed us,' Billa says much later.

Dom has come back late from Treliske Hospital, where Tris is not expected to last the night, and he and Tilly have gone home.

'I explained the relationship to the duty doctor,' Dom told them. 'Said we hadn't seen Tris for fifty years but assumed he'd made the visit just to tie up loose ends. There's nothing suspicious about his death, nobody will know about the miniatures, though there might be a copy of the will somewhere. I can't say I'm too bothered about that. It was never going to stand up and, anyway, it was a smoke screen. He wasn't after the money, it was the miniatures he wanted. The box was made specially for them.'

Billa and Ed were still too shocked to react and Dom and Tilly left them alone to recover.

'I feel such a fool,' says Ed, after they've gone. 'Just letting him walk out with them. And I'd had them reinsured last year because the value had suddenly shot up.'

'He took us all in,' says Billa bitterly. 'Telling us about his mother and his half-brother and talking about dying.'

'Well, that at least is true,' offers Ed. 'Did you hear Dom say that, apart from the tuberculosis, his body was destroyed by drug abuse? Those capsules were cocaine.' He nearly adds 'poor

314

fellow' but at the thought of his father's miniatures, taken so cleverly from under his nose, the words are stillborn. 'What a miracle that Tilly was there,' he says. 'My God, it was a close shave.'

'Lucky he collapsed,' says Billa fiercely. 'If not, he'd have been long gone by now.'

She feels so angry that she could burn up with it. She feels disgusted with herself when she remembers how she felt yesterday, watching Tris get out of the car, when he held her wrist; how for a while she was able to identify with her mother and to allow some kind of forgiveness and understanding to comfort her. Now she feels as if she has been emotionally mugged. How he must have laughed behind their backs; to be able to walk into their lives for a second time and wreck them. She knows that this is an extreme reaction—Tris has not wrecked their lives—but at some deep level she recognizes that this hatred of him could destroy her. Yet she clings to it, allowing it to feed her rage and self-pity.

'I suppose it was right of Dom to go to the hospital,' Ed is saying. 'It would have been awkward if they'd begun to ask questions at the pub. Best that it's in the open. Though I don't know how it will be explained that he was using another name. Another of his little jokes, I suppose. Tristan Carr. Christian Marr.'

'Dom says his passport was in his jeans pocket

in the name of Tristan Carr. I don't suppose that Carr was ever their real name anyway. Oh, what does it matter? There might be a bit of local gossip but nothing's happened. Dom has defused it all by acknowledging him. Well, don't expect me to go to his funeral, that's all.'

Ed looks alarmed. 'Would we be expected to?'

'Dom says he'll go. That it'll draw a line under the whole thing.'

And a few days later, when Dom brings back Tris's ashes in a plastic box, Billa stares at them with distaste.

'What are we supposed to do with that?' she says, wrinkling her nose.

'I don't know yet,' he says. 'But I thought you might want to know that I've got them.'

'Won't his family want them? This nephew, Léon, he's so proud of?'

'According to Sir Alec, any ashes sent out of the country have to be accompanied and it's a very complicated procedure. I've taken the executive decision that we'll deal with them here.' Dom stands the box on the dresser, pushing it under the lower shelf. 'Forget it for the moment, Billa. Come out for a walk round the lake.'

One morning, at the end of her first week at Chi-Meur, Tilly comes downstairs just in time to see a few people going quietly into the chapel for Terce. She hesitates, then on an impulse she

316

follows them in and sits just inside the door at the back. The Sisters have already come in through their own private entrance: Sister Nichola sits at the end of a pew in her wheelchair with Sister Ruth beside her. Mother Magda and Sister Emily sit together.

There is a sense of deep-down peace here and Tilly relaxes into it, welcoming it. She stands and sits when the nuns and the visitors do, half-listening, half-dreaming. Someone has given her an Office prayer book but she doesn't know her way around it and simply listens. She is aware of Sister Emily's voice, rising and falling, those delicate inflections she places on certain words, and suddenly Tilly's attention is caught by a new emphasis; a lilting joy:

> The Lord is my strength and my song:
> He has become my salvation.
> I shall not die but live,
> and declare the works of the Lord.

Tilly can hear a blackbird singing in the lilac tree, and finds herself thinking about Tristan Carr, who died a week ago in Treliske Hospital. He never recovered consciousness, Dom said. He'd been cremated, disposed of, with only Dom to say goodbye to him. Tilly thinks of Tris looking so alive, so vital; chatting to Harry in the bar; nothing now but ashes. She feels a terrible sadness but

Sister Emily's voice is breaking through it, lifting her: 'I shall not die but live . . .'

Now, Mother Magda is speaking the blessing: 'May Christ dwell in our hearts by faith,' and Tilly gets ready to slip out, to hurry away to her office.

She is settling in very quickly, loving the Priest's Flat, getting used to the way everything is held within the structure of the Daily Offices. From the back gates of the convent the cobbled road leads directly into the village and she can walk down the steep hill to see Sarah or to see Sir Alec, and, of course, Clem and Jakey.

Yesterday, she and Dossie broke the news to Jakey that they won't be having a puppy. Tilly sat beside him on the sofa while Dossie cleared up the tea, and they discussed it together.

'Just to begin with,' Tilly said, 'it would be too difficult. We need a dog who can be with me, and with you, and with Dossie. That would be a bit confusing for a puppy, don't you think?'

Jakey looked downcast: he'd set his heart on a puppy.

'It's better to have an older dog,' Tilly went on, noticing the downturn of his mouth, praying for wisdom, 'so that we can have lots of fun without worrying too much.'

'I did want a puppy, though,' he says wistfully, testing her.

'A puppy is very hard work and makes a lot of

mess,' said Dossie firmly, appearing in the doorway. 'You need to have someone practically full time with a puppy. Daddy's much more likely to agree to an older dog, so don't push your luck, Jakes.'

Jakey looked resigned and Tilly glanced at Dossie admiringly. Dossie gave her a little wink.

'There's a nice little black Lab at Blisland looking for a home,' she said casually. 'You might like to go and meet her. See what you think.'

Jakey looked up at Tilly. 'Have you seen her?' he asked eagerly.

Tilly nodded. 'She's an absolute sweetie. I think she'd be just the thing for us.'

'Has she got a name?'

Dossie laughed. 'She's called Bellissima Beauty of Blisland,' she says, and Jakey and Tilly laugh, too.

'But they call her Bells,' Tilly says.

'Bells,' repeats Jakey. Bells is a cool name; a name Harry might have used.

'When can we go?' he asked. 'Can we go now? Can we?'

Dossie glanced at Tilly: they'd been leading up to this.

'If Tilly doesn't mind taking you,' said Dossie, 'you could go and see her now. But I've got to get back to Mo and Pa. Could you manage it, Tilly?'

'Oh, I think I could,' said Tilly, smiling at Jakey's expression. 'If you really want to?'

But Jakey was already on his feet, yelling with excitement, ready to go.

And it was good. He was a cheerful companion, he adored Bells, and so the first step was taken.

Now, full of happy anticipation at the prospect of being a part dog-owner, Tilly switches on the computer and prepares to work.

It is Dom who suggests that they should consult with Sir Alec about the will. Alec is rather nervous, unwilling to act as any kind of judge in such a personal family matter, but Billa and Ed agree. So he drives to the old butter factory with great trepidation and praying for wisdom.

'Alec's checked Léon out,' Dom says when they've all gathered around the big slate table. 'There is a Léon, living with his mother in the Rue Félix Pyat, who works at the marina. Apparently he's a decent hard-working boy, very popular locally, and he's lived there all his life.'

'And are you seriously suggesting,' Billa asks incredulously, 'that we should send him ten thousand pounds? For simply being a decent, hard-working boy who looks after his mother?'

There is a little silence whilst Alec thinks about things and takes the temperature of the meeting. He guesses that Ed has had a shock, been made to feel a bit of a fool, but has already put it behind him. His miniatures are back, no harm done, and he wouldn't object to helping Léon financially.

Dom has seen the whole thing as a contest in which death has come to his aid; part of him can't help doffing his hat to Tris's quick thinking and audacity. He is probably in two minds about whether the will should be honoured. Billa, however, is another matter; Alec feels Billa's boiling anger, sees her bitter expression, and it saddens him.

'The first thing we should get straight,' he says cautiously, 'is whether you feel that the wishes of the dead should be honoured. Your mother wanted Andrew to have ten thousand pounds, which would have been Tris's and now Léon's.'

'But she didn't really know Andrew,' bursts out Billa. 'He completely deceived her. She didn't love him. It was a kind of physical madness and if she hadn't become ill she would have changed her will.'

Alec glances at Ed, who is watching Billa with something like compassion. With a flash of insight Alec wonders if some of that same physical madness edged into the brief time Billa and Tris have shared recently. She is too intense about it; so hurt that she cannot remain unaffected even by the mere mention of his name—which might be explained by the theft of the miniatures or might not.

'At least, according to you all,' Alec says, 'he loved the boy. I find that comforting.'

'Why?' asks Billa sharply.

'Because it is a redeeming feature. It shows Tris wasn't an utterly lost soul. If his mother hadn't been killed and his life fractured, if he hadn't been dragged from pillar to post and been forced to live with fear and exposure to danger, who can say what he might have been? What would we have been like in his shoes?'

Dom stirs, his eyes fixed on the table, and Alec suspects that he has already made this mental leap. Ed's face is beginning to soften with his ready sympathy, but Billa's remains stony. She stares at him.

'So what are you saying?'

Alec debates with himself. 'Tris's life was ruined before he could begin it,' he says. 'He was weakened, damaged, and he acted accordingly. Perhaps he longed to be free of it but didn't have the courage or the genetic make-up to make the leap for freedom. We often allow ourselves to be confined like that, don't you think? Clinging to past hurts, rejections, cruel words. Hugging them to us, rooting around in them, and reigniting our anger and self-pity at regular intervals rather than casting them away from us. All those angry conversations we have in our heads that we choose to engage in. Tris couldn't make the break and now he's dead, and his body is confined to a small box of ashes, poor devil. Perhaps Léon might make a better fist of things. From what we've heard about him, it sounds like he's made a good start; that he'd be a son we could all be proud of. Perhaps Léon makes sense of Andrew and Tris.'

Another silence.

Alec leans back in his chair and looks around at them. 'None of my business, of course,' he says mildly. 'But you asked my opinion.'

'And what would you do?' asks Billa, but her eyes are less fierce now and her voice is quieter.

Alec gives a little shrug. 'I'd do a few more checks, then I'd decide what I could afford and ask my lawyer to send the boy a cheque with a letter telling him how his uncle died and explaining that he has been cremated, his ashes disposed of and his estate has been wound up. Nothing else; no names, no pack drill. End of story.'

The St Enedocs look at each other.

'I rather like that idea,' says Ed cautiously. 'What do you say, Billa? Dom? Shall we give Léon the benefit of the doubt?'

'It sounds like an honourable conclusion,' says Dom cautiously. 'Do you agree, Billa?'

Billa takes a deep breath; her shoulders relax. 'If you all think it's the right thing to do,' she says wearily. 'Why not?'

CHAPTER TWENTY-EIGHT

Postcards arrive from Harry: high snowy mountains for Dom, deep tranquil lakes for Ed and Billa; a pretty market square for Tilly and a handsome Bernese Mountain Dog for Jakey.

'Hi, mate,' he writes to Jakey. 'You'd love these fellows. Nearly as big as Bear but not quite. The snow is good. You must come out here one day. When you've learned to surf then I'll teach you to ski. Smile and wave. Smile and wave. Love Harry xx.'

Jakey keeps the postcard on his little desk in his bedroom with the photograph of the dogs' tea party and a photograph of Bells. Now he picks up the postcard to read it again and he glows with pride. He's taken the card to show at school, and he's shown it to Tilly and to Sir Alec, and the excitement precipitated another dogs' tea party. It wasn't quite such fun without Harry, but Tilly was nearly as good, and now he has Bells to tell Ed and Billa and Dom about. Tilly has taken a photograph of Bells, which Jakey showed to them, and they were suitably impressed and agreed that once Bells was part of the family then she would certainly be invited to the next dogs' tea party. Jakey kneeled beside the sofa to show the recumbent Bear the photograph. He sleepily opened one eye and beat his tail once or twice.

'There you are,' said Tilly. 'You have the official Bear "Seal of Approval",' and they both laughed and did a high-five.

He and Tilly have taken Bells out twice now. Her owner thought it was a good idea for her to adjust slowly to her new family so they'd driven Daddy to Blisland to meet her and then the three of them took Bells for a walk on the cliffs. Jakey ran ahead with Bells, while Daddy and Tilly wandered along behind, and Jakey felt proud and grown up, as if he were in charge of Bells. She was really good. She knew how to 'Sit' and 'Stay' and walk to heel, and he felt very responsible. He hated it when they took her back but Tilly promised they'd take her out again soon and he decided that he wouldn't make a fuss.

'You must write to Harry and tell him all about Bells,' she said. 'You could send a photograph. I'll help you if you like.'

So they settled down after school one afternoon and he wrote to Harry and put in a photograph of Bells.

'Hi, mate,' he wrote in careful letters. 'This is me with Bells.'

And at the end he'd written, 'Smile and wave. Smile and wave,' just like Harry had on the postcard.

On the next outing he and Tilly took Bells to meet Mo and Pa and their little terrier, Wolfie.

'Wolfie really misses old Jonno,' Mo said.

Years and years ago, before Jakey was born, she said, Jonno had come from Blisland too, and he was Bells' great-uncle. This made her even more like one of the family and Mo and Pa were really happy to meet her. They'd both hugged Tilly when it was time to go home and Mo had suddenly looked as if she might cry, but the next minute she was laughing, which was a bit odd, Jakey thought.

'Are you all right, Mo?' he asked her, and she smiled at him and kissed him.

'I'm very, very all right, darling,' she said, and she and Pa smiled at each other in a very excited kind of way. Jakey wondered for a minute if they were going to do a high-five, but they didn't.

On the way home he noticed that Tilly was looking happy, too, smiling to herself as if she'd been given a present or something like that.

He really likes Tilly, and he likes it that Tilly and Janna are friends. He loves Janna, loves going to see her, having tea with her. She's very excited about Bells too, and when he and Daddy are back in the Lodge they're all going to walk the cliff path to Trevone.

'But we must make sure she doesn't fall down the blowhole, my lover,' Janna said.

Then Tilly said, 'What's the blowhole?' and he and Janna promised to show her on their next walk.

Now, Jakey props the photograph of Bells next to Harry's postcard and the dogs' tea party photograph, and stares at them. Soon he and Daddy will be back at the Lodge, Bells will belong to them properly and Harry will be coming home. He can hardly wait.

Sarah gives a little farewell party when Dave comes home. She invites some parents from Ben's nursery school, Clem, Tilly and Sir Alec. His ankle is much better now and he and Clem walk up to the cottage together.

'Good to see you out and about again,' says Clem.

'Can't stand being grounded,' says Sir Alec. 'Get cabin fever. So, this is very good news about the dog.'

'She's a connection, our Bells,' says Clem. 'She's an absolute godsend.'

Sir Alec smiles to himself. 'She's going to be a great addition to our dogs' tea party. When am I going to meet her?'

'We're not taking possession until we've moved,' Clem says. 'Her breeder thinks it's wise not to confuse Bells too much with lots of different homes. Generally, we just take her out for walks. Tilly and Jakey do most of it.'

'Splendid,' says Sir Alec. 'Just what was needed. As you say: a connection.'

They go into the cottage where a few people

have already gathered. Dave shakes Sir Alec's hand, passes him on to Sarah, and claps Clem on the shoulder.

'Thanks for looking after Sarah,' he says. 'Sounds like it's been a bit stressy while I've been away. What will you drink?'

'It's quite a lot to cope with,' says Clem. 'Two small children and trying to run a business. Thanks, I'll have a beer, if you've got one.'

There is no sign of Tilly but Sarah waves to him and he's pleased to see that she's looking happier. She edges her way through the knot of people and smiles at him. He bends to kiss her.

'How are you doing?'

'I'm better now Dave's back,' she says. 'Quite looking forward to the move. But I shall miss you all.'

'Will you come for Easter when your mum comes down?'

Sarah makes a little face. 'I think it might be too soon. Ben needs to settle into Yelverton, make new friends. I think it will confuse him if we come back quite so quickly.'

Clem nods. 'That makes sense.'

'You must come and see us when we've got settled,' she tells him. 'You and Jakey. And Tilly, of course,' she adds, with just the faintest edge of malice.

Clem smiles. 'Thanks,' he says non-committally.

Dave comes back with his beer and Clem raises

it in a toast to the move and their new house. Some more people are arriving and Clem strolls away, chatting to the other guests, waiting for Tilly.

Billa has been picking daffodils. The woodland floor is a mosaic of gold and cream and white and she's been out for an early walk, unable to sleep once the light begins to slide over her bedroom windowsill. Ever since the dogs' tea party, Billa has been restless. Jakey unsettles her. He is so eager, so confiding, so natural in his sudden displays of affection. She is beginning to love him, and she misses him when he goes; his bright little face beaming from the car window, hand waving furiously.

We are lucky, she tells herself. Lucky to have Tilly and Harry—and now Clem and Jakey to add to the family. It's good to have the young around, making us laugh, keeping us up to the mark.

When she ruffles Jakey's hair, treasuring those rare moments when he reaches unselfconsciously for her hand, Billa thinks about her lost children and what she has missed and her heart aches.

'I shall want babies,' Tilly said a little anxiously, in a moment of confiding.

'Of course you will,' she answered firmly. 'And you needn't worry about Jakey. He's old enough and secure enough to be quite sensible about it.'

Tilly nodded. 'I think so too. I think he'll be very fraternal, and rather strict, but very loving.'

329

They'd laughed together, imagining it.

'He'll be old enough to be a proper part of it all,' agreed Billa. 'He'll be very useful. Like having a reliable older dog to help bring up a puppy.'

'I feel so lucky I can hardly dare believe it,' Tilly said. 'Did Dom tell you that Mum and Dad are coming over for Easter? They want to meet Clem and Jakey. And Dossie and Mo and Pa. And isn't it weird that Dom knows Pa—you know, Clem's grandfather? He was a mining engineer, too. They don't know each other very well but it's another tiny connection. Dad'll be thrilled. I'm taking Dom to meet them.'

Now, as she fills the vases with fresh water, trims the daffodils' thick stems, Billa remembers Dom talking about it.

'He's a bit older than I am,' he said, 'but the name rings a definite bell. Everything's falling nicely into place for our Tills, isn't it?'

And so it is. For a little while, after that meeting about Tris with Alec, things were a bit strained between her and Dom but, after some more talks, she and Ed decided to abide by their mother's wishes and arrange for their lawyer to send Léon ten thousand pounds.

'I'd like us to go thirds,' Dom insisted when they told him. 'After all, I might so easily have been like Léon, mightn't I? If our father had refused to acknowledge me, if he hadn't provided for me, I might have finished up in a few rooms in a shabby old lodging house looking after my mother when she fell ill. Let me pay a share.'

When he brought Tris's belongings back from the hospital and from the Chough, Dom showed Billa the photograph of Léon. She stared at the young, smiling face, searching for some evidence of Tris or Andrew, but there was none.

'Perhaps he looks like Tante Berthe,' Dom said. 'And perhaps he's taken after her in more ways than one. After all, she took Andrew in when he was on the run and she looked after Tris. He wanted to stay with her, remember? He told me that he felt he had a family again and he wanted to look after Tante Berthe and his half-brother. What a shame he couldn't keep it up. Maybe Léon is made of different stuff. Anyway, it's all over now.'

Billa places the daffodils into the vases with quick stabs. She wants to let it go; to chalk Tris's visit up to experience and put it behind her. But she can't quite manage it. She remembers Alec's words about clinging to hurts and rejections, and knows that it will take some action, some gesture to free her; but she doesn't know what it is. It is easier to think about her mother more kindly now, with a greater understanding, though she still suffers spasms of humiliation when she thinks of the way Tris looked at her, holding her wrist.

Let it go, she tells herself silently, angrily. Just let it all go. Step free of it.

She finishes the vases and carries one into the hall and another up to the gallery, where she can hear Miles Davis playing 'Old Devil Moon' and Ed's computer keys tapping away. One of his publishing friends has promised to look at the manuscript, and Ed is completely committed to his story now.

Billa goes back down to the kitchen and lifts the remaining vase on to the dresser. It doesn't quite stand properly, something is blocking it, and she reaches behind it and brings out an ugly plastic box. She stares at it for a moment, puzzled, and then realizes what it is: it is Tris's ashes. She remembers Alec saying: 'Tris couldn't make the break and now he's dead, and his body is confined to a small box of ashes.'

She sits down at the table, holding the box, and quite suddenly, quite unexpectedly, she begins to weep. She weeps for her babies who had no burial, no formal grieving, for Bitser who vanished out of her life one day so many years ago. She weeps for her mother, wishing she could tell her that she was sorry, and for her father whom she'd loved so much. And at last she weeps for Tris. She folds her arms on the table and lays her head on them and it seems the tears will never stop. But they do, and when she sits up she knows now how she can weave all these threads together into one final gesture of release.

• • •

A few days later, on a bright blowy March morning, Tilly arrives at the old butter factory to find Billa getting ready to go for walk.

'It's a bit early,' says Tilly apologetically. 'I was hoping to surprise Dom but he's out so I thought I'd just come along to you anyway.'

'Walk with me,' says Billa. 'I'd like some company. I'm not bringing Bear on this one because I don't know how far I'm going.'

So they set out together, passing around the lake's edge where the wild cherry tree is in blossom, skirting the thickets of scarlet and yellow dogwood that guard its northern shore. They walk on beside the turbulent stream and into the woods. Presently Billa turns inland, climbing the hill that leads to the moors, until they are looking down on the grey slate roof of Dom's cottage and they can see the stream winding away, disappearing amongst the high banks of azaleas and rhododendrons. They are high up, unprotected, and the cold west wind is strong.

Billa hesitates, looks around her. 'This is a good place, I think,' she says. 'Do you mind waiting for a moment?'

She walks a little distance away and pauses beside a blackthorn tree whose buds are just breaking into creamy white stars. Taking a plastic box from her pocket, Billa fumbles with the lid and stares down at the contents. She remains quite

333

still for several moments, then suddenly she raises the box with a tossing movement, so that the ashes scatter into the wind and stream away towards the moors. She continues to hold the box high above her head as if to make certain it is completely empty; waiting patiently in the cold cleansing wind.

Watching her, Tilly thinks that somewhere beyond the sound of the wind and the distant water she can hear Sister Emily's voice, jubilant and full of hope.

> The Lord is my strength and my song:
> He has become my salvation.
> I shall not die but live . . .

Billa is coming back towards her now: her eyes are bright with tears but her face is serene, peaceful. She smiles at Tilly.

'Perhaps he's free now,' she says. 'Come on, let's go home.'

ABOUT THE AUTHOR

Marcia Willett's early life was devoted to the ballet, but her dreams of becoming a ballerina ended when she grew out of the classical proportions required. She had always loved books, and a family crisis made her take up a new career as a novelist—a decision she has never regretted. She lives in a beautiful and wild part of Devon.

Find out more about Marcia Willett and her novels at www.marciawillett.co.uk

Center Point Large Print
600 Brooks Road / PO Box 1
Thorndike, ME 04986-0001 USA

(207) 568-3717

US & Canada:
1 800 929-9108
www.centerpointlargeprint.com